Berkley Prime Crime titles by Julia Buckley

Writer's Apprentice Mysteries
A DARK AND STORMY MURDER
DEATH IN DARK BLUE
A DARK AND TWISTING PATH
DEATH WAITS IN THE DARK
DEATH WITH A DARK RED ROSE

A Hungarian Tea House Mystery
DEATH IN A BUDAPEST BUTTERFLY

Undercover Dish Mysteries
THE BIG CHILI
CHEDDAR OFF DEAD
PUDDING UP WITH MURDER

Death with a
Dark Red Rose

Julia Buckley

BERKLEY PRIME CRIME
New York

BERKLEY PRIME CRIME
Published by Berkley
An imprint of Penguin Random House LLC
penguinrandomhouse.com

Copyright © 2020 by Julia Buckley
Penguin Random House supports copyright. Copyright fuels creativity, encourages
diverse voices, promotes free speech, and creates a vibrant culture. Thank you for buying
an authorized edition of this book and for complying with copyright laws by not
reproducing, scanning, or distributing any part of it in any form without permission.
You are supporting writers and allowing Penguin Random House to continue to
publish books for every reader.

BERKLEY and the BERKLEY & B colophon are registered trademarks and
BERKLEY PRIME CRIME is a trademark of Penguin Random House LLC.

ISBN: 9780451491930

First Edition: February 2020

Printed in the United States of America
1   3   5   7   9   10   8   6   4   2

Cover art by Bob Kayganich
Cover design by Sarah Oberrender
Book design by Laura K. Corless

For Velda Johnston

Acknowledgments

Three wise, wonderful women helped these books exist: Kim Lionetti, Michelle Vega, and Katherine Rohaly. Kim, thank you for sharing my vision and helping it come to fruition. Michelle, thank you for being the enthusiastic champion of the Blue Lake saga. And, Mom— thank you for instilling the love of a good story in me, especially a good Gothic suspense novel. I wish you had been able to read this series, but if the universe is just, then you know, somewhere, how much love for you is inscribed on every page.

Some other wise women must be thanked here. Lydia Brauer, thank you for being my friend. Cynthia Quam, Elizabeth Diskin, Martha Whitehead—thank you for your writerly support over nearly twenty years. Linda and Claudia, thanks for being my sisters: slightly older but infinitely wiser, and always supportive.

Finally, thank you to Velda Johnston, unsung hero of Gothic romantic suspense. Your books were among the best in the genre.

Bestselling Books by Camilla Graham:

The Lost Child (1972)
Castle of Disquiet (1973)
Snow in Eden (1974)
Winds of Treachery (1975)
They Came from Calais (1976)
In Spite of Thunder (1978)
Whispers of the Wicked (1979)
Twilight in Daventry (1980)
Stars, Hide Your Fires (1981)
The Torches Burn Bright (1982)
For the Love of Jane (1983)
River of Silence (1985)
A Fine Deceit (1987)
Fall of a Sparrow (1988)
Absent Thee from Felicity (1989)
The Thorny Path (1990)
Betraying Eve (1991)
On London Bridge (1992)
The Silver Birch (1994)
The Tide Rises (1995)
What Dreams May Come (1996)
The Villainous Smile (1998)
Gone by Midnight (1999)
Sapphire Sea (2000)
Beautiful Mankind (2001)
Frost and Fire (2002)
Savage Storm (2003)
The Pen and the Sword (2005)
The Tenth Muse (2006)
Death at Seaside (2008)
Mist of Time (2009)
He Kindly Stopped for Me (2010)

(a four-year hiatus)

Bereft (2015)
The Salzburg Train (2016)
Death on the Danube (2017)
Death at Delphi (2018)
Danger at Debenham Station (in progress)

And now, whatever way our stories end,
I know you have re-written mine
by being my friend.

—From "For Good" by Stephen Schwartz

Sender: Cliff Blake
Recipients: Sam West, Lena London, Doug Heller, Belinda Frailey, Allison Branch, John Branch, Camilla Graham, Adam Rayburn, Isabelle Devon

Hey, gang!

Do any of you have inside information about that monstrosity that's going to be blotting out the sun at the intersection of Green Glass Highway and Route 14? I saw it today while I was driving to work, and I think the architecture must have been inspired by a 19th-century prison. There's a little sign at the edge of the road that reads "Coming soon: Plasti-Source." What the heck is Plasti-Source? Does plastic *have* a source? Doug, have you talked to the mayor about this? Do they have all the proper permits and such?

I know I just got to this town, but it breaks my heart to see that big ugly thing going up in that gold field that provided my morning Zen experience for the last several months. Lena and I like to jog past it, too. Lena, when you see this you'll want to change our route. It is truly ugly. Maybe you and I can come up with some Scooby-Doo–inspired plan to drive them out of town.

Who's with me?

Meanwhile, I'm going to do some digging into this company (and by that I mean I asked Belinda to do it); a quick Google search has told me only that "Plasti-Source is your source for polymer materials, for the next century of construction, electronics, aerospace, and transportation."

I think I'll just get my polymer materials at Bick's Hardware.

Sender: Doug Heller
Reply All

Funny you should ask. I asked to see a permit from someone at the site just yesterday, and I was referred to a "Mr. Randall," who is so far not answering my calls. Lydia at the town hall says that they have four other locations but decided on Blue Lake as the site for their new and bigger plant, apparently because they realized we had a landscape worth ruining.

If anyone had obscure "polymer materials" stowed away on some dusty shelf, it would be Horace Bick.

Sender: Sam West
Reply All

I think Cliff's ties are made of polymer materials. Also, Doug's various implants (you thought he was naturally good-looking, ladies? Think *polymer*).

Sender: Allison Branch
Reply All

How did you guys ever live without each other?

Sender: Lena London
Reply All

Within hours they will all be in Sam's yard, drinking beers and telling lies. John, I'm sure they'll be trying to lure you in, as well.

Cliff, I saw that ugly structure yesterday when I drove to the dentist (no cavities!). It looks like something a kid made with an erector set. I hate it. I'm on board for chasing them out of town. I need my big Blue Lake sky!

Sender: Adam Rayburn
Reply All

Camilla and I are enjoying your conversation; she asked me to tell you, because she is off to the hairdresser's, that you remind her of the three sparring brothers in *They Came from Calais*. She said Lena would understand. She forgets that her loyal and devoted Adam has also read all of her books. I agree with her, though—the three brothers argue their way into a happy resolution, solving a mystery and fending off evildoers in the process. Perhaps life can imitate art.

While I have you all here, I will mention that Camilla and I are going away for a couple of days to take in the fall color and do some sightseeing. I know I can count on all of you to keep an eye on the house; Lena and Sam have agreed to be the caretakers of Camilla's beasts.

Sender: John Branch
Reply All

Just saw this text chain. Cliff, there was a Plasti-Source in Chicago where Allison and I used to live. It was also an ugly building with a chain link fence around it and lots of warning signs. It got shut down twice for breaking EPA laws about whatever toxic smoke was coming out of the plant, or maybe the toxic sludge that came out of some chemical process they were using. It is *not* a place we want setting up shop in Blue Lake.

Have a great trip, Adam. You and Camilla deserve a little romantic getaway.

Sender: Belinda Frailey
Reply All

I will start a research file on Plasti-Source. Sounds like we need to have a meeting soon! I'll bring chips and dip.

Sender: Isabelle Devon
Reply All

I don't have anything to add; I just wanted to be in on the conversation. Thanks for copying me, Cliff. :)

A reader wants a heroine she can understand, admire, aspire to be. But a reader also wants to see that main character as an extension of herself. If the heroine confronts a murderer, the reader does so as well, as the heroine's loyal companion in that story. The average reader is just as good and clever and brave as the person she chooses to follow into a literary adventure, and a good book helps her (or him) come to that realization.

—From the notebooks of Camilla Graham

NOSTALGIA ISN'T A phenomenon reserved exclusively for those in later life; it can take a person of any age by surprise, simply by reminding her of what once was, and is no more. Walking through Blue Lake, Indiana, on a crisp October morning made me feel nostalgic for a Lena London of the past, a Lena who would never exist again. That Lena had entered town under a dark cloud, full of fear and wonder at the idea of meeting her new employer (and idol), Camilla Graham. That Lena had been surprised to meet a young police detective on the side of the road, and then later at the site of a murder, and had been initially suspicious of his charm. She had disliked the local recluse, Sam West, on sight, but grew troubled when she learned his tragic story. And she had been glad to know that at least one person in town, her best friend from high school, Allison Branch, would always love and protect her.

Now, almost a year later, standing on a scenic overlook that let me admire the sun-dappled town and the glorious lake (which did in fact look very blue today), I realized how different my life had become—drastically, irrevocably different. Camilla Graham, my unknown employer, had become my family, my dear friend and confidante. Doug Heller, too, that wonderful police detective who had solved several mysteries in town since my arrival, was like my brother, and his girlfriend, Belinda, a genius of a research librarian who had helped me solve two very personal mysteries, was like a sister. Allison had proven her friendship to me time and again, most recently when I was recovering from a terrible injury; she had nursed me both physically and emotionally. All of my Blue Lake friends had become a sort of family in one way or another. Most significant of all, Sam West, the scowling, unfriendly neighbor of one year ago—the man who had been accused of murdering his own wife, and later of murdering his wife's friend—was in fact a kind, gentle, generous, and sexy man. He stood beside me now, not as a friend or a neighbor, but as my fiancé. I glanced down at the ring on my left hand, and at the scar on my left arm, partly visible now that I had pushed up the sleeve of my sweatshirt; the scar, white and almost pearlescent, was more than six inches long when totally uncovered. Some memories stayed with you, imprinted on your very skin . . .

"Are you having one of your deep-thoughts meditations?" asked Sam, studying me with his exquisite blue eyes. "Because you've been awfully quiet, and I thought we were going to make some wedding plans while we walked."

"Sorry. It's been almost a year, did you realize that? It struck me this morning when I put Lestrade's vet appointment on the calendar. Almost a full year in this town, and a lot of turbulent water under the bridge."

"Very true." Sam looked out at the lake but reached out his right arm and pulled me against his side. "But it's also true that sometimes you can come through adversity and find life even better on the other side. How can I complain when I have you? And Cliff? And all these new friends?"

"You can't," I said.

"Then I won't." He leaned over and kissed the top of my head. "Do you want to get married here? Or in Chicago, where you grew up? Or in Florida, near your dad? Or in Indianapolis, where we've escaped for some very romantic dates? Or on some far-flung island, like all those trendy people who have 'destination weddings'?"

"How do you know about destination weddings?"

"I've done my research. I'm a very thorough person." He looked at me, all windblown brown hair and deep smile lines and intense blue eyes, and his second statement seemed somehow suggestive. I blushed, and he smiled.

I shook my head and looked back at the lake, taking a deep breath of fall air. "Mmm. Someone is burning leaves. I have to tell you—despite everything we've been through in this town—I can't imagine getting married anywhere but here, can you?" I glanced back his way.

He shrugged. "Not really."

"Okay. One wedding plan decided. It will happen in Blue Lake."

"Actually, two plans. The first was that we decided who to marry."

"That goes without saying."

"I just like to say it," said Sam. "I'm going to marry Lena London."

I hugged him and kissed his newly shaven cheek. "I like it when you say it, too."

"It's a good thing Cliff and Doug aren't here. They would find our dialogue disgusting."

"Only because they're jealous, though God knows why. They both have women in their lives. At least Doug does. Has Cliff finally asked Isabelle to go out with him?"

"I don't know. He's been very closemouthed about it, which is not like Cliff. I know they both work weird shifts, which probably makes it harder."

"Love conquers all," I said.

"Ours did."

I squeezed him more tightly. "That should be in our vows, don't you think?"

"Absolutely. Along with something about not believing in first impressions, and the importance of cats and dogs in forming a strong relationship."

I giggled. Sam had recently become the adoptive parent of four cats, two of whom he had given to his half brother, Cliff (another new addition to his life). Now, between his two cats, my spoiled feline Lestrade, and Camilla's two dogs, we made animals a big part of our daily routine.

Sam's phone buzzed in his pocket, and he pulled it out and answered after kissing my cheek. "This is Sam . . .

Hey, Doug, we were just talking about you! What? Okay—yeah, we can do that. No, that's fine. We'll be there in ten minutes." He ended the call, his expression suddenly sober. He stared for a moment at the gold-orange vista before him, thinking his thoughts.

"What's wrong?"

"I'm not sure. Doug said he needs our help, and he wants us to come to Belinda's house."

"What—? That's weird. Is he on duty?"

"I don't know—wait, yes, I do. Cliff told me last night that he, Cliff, was on duty today because Doug had the day off and was going to take Belinda to Daleville for their Oktoberfest."

It was unlike Doug Heller to ask for help, and a gray, miserable feeling started to worm its way into my consciousness. "Okay, let's go. We can take my new car—it's closest." We moved quickly back down the path until we reached the pebbled driveway of Graham House, where Camilla lived. She was outside now, throwing tennis balls for her German shepherds, Heathcliff and Rochester, who cavorted in the fall air like happy lambs. Camilla looked good. She had new glasses that accentuated her delicate bone structure, and she had been taking daily walks with her devoted boyfriend, Adam, leaving her looking fit and contented. She and Adam were about to leave on a short trip in search of togetherness and fall color.

"Hello," she said. Then, ever attuned to our feelings, she said, "Something's up?"

Sam shrugged. "Doug called and asked us to come to Belinda's. He sounded a little—out of sorts."

The dogs were back; they laid slobbery balls at Camilla's feet, and she picked them up and threw them again. "Go, by all means. Lena knows I was going to have lunch with Adam on the way out of town, anyway. But please do keep me apprised. You know I'll worry if you don't."

I think Camilla saw us all as her Blue Lake children—Sam and me, Doug Heller and Belinda, and my best friend, Allison, and her husband, John. We were all around the same age, and we all looked up to Camilla and Adam. If Blue Lake was a kingdom, then they were the king and queen, with their castle at the top of the bluff. "We will, of course," I said. "And I know we're back on our writing schedule on Monday, correct? I assume you'll be back by the weekend and Adam isn't driving you all the way to Maine or somewhere." Camilla laughed. "Meanwhile, Sam and I will keep an eye on things here."

"Thank you. Yes, back to work on Monday, but for now we can all go play in the leaves. It's a perfect time to witness some autumnal splendor, isn't it? I think Adam wants to leave by noon. But I'll have my phone on, and I want to hear everything."

"Yes, all right. Have a great time." I gave her a quick hug, then ran inside to get my keys and purse, and then Sam and I climbed into my new car—a green Dodge Caravan. My father had approved its safety rating (since my last car had been totaled in an accident) and my insurance company had approved the price. I waved to Camilla as we pulled away; the dogs stood at her feet, staring at me with wide, panting mouths.

Navigating the pebbly downward road that was lined with trees dressed in yellow and rust-colored leaves, I stole a glance at Sam. "Any guesses what this could be about?"

He shook his head. "Truly not a clue. Everything seemed fine last night, didn't it?"

We had dined with Doug and Belinda the evening before; Sam had barbecued steaks on his back patio and we ate them in his large kitchen. Belinda had been proud of the potato salad she made from scratch, and Doug's eyes had drifted to her often, just as his hand often found its way into her long blond hair. He smiled at her whenever she addressed him. It had been comforting to see them so happy together.

We drove down Lake Road, bound for Belinda's place, and I gazed at the scenery that flitted past in bursts of color. What a sensory experience fall was—the red trees, the fragrant wood smoke, the taste of hot chocolate, the sound of the cold lake water lapping the dock, the feel of soft fleece when I donned a favorite fall jacket. I loved it all.

I reached for Sam, still looking out the window, and as always, he understood. His warm hand enveloped mine as my gaze lighted on two men walking on the side of the road. Workmen, by the look of them, with sturdy jeans and plaid flannel jackets. One of them held a camera and some tool I didn't recognize. The taller of the two turned and made eye contact with me as we drove past; his face was particularly unfriendly, almost *villainous*. But that was one of Camilla's words, and I was probably half writing the men into some future book.

They turned suddenly down a dirt path and disappeared into the woods.

"What are they up to?" I asked.

Sam made a sound of agreement. "I was just wondering that. I'm using process of elimination. They don't look like brothers or friends going fishing. No poles, and not much interaction between them."

"No, they look official somehow. Blue Lake Township Office?"

Sam shook his head. "I don't think so. Why would anyone from the township be out here?"

"Surveyors, maybe?"

"Maybe." Sam's brows furrowed. "But they didn't have surveying equipment."

I squeezed his hand, then put mine back on the steering wheel. "I guess we should stop looking for mysteries everywhere. We've had enough of them."

"God, yes. Enough to last a lifetime."

"Including this thing with Doug. Why would he want us to come to Belinda's?"

"We'll find out," he said, as I flipped on my blinker and turned left on One Shoe Road.

Sam drummed his fingers on his armrest. "Why's it called One Shoe Road, anyway? And why are all these shoes always lying here? I assume there's a story behind it."

"There is! Camilla told me that years ago a shoe appeared near the stoplight—just one shoe, as sometimes happens, making travelers wonder how it got there. Same with those shoes you see hanging from telephone poles and electric wires and stuff."

"Okay, back to the story."

"So apparently no one came to remove the shoe—no cleanup crew, no police officer. Maybe everyone thought it was someone else's job. So finally, locals decided it was funny, and someone put up a handmade sign next to the shoe that said, 'I'm lonely.'"

Sam laughed. "Don't tell me. Mr. Shoe started getting friends."

"Yup. A few appeared the same week as the sign, and then more and more, until the story about shoes at the intersection of Lake Road and Longwill, as it was called then, made the local newspaper."

"Huh."

"It became a part of Blue Lake tradition. People tend to put shoes out there as a rite of passage. Birthdays, graduations, engagements. You have to admit, they're lined up pretty neatly. I've seen tourists ask Marge Bick where they can find Shoe Corner, which I guess is what people call that intersection."

"We're famous. And when exactly did they change the name?"

"Camilla says it was about ten years ago, and it coincided with the town's centennial celebration."

"Huh. So Blue Lake is more than one hundred years old. I guess that makes sense. Although in the early 1900s Blue Lake was probably three houses and a barn. Hey, look at that." Sam pointed to a sign near the roadway and I glanced at it. A homemade poster nailed to a stake read, in dark black marker, "Keep Blue Lake Clean! Down with PLASTI-SOURCE!!"

"Wow," I said. "What does it say underneath there?"

"The Blue Lake Ecology Commission."

"But there is no such thing, and if there were, I think they'd spring for more expensive signage. Probably just an angry citizen wanting to add some drama to the protest."

I was still pondering this as we drew closer to our destination. I knew the way to Belinda's house well now; I had visited it first at a July Fourth celebration (not a happy evening) but had been back several times since, sometimes in a gathering of couples, sometimes just when Belinda and I wanted to chat. On those latter occasions, my friend Allison occasionally joined us. We all had different work schedules, so our social meetings had to be timed carefully. We did a lot of texting.

By the time we reached Belinda's subdivision, the sky had become overcast. I waited until Sam met my gaze. "Why am I nervous?"

"I'm sure it's fine." He brooded for a moment before he said, "Although it's very unusual behavior for Doug."

I pulled into Belinda's driveway, covered in yellow leaves that had drifted down from a tulip tree in her front yard. I wondered why the meticulous Belinda hadn't been out raking them. They were even scattered across the windshield of her car, which sat just in front of the closed garage.

We got out and went to the door, only to find it ajar. "Doug?" I called, pushing the door open. We entered Belinda's familiar, airy living room and moved toward the kitchen, where we heard rustling. Doug stood at Belinda's kitchen island, opening drawers and rifling through the contents. The room was in disarray. Sam looked as surprised as I felt. "Doug?" he said.

Doug looked up at us, his brown eyes troubled. "Hey—thanks for coming. I need your help."

"What's going on?" I said, setting down my purse and giving him a quick hug.

"I came here to pick up Belinda. Her car is there, and her door was unlocked."

"Maybe she ran a quick errand with a friend?"

He frowned. "I tried to text her, ask her where she

was. That's when I realized her phone is still here, along with her purse." He pointed to a little side table, which held those items. "And this." He went to her counter and held up a single long-stemmed dark red rose, fresh and perfect. "This wasn't here last night when I dropped her off," he said. "And if Belinda had bought it, she would have put it in a vase."

That was true. We all knew Belinda.

"So if she's gone on an errand, she's doing it without money or identification?" Sam asked.

"Something's not right," Doug said. "Nothing's been ransacked—I made this mess. The house was perfectly clean when I got here, just with a rose on the counter. But she hasn't been in touch. We should have been in Daleville now, drinking beer and listening to polka music." He glanced out at some crimson trees rustling near Belinda's kitchen window, his eyes creased with concern. Then he looked back at us. "I have a bad feeling."

My heart plunged into my stomach. Surely this moment wasn't real.

But Doug's brown eyes were looking into mine, and those eyes held fear. "I know this sounds extreme, but I think someone took Belinda."

· 2 ·

I have one goal when writing a story—to make it an adventure the reader cannot resist.
  —From the notebooks of Camilla Graham

I FELT COLD. "You think—someone abducted her?"

"I'm leaning toward that," Doug said.

Sam clamped a hand on Doug's shoulder. "I don't think so. No sign of a struggle, so she's okay."

Doug turned to him eagerly. "I hope so. I don't want to think the worst, but—this looks suspect."

I leaned toward him. "Doug, remember when Belinda and Allison and I took that self-defense course, right after the whole Nikon Lazos scare?"

"Yeah."

"Belinda was the best in the class. Really alert, and strong. She mastered all the moves. No one is going to take her by surprise."

"Right." He looked slightly heartened, but pale. "She's not—officially missing. I've only been here about half an hour, and there could still be some logical explanation. I wish she would walk in right now and give it."

"What about her family?" I said. "Does she have any in the area?"

He shook his head. "Her parents are retired; they live in San Diego. She has an older brother named Mark, doing some park ranger job in Alaska, and there's a younger brother—I forgot his name. I think he lives with the parents. He's several years younger—still just a kid. That's all. She's never mentioned anyone in the area. But I mean—she is renting this house from her parents. I suppose one of them could possibly have a key . . ." He scratched his head in the classic gesture of confusion. "But my instinct is to pursue this as a missing persons case. I don't want to lose time."

Sam moved in, ready to take charge. "First of all, have a seat." He gently guided Doug onto a stool in front of the kitchen island. "Lena, could you get him some coffee?" He went to the side table and retrieved Belinda's phone. "Have you ever talked to her parents before?"

"No," Doug said. "I mean, not by myself. Sometimes when Belinda's talking to them she has me say hello."

Sam put the phone down in front of him. "Do it now. Call them, introduce yourself, ask if they've heard from her, or if any family is in the area."

"Right," Doug said.

I poured some coffee from a carafe on Belinda's counter and put the mug in the microwave. "Did you call Cliff? Can't he put out an APB on her car?"

Doug shook his head. "That's her only car, in the driveway."

Sam's voice was calm and comforting. "I'll call Cliff

anyway. Ask him what he would do next. We need all great minds on this." He took his cell phone into the next room to call his brother.

The microwave beeped and I took out the coffee; I walked a few steps and set it before Doug, who had entered Belinda's passcode and was scrolling through messages on Belinda's phone. He looked up at me with miserable eyes. "I'm scared," he said.

"Of course you are. But we'll find her. I promise we will."

He found her parents' number and pressed Belinda's speed dial. He put the call on speakerphone and set the phone down so that he and I could both hear. "Hi, sweetheart," said a woman's voice. Of course—Belinda's name would have come up on her caller ID.

"Hello, is that Mrs. Frailey?"

"Yes." Her voice sounded uncertain and slightly suspicious.

"My name is Doug Heller—Belinda's boyfriend. We spoke briefly a few weeks ago when you and Belinda were Skyping."

"Oh, of course, Doug! How are you? How is my daughter today?" Her voice was suddenly full of warmth.

"That's why I'm calling, actually." Doug put his face closer to the phone. "We were going to drive to Daleville today for Oktoberfest, but when I got here Belinda was gone. She's left her purse and her keys and her car, and I can't figure out where in the world she could be. I just—I guess I wondered if you had any insights, or if you'd heard from her."

Belinda's mother's voice was concerned, yet comforting. "Well, that's odd. But our Belinda is such a private person, isn't she? Maybe she took a walk in the woods and lost track of time? She did that once when we were visiting."

A brief glimmer of hope appeared in Doug's eyes. "That's a possibility, I guess. We'll certainly have a look around. Did she happen to mention anything to you? Anything about going somewhere, or—?"

We could hear Mrs. Frailey talking to someone in the background, seemingly her husband. Then she was back. "Did she possibly go in to work? Maybe a last-minute task she wanted to do?"

"I would have thought that, too, but again, her car is in the driveway, and her keys are here. She would need them to get into the library, because it's not open until ten."

"Oh, yes—I see. Well, you do have me a bit concerned, Doug. I wonder—" She disappeared into a side conversation again. Her voice mingled with a deeper one, and they seemed to consider and discard several options while Doug's anxiety grew. He drummed his fingers on Belinda's counter and chewed at his lip.

Mrs. Frailey came back. "Doug, do you know—has Carl contacted Belinda at all, since he's been in town?"

Doug blinked. "Carl? No, I don't know anyone by that name."

"Carl is Belinda's brother," she said.

"Oh—right. But I thought he lived out there with you?" Doug asked.

"No, hon. Carl moved back to Indiana about three months ago. He grew up out there, you know, where you all are. He was excited to connect with Belinda again, but he said he would get settled first. He wanted to tell her he had a job, to make her proud of him. He—he's funny that way."

"Okay," Doug said, uncertain.

"Anyway, I don't know if Belinda has ever told you about Carl. He's a dear, and they get along quite well, but Carl has moments when he's a bit—unpredictable. He's on medication, actually. But I can't monitor it from out here. I had his promise that he would take it regularly."

Doug's eyes met mine, and I saw his alarm. "Does he get violent when he goes off his meds?"

Mrs. Frailey made a distressed sound. "Oh, goodness no. He just—becomes a bit manic. Does extreme things. Once he had a whim about wanting to see Vegas, and he got in the car and drove there. Didn't even check how much gas was in the car. You see? Another time he wanted cookies, so he started baking them at two in the morning. It's more about impulse control. Belinda understands; she was always the best at corralling her brother."

"Would Carl be likely to bring her a red rose?"

"Well, I mean—if Carl came to visit, then, yes, I think he would. He loves giving gifts and he always did like to give Belinda flowers, when he could afford it. Carl has looked up to Belinda all his life. And I'm afraid deep down he felt he could never live up to her standards. He's spent a lot of time trying to sort of win her over. Which he doesn't need to do, because Belinda loves him," Mrs. Frailey assured Doug in a breathy voice.

Doug cleared his throat. "I don't suppose you have any idea where I might find Carl?"

"Well—no. He called us when he got out there, said he was staying with a friend and he'd send his address when he got a place of his own. He hasn't sent that yet, so I assumed that he and the friend were sticking together for the time being. He texts me all the time, so I haven't had need of the address yet. I think he's staying in Stafford."

Doug tensed. "That's just half an hour from here."

"Yes. He's working at a company called Plasti-Source."

Plasti-Source.

I sent Doug an urgent message with my eyes, and he held up a hand to acknowledge it. "No idea of his address at all, or the friend's name?"

She sighed. "No. But I will also tell you that our family owns a little cabin in Michigan. I gave Carl the key, in case he ever wanted to spend a weekend out there. It's only about an hour from you. It's up in Allegan County— very beautiful."

"Yes, I'm familiar. Belinda has told me about that place, but we haven't been there yet. Can you give me the address of that cabin?"

Mrs. Frailey rustled around, perhaps finding an address book. "Of course. And if he's not there, and you need to rest, you'll find a key in the blue birdhouse."

Doug jotted down the information that she recited to him. "You said Carl texted you. Has he done so today?"

"No. And he seems to have his phone off, because I called him this morning, and it went straight to voice-mail. It might be out of battery power, too. He forgets to charge it sometimes."

"Give me his number, just in case."

She did so, and Doug jotted it down. "Thank you, Mrs. Frailey."

Her voice was breathy again, and a bit tremulous. "You will let us know what you find, won't you?"

"I will."

"Doug? I want you to know—I just spoke with Belinda two days ago, and she was very, very happy. She said that you were the love of her life."

Doug's knuckles whitened on the phone, and his face remained blank. "Thank you, Mrs. Frailey. We'll call you soon."

He ended the call and looked at me. Sam, who had come in midway through the call and understood the gist of things, said, "Let's go."

Doug turned, surprised. "You guys don't have to go anywhere." But his hands were shaking when he put Belinda's phone in his pocket, and Sam saw it.

"We're going, and I'm driving," Sam said. "Lena, call Camilla and tell her what's up."

Moments later we were all in my car; Doug sat in front to give directions to Sam, while I sat in the back to offer moral support.

I called Camilla, filled her in, and wished her a nice trip.

"Oh, find Belinda immediately, or I'll worry the whole time," she said.

"I'll contact you as soon as we know."

I ended the call, but on an impulse I searched for Plasti-Source on my phone's Google app. "There is another Plasti-Source location in Stafford," I told the men. "I'm going to see if Carl is working today."

I pressed the "call" button on the business page for the company, and a woman's voice answered after two rings. "Good morning, this is Plasti-Source. I'm Jeannine. How may I direct your call?"

"I'd like to speak with Carl Frailey," I said. "I understand he is one of your employees."

She said, "That's the IT Department. One moment, please."

Doug was staring at me from the front seat; I held up a finger. The woman's voice returned. "Carl is not on the schedule again until Monday, I'm afraid. You'll want to try him at home."

I thanked her and ended the call. "Not scheduled until Monday," I said.

Doug nodded. "Which would give him some time to finally visit his sister. What would make him wait for three months before seeking her out?"

"It sounds like Carl marches to the beat of his own drum," Sam said. "So he's probably involved in her AWOL status somehow."

"Maybe," Doug said. "I actually hope you're right, Sam. Although I might have to punch Carl in the face, if that's the case." We were passing the hulk of the new Plasti-Source plant, black and forbidding against the gray-blue sky. It had the look of a villain's lair, and Doug glared at it. I was pleased, though, to see that Doug looked a bit less pale and that Sam's calm logic was helping him regain his usual composure.

Sam flipped on the radio, perhaps hoping for a good distraction, but I had left the dial on a classic rock station, and we heard Paul McCartney's plaintive voice singing "The Long and Winding Road." Doug's shoulders tensed again, and he looked out his window with a restless expression.

Sam swore under his breath and flicked the radio off.

"We had a little argument last night," Doug said to the trees outside his window. "Nothing earthshaking, but—

a disagreement. And now I feel bad about it. About some of the things I . . ." His voice drifted off.

How terrible it would feel, worrying about a person's welfare while struggling with the memory of words that would have been better left unsaid. "I'm sure it wasn't as bad as you think," I said. "And I know we'll find her soon."

Doug sighed. "A few nights ago, we were having dinner together at my place. I was at the stove, stirring a pot of soup and telling her about my day, and I realized she wasn't paying attention. She was looking down at something in her lap. I went over to see what was stealing her attention from me. It was a book; she was hiding a book and trying to read it while we were talking." He was both amused and surprised by the memory. "She apologized but told me it was a really good part. And she looked up at me with those big green eyes and pushed her glasses up on her nose, and I just—I realized I was in love with her."

"Oh, Doug!" I said.

"I told her last night. But she wouldn't say it back to me. I think she wants to, but she's so careful. Everything has to be crystal clear." He stared out the window again and wiped at his eyes.

Sam touched his arm. "She's at the cabin, Doug. You have time to talk, to work things out. You'll get your chance to go to Oktoberfest and a million other things with her. You're going to feel such relief. Not long now."

Doug turned to him, eyes wide. "And what makes you so sure?"

Sam shrugged, both hands back on the wheel. "Because I've almost lost Lena any number of times, and a few months ago I saw her pulled from the wreckage of her car looking like a broken doll, but I got her back. And before that she and I walked away from that monster house across from Allison's place, intact, and I learned that you and Cliff would both survive, and that's when I knew that no troubles could bring me down as long as all of you were alive. That's what you'll feel, because we're all under some weird Blue Lake spell, some mixed curse, that brings us great misfortune, but corresponding great blessings. The same paradox, again and again. Belinda is missing, but your reunion will be the blessing. That's how it is in this place."

Doug stared at him for a while, thinking about this. Finally, he said, "It does kind of seem that way, doesn't it? A pendulum swinging back and forth, for at least a year now."

"Yeah." Sam stole a glance at him. "Take heart."

Even Sam's voice was a bit nervous, though. Because beyond our shared hope that we would find Belinda at the end of our drive, there was an unspoken fear in the car: that Belinda's disappearance had nothing to do with her brother, and that some other person was currently getting farther away as we drove into a wild-goose chase.

The Beatles song kept playing in my head as the miles flashed past. *"Don't leave me waiting here . . ."*

It was a peak color weekend, as Doug had said, but I don't think one of us noticed the trees as Sam sped down the interstate, waiting for the sign that said, "Welcome to Michigan."

3

My parents filled our house with books. I don't suppose they knew just how influential that choice would be, but I'll be forever grateful to them for that early gift of literacy. For a paradise of volumes, with story after story at my eager fingertips.
—From the notebooks of Camilla Graham

IT TOOK A while to locate the cabin. I had nervously been regaling them with some of the plots of Camilla's novels. "You would love *Absent Thee from Felicity*. In that one, a woman leaves her family to follow a clue in an old letter, hoping to find out what happened to her father. Kind of a similar theme in *For the Love of Jane*—a man arranges his own death to protect his family. Actually, you would both probably like *Savage Storm* the best. That's about two cops who are pursuing the same criminal. And of course they just so happen to fall in love."

"I'll read them all eventually," Doug said, only half listening.

We were on a dirt road with woods on one side and Lake Michigan on the other; the waves tossed restlessly against an ambivalent sky. Everything looked gray, but the sun was shining, and Doug had to squint to read the numbers on the houses tucked here and there into the trees.

"She said 488," Doug said. "This place up here has a little wooden placard—I think she told me about that— yes! It says 488, Sam!" His voice was loud in the quiet car, and he couldn't hold still in his seat. Sam had done a commendable job of calming Doug for the majority of the ride, but after we hit Allegan County, Doug's anxiety was back. Even from my vantage point behind him, I could see his tension in the stiffness of his shoulders and the routine clamping of his jaw.

"Doug," I said. "You have to take some deep breaths. Get control over the situation."

He didn't take offense; he turned to look at me, his brown eyes studying mine. We had our own sort of connection—not the same as Camilla's and mine, which Sam called "writer telepathy," but a kind of sympathy of souls. I had realized it fully back in July when I had hinted to Doug that I knew who was vandalizing certain areas of Blue Lake. He had looked at my face and then figured it out himself. Now he read my message: that he would be a better help to Belinda if he could reclaim his usual calm.

He puffed out a few breaths as Sam pulled into the driveway. "There's a car here," Sam said. "That's good, right?"

Doug had closed his eyes to aid his deep breathing. Now he opened them and said, "I hope so." His door was open before Sam had even put the car in park. Sam and I were close on Doug's heels as he moved up a narrow walkway to a little wooden door. I saw the blue birdhouse that Belinda's mother had mentioned; it sat in the middle of a neglected wildflower garden. If need be I could claim the key for Doug, who rapped loudly on the door.

We stood for a moment. A curtain in the window to the left of the door twitched and was still. A moment later the door opened just wide enough for a young man to thrust his face out of it. I knew at once that this was Belinda's brother; he had eyes the same color and shape as hers, and he shared what I had thought her distinctively shy expression. Doug seemed to see it, too. "Yeah?" the young man asked, his eyes scanning to study the three of us in turn.

Doug took out his ID. "I'm Detective Heller from the Blue Lake Police Department. I'm looking for Belinda Frailey."

The young man's face became expressionless. I realized he was quite young—only twenty-one or -two, and he looked suddenly like a teenager. "She's not here."

"Who are you?" Doug asked.

"None of your business," the boy said. I read something protective in his tone; did he think Doug was here to arrest Belinda?

Doug's jaw tightened, but he kept his voice level. "It *is* my business because Belinda Frailey is my business. You want to tell me who you are, or do you want me to call for some backup so we can search the premises?"

"Belinda's not here. I don't know anyone named Belinda." He was clearly lying, and his face looked so miserable that I actually felt sorry for him.

I touched Doug's arm, pushing slightly, and he moved over with an impatient sound. I stepped forward and smiled at the man in the door. "Carl?" I said. "Your mom told us you might be here. Belinda is our friend. We just want to talk to her."

Something flickered in his face, and I thought he looked a bit less unhappy. "Talk to her about what? Maybe if she shows up I can tell her," he said. He scratched at some peach fuzz on his cheek. The door opened a bit more and he became fully visible. He was quite thin; he wore hiking boots, sturdy blue jeans, and a blue flannel shirt.

Doug edged back to his original spot, pushing me into Sam, whose arms wrapped around me. "About her disappearance from Blue Lake. She had an appointment with me this morning, and it's not like her to break *any* appointment," Doug said. He tried to peer past the boy, and the latter instinctively narrowed the opening again.

"If I see her I'll be sure to tell her."

Just then Belinda herself came around the corner of the house, holding a handful of colorful leaves. She saw us and her face brightened, then creased into a huge smile. "Doug!" she cried as she ran toward him.

"Oh God, Belinda!" Doug said, closing the distance in two strides, crushing her against his chest and kissing her blond hair. Her leaves fluttered to the ground in a burst of orange, red, and gold. Doug held her away from him for a moment. "Where have you *been*? Why didn't you take your phone? I've been going nuts."

"I'm so sorry, hon," she said, laughing a little as he covered her face with kisses. "It's a long story. It involves my little brother there, who is in the doghouse, to say the *least*."

I spared a glance at Carl, still just a face in the doorway. He scowled, but I read some shame and unhappiness beneath the veneer of anger.

Belinda peered over Doug's shoulder at Sam and me, still smiling. "It was nice of you guys to come. I know Doug must have appreciated it."

"I did," Doug said, finally letting go of Belinda and turning back to us. "They kept me sane while I was worrying over you." He looked at Carl's narrow face, red now with some emotion. "I think you need to introduce me to your brother. And then I have a *lot* of questions." He was wearing his no-nonsense face, and Sam said, "Uh-oh," under his breath.

"Let's go inside," Belinda said. "Carl, open the door. We're going to have a little chat at the table. You can share your caramel apples with everyone."

Carl backed up into the house and opened the door, as instructed. He kicked at the door frame. "I don't know if I have enough."

"You do. Go get them," she said. Carl disappeared, and Belinda shook her head. Even in her apparent disappointment, I saw something very clearly: she loved and even doted on this boy.

Doug and Sam moved into the room, and I grabbed Belinda's hand. "We were really worried about you," I said.

To my great surprise, her eyes filled with tears. "I am so—surprised, and—happy—to see you guys. I didn't know how to contact you. I can't believe you found me so quickly."

I stared at her for a minute. Doug was right: her green eyes really were big. "Well, I should think so. Doug is *in love* with you. You're one of my *best friends*. Sam's, too. We all love you, and we were terrified."

She moved forward and threw her arms around me. "I love you, too."

I hugged her tightly, then pulled back to study her face. "Are you okay?"

She nodded. "I'm fine. Carl was totally irresponsible, but there's—a backstory to it all. In fact, I'm so glad you guys are here for another reason. Carl has a problem, and I've been trying to help him with it. I told him he had to take me home, but while we were here, I just wanted to take a quick walk on the property. It's been a long time since I drove out. I wanted to bring Doug here soon, but not this way."

"No, of course not."

"Anyway, now that you're here, maybe you can help Carl. Or give me some ideas how to help him. He's—got himself embroiled in something."

"Belinda?" Doug called from the cabin.

"Come on," she said to me. "Help me pick up my leaves—I wanted to make a centerpiece. Then I'll tell you inside." Together we retrieved the leaves that had fallen during her reunion with Doug; they were a spectacular mixture of large and small, bright and muted examples of fall color. Belinda led me into a quaint little kitchen, quite simple, yet distinguished with its wood-framed walls and bright white paint. A long farmer's table dominated the room, and Doug and Sam had already taken seats there. Carl, suddenly transformed into a host, was pouring coffee into large brown mugs, avoiding the gaze of the two men. A quick glance into the next room showed me a small but cozy space, lined from floor to ceiling with books. Belinda's love of literature had obviously been encouraged by her family. And what a paradise for a child who loved reading!

We set our leaves in the center of the table in a decorative wooden bowl. Belinda sat next to Doug, and I tucked in next to Sam. Belinda said, "Everyone, this is

Carl Frailey. He's a good guy and a great brother, but today he did something really impulsive and pretty self-centered, so I've spent part of the morning not speaking to him," she said.

Carl's mouth tightened with displeasure, but he put out mugs for Belinda and me and poured coffee into them. He was surprisingly dexterous with his movements; he arranged everything quickly and didn't spill a drop of liquid.

"Nice to meet you, Carl," Sam said, offering his hand. Carl shook it, nodding. "How exactly did the two of you end up here this morning?"

Belinda sighed and stroked Doug's cheek. "Carl showed up at my door. I hadn't seen him in almost a year, so I was of course very excited and pleased. He gave me a red rose and told me he had missed me."

Doug was still alternating between glaring at Carl and gazing at Belinda. He spared a glance for Carl now, saying, "Haven't you been in town for months?"

Carl's eyebrows rose, and he grew defensive. "Yeah, but I had to get settled. I need to get settled in a place. I wanted to tell Belinda that everything was all set up. But I couldn't wait anymore, because—well, I had to see her." He turned abruptly and went into a little pantry area, where he opened a refrigerator and took out a small tray. He came back to the table with the caramel apples Belinda had mentioned, clearly fresh, and fragrant.

"I just made these," he said. "I'm good at making things in the kitchen. You can all have one." He set down the tray and then started to walk into the next room.

"Carl," Doug said, his voice mellowed by perhaps one degree. "Come back and sit with us. I want to talk to you."

Carl hesitated, then looked at Belinda. She nodded. "Come on back and meet my friends."

He strode back to the table, looking uncomfortable. He sat down at the far end, and Belinda took up her story. "Carl said he wanted to show me something, and could I come with him. He implied it would only take a minute, which is why I didn't leave a note or anything. I'm so sorry," she said to Doug, who was playing with her hair and kissing her cheek every now and then.

"I was telling the truth," Carl said. "I was going to just take you over to Plasti-Source, but then I felt like they'd be watching us, and I tried to think of someplace private. So I drove here."

Belinda frowned. "Yes, Carl drove here, despite my protests, and we are still working that out."

Doug scowled in Carl's direction. "Something you should know, Carl, is that I love your sister, and you scared us all to death. We thought someone had kidnapped her. And essentially that's what you did. I could charge you with abduction."

Carl's mouth opened, but no sound came out. Clearly, he had not anticipated this response, and he looked genuinely surprised. "I didn't mean to scare anyone. I guess I just figured—I'd have her back by afternoon, so what was the big deal?"

Doug's frown was Olympian in scope, but Sam held up a hand. "You were picturing Belinda living alone, being kind of an introvert, right? But she's made a lot of new friends over the last year." He pointed around the table at Belinda's new friends. "And when she's not with her real family, *we're* her family."

Belinda's eyes widened, and the smile she sent Sam

was full of gratitude. Then she frowned at her brother. "But aside from that, I told you I had to be back, and you simply disregarded me. That's not okay, Carl."

Carl shifted in his chair, restless as the princess on a pea. Doug frowned. "Why did you lie when we got here? Why did you say Belinda wasn't here?"

The boy shrugged. "You said you were the police. You didn't say you were her friends or anything. I didn't want the police bothering her."

"Oh, Carl," Belinda said, her tone a mixture of frustration and indulgence.

Doug had sliced off a piece of his caramel apple with a pocketknife and put it in his mouth. His eyes widened, and he said, "My God, that's good."

Carl smiled for the first time and I realized what a handsome boy he was. "I'm a really good cook," he said. "I watch all the cooking shows."

"Carl's trying to get on one of them," Belinda said, her pride overriding her anger. "One of those shows like *Top Chef* or something."

Sam and I both tried our apples, and Doug was right. They were amazing; Carl had obviously made his own caramel mixture, and it was like nothing I'd ever tasted— buttery and fruity all at once. "Oh wow, Carl!" I said, and he bestowed his handsome smile on me as well.

Doug took another bite, then held up a hand. "Okay, I'm glad to have found Belinda, and I appreciate the snack, but I think you owe us all an explanation, Carl. Why did you bring Belinda here, and what does it have to do with Plasti-Source?"

Carl shifted in his chair and sent a look to Belinda. He

seemed to be seeking guidance. Belinda nodded, her green eyes calm and wise. "Tell him, Carl. He can help."

"Help with what?" Doug said.

Carl got up, poured himself some coffee, and sat back down. "I have a problem about one of my friends. A mystery, I guess you'd say."

"We're good at solving those," I said.

Carl looked at me with the face of a worried boy. "He's a guy I work with at Plasti-Source. His name is Luis. We like to hang out at lunch and just shoot the breeze. He doesn't care that I'm younger than he is. We both like the same stuff: reading history books, really *all* books for Luis, and cooking, and playing video games, and working in the garden. We just hit it off right away."

Sam put a friendly hand on Carl's thin arm. "And what's the problem with Luis?"

Carl frowned into his coffee, then looked at Sam with troubled eyes. "He's disappeared."

$$\begin{array}{ccc} \text{❧} & \cdot \ 4 \ \cdot & \text{❧} \end{array}$$

*Readers ask me where my ideas come from. I've
never quite known the answer to that, but I can
assure you that they come in droves. They always
have.*

—From the notebooks of Camilla Graham

DOUG WAS CUTTING another piece of his apple. "What do
you mean, he's disappeared? If he didn't show up to work—"

"He didn't," Carl said. "Which isn't like him. He's got
what my dad calls a good work ethic. He's always early,
and he stays until no one needs him. And he's real devoted to his wife and stuff."

"Maybe he's home with his wife," Sam suggested gently, studying his coffee cup.

Carl turned to him, thin and nervous. "I went to his
house in Blue Lake, days ago. His wife was there; her
name is Elena. She said he wasn't around, but she didn't
expect him because they had a fight."

This seemed like a strange echo of what Doug had told
us about his fight with Belinda and her subsequent disappearance; he and Belinda exchanged a secret glance, perhaps in acknowledgment of this.

Doug looked troubled. "Well, it's his wife who would have to report him missing, Carl."

"She's lying," Carl said, thrusting out his chin.

"Why do you think that?" Despite himself, Doug seemed intrigued by Carl's story.

Carl jumped up again to retrieve the coffeepot; he returned and started topping off everyone's cup. His brows were furrowed with anger or concentration. "I don't think it, I know it. You have to know Luis. He's the nicest guy, really soft-spoken and kind. He and I sometimes played video games together at this place in Stafford, and he was always spotting me tokens and stuff. He knew I liked cooking shows, so he got me a cookbook once with recipes from *The Great British Baking Show*. For no reason, just because I liked it."

My eyes went to Belinda, who was studying her brother with a mixture of love and concern. Then I said, "Carl, he sounds like a great guy. But why does that mean his wife is lying?"

Carl looked at me with interested green eyes. "My boss at work says he's not going to hunt Luis down. They're all saying it—the big bosses and even the guys we work with from day to day. Joe and Gino said Luis has pulled stuff like this before, and so Phil Enderby said as far as he's concerned, Luis is fired. So I went to Elena, and she said Luis and she fought, and she's not expecting him back in the near future. It seems like the only one who misses Luis is me. That's fishy."

To my surprise, Doug leaned forward almost eagerly. "You know what, Carl? That *is* fishy. Did you think he was the type to wander off?"

Carl shook his head. "No. He liked going home and

watching TV every night, just like most people. Elena is a great cook, he said, and he looked forward to eating her dinner and watching cop shows on TV. He even told me once he hated traveling. He said it was lots of driving or flying just to see a few things far away, and the whole time you're wishing to sit in your own house and relax. He just likes being in his own space, but suddenly he's gone."

Sam was starting to look interested, too. "You said Luis lives in Blue Lake?" He turned to the cop at the table. "That's your jurisdiction, Doug."

Doug nodded. "But clearly I won't have a missing persons report. Still . . . it would give me a great reason to march into Plasti-Source and get the lay of the land in there." He turned to Carl. "What's that company like?"

Carl shrugged. "They're okay. They pay pretty good. No one's super friendly. It's not one of those companies where everyone is encouraged to go out together after work or anything. Luis was the only friendly one to me. He and I both work in IT. When I got hired I was just an entry-level clerk, but they kept needing me to solve their computer problems. So I got promoted."

I was almost finished with my caramel apple and wondering if I could ask Carl for another one. Sam saw my yearning expression and grinned at me. "Carl," I said. "Does Luis have a phone? Have you tried texting or calling him?"

Carl sighed. "Yeah. It just goes to his voicemail over and over. Which is also weird. Luis loves his phone. He was always playing games on it, and whenever I sent a text, he answered it."

Again, this seemed like a repetition of what we had gone through with Belinda. "And his wife didn't seem concerned about him? Even if she was angry, she would want to know where he was, wouldn't she?"

Carl nodded. "I know something is wrong. Because even if he didn't contact his wife, I think Luis would contact me. We're always texting each other jokes and GIFs and stuff. He has this funny laugh, and he loves jokes. I sent him a couple on the first day he lost contact and never heard back. Now I haven't heard from him in five days. Almost a week. It's just weird."

A sudden thought struck me. "Belinda. Wasn't there a guy in our last Blue Lake book club meeting named Luis? The dark-haired guy who sat by the door? We were discussing *Great Expectations*. He had found all the humorous parts and laughed about them."

Belinda's eyes widened. "I think you're right. I can look him up—we all signed in. I think we had a total of fourteen people for that discussion."

Carl leaned forward. "That sounds like him. He loved to read; he always had a book with him. Sometimes he listened to them on his phone. But he said he read less since he met me because we were always talking."

"Camilla is going to be sorry she wasn't here," I murmured to Sam. "She loves a good mystery in real life, too, not just in the books she writes."

The words elicited a shocked look from Carl. "You know a writer named Camilla? What's her last name?"

"Graham."

Carl slapped the table. "I read her books. I've read a ton of her books. I was getting Luis to read them, too."

"Aren't they great?" I said.

Carl nodded. Then he said, "Are you Lena London? That new lady who writes with her?"

"Yes."

"Wow! You guys are famous!"

I smiled, and Sam touched my hand. "Camilla is," I said. "Very famous."

Doug studied the wood table for a while. Finally, he said, "I'm going to look into this, Carl. I'm very curious about Luis as well. And about the company where you both work."

Carl's face melted into relief, and suddenly he was emotional. "I'm sorry," he said in a rush. "I'm sorry I took away Belinda and didn't let her call anyone. I was worried about Luis and I didn't take my pills. I've taken them every day, but I didn't take them this week, and then I got caught up in wanting her help and wanting to talk to her alone and thinking about the cabin. I got caught up in it." His lashes held tiny pinpricks of tears; I felt answering tears forming in my own eyes.

Belinda said, "It's okay, Carl. But you have to take the pills when we get back. I mean right away."

"I know." Carl wiped at his eyes. "I'm sorry to everyone."

Doug offered a genuine smile. "Carl? I didn't want to meet you this way, but it's nice to meet you." He stuck out a hand, and Carl shook it with a shy smile. "I don't suppose you have any food that resembles lunch in that fridge?"

Carl beamed. "I do! I stopped at Peabody's on the way into town. Belinda was so mad at me. But I can make a real good lunch that I saw Gordon Ramsay make."

"Well, if *Gordon Ramsay* made it," Sam joked.

And just like that the tension was defused. I texted Camilla to tell her that all was well, and Doug made Belinda call her parents to tell them the same. Carl practically skipped into the kitchen and wrapped an apron around his waist. I wandered to the giant wall of books and saw that one of the Fraileys (and I thought I knew which) had arranged the books in order of genre, and then alphabetically within those sections. I was drawn to the mystery section, which contained three old Camilla Graham titles, and to the classics section, which was well stocked with Shakespeare, Dickens, Austen, and the Brontës.

"Hey, bookworm," Sam said behind me. "Want a caramel-flavored kiss?"

"When *don't* I want that?" I said.

Sam bent to press his lips to mine. "Mmm," he said.

"You were right about everything," I said. "You told Doug that she would be here, that everything would be fine, that he would feel relief and joy. Look at him."

We turned to look out the window, where Doug and Belinda were talking animatedly in the front yard. Doug impulsively picked her up and spun her around, and they both laughed like children. "That's joy, all right," Sam said.

"You're like a wise old mariner," I said.

"I *am* old," Sam said.

"Oh yes. Old man of thirty-six."

"The pendulum has swung back." Sam continued to study Belinda and Doug out in the bright yard. "But this story has me troubled. Things don't sound good for Luis."

"I don't know. We learned today that missing people can be found."

"Let's hope so." He turned and shifted his attention to the bookshelves. "What looks good?"

"Everything! I wonder if the Fraileys have a lending

library. They have a great history section over on the last shelf. A couple of books about the Native Americans. And one huge one about World War I."

"Sounds intriguing." He scanned the room. "Between the books and Carl's food, a person could spend an enjoyable weekend here."

In fact, a delicious aroma was emanating from the kitchen, along with the sounds of pots clanging and Carl's melodic humming. "I did not expect to be dining in Michigan today. But I'm glad. This was the most positive outcome we could have imagined."

Doug and Belinda came back in and stomped their feet on the doormat. Their cheeks were rosy, their eyes bright. Sam and I exchanged a glance and silently agreed that whatever argument had existed between them had now been resolved.

Soon we were again seated at the table, and again Carl was feeding us—this time chicken parmesan sandwiches on crusty bread. "I don't have beer or anything," Carl said. "I don't really drink. But I have fresh cider."

"That's perfect, Carl," Belinda said.

Carl stood over us for a moment, looking around the table. "I'll just say a basic blessing over you," he said, and murmured a prayer that we could barely hear. Then he went back in the kitchen.

Belinda said, "For a while Carl thought he might want to be a priest. He's very spiritual."

"He's great, Belinda, and very handsome. And he looks so much like you! Does your other brother resemble you, too?" I asked.

She nodded. "We all look kind of similar, we Fraileys."

Sam was already eating his sandwich. "This is amazing," he said. "Adam should hire this kid at Wheat Grass."

Belinda's eyes brightened. "Oh my gosh, that's a perfect idea! Wheat Grass is such a sophisticated restaurant—Carl's always admired it."

"I'm sure we could arrange an interview, since we are all good friends with the proprietor," I said. "By the way, I need to tell Camilla that I saw her books on the shelf here. I hope she doesn't mind that I keep bugging her. I know she and Adam are having their little romantic getaway."

"She loves it when you text her," Sam said.

"I need to text Adam, too. We're right in the midst of planning Camilla's party. You all know it's at the end of the month, right? I came here last year right after she turned sixty-nine. This year—seventy—is such a momentous birthday, and Adam and I want to make it special."

"Do you need us to help with anything?" Doug asked, looking at his plate. He, too, seemed quite enamored with his sandwich.

"I think Adam and I have it covered. He's providing the Wheat Grass main room, of course, and we have been planning all sorts of little surprises. It gave me something to do while I was recuperating." I pointed vaguely at my arm. Doug and Sam grew solemn; they both hated to think of the car crash that had nearly killed Camilla and me in the summer. I realized it might be best to change the subject.

"I have a lot of texting to do, and not just to Adam. I'll do that while you drive home, Sam."

Doug finished his last bite and cast a longing expression at his empty plate. "That was amazing. And speaking of driving home, we need to do that. My fall outing is ruined, but I can still treat my Belinda to a nice evening in Blue Lake."

"That sounds great," Belinda said with a smile.

Moments later we were helping to clear the table and carrying dishes into the kitchen, where all five of us collaborated on washing, drying, and putting away. We had made it our unspoken goal to put Carl at ease, and by the end of our KP duty he was laughing and joking with Sam and Doug as though they had grown up together.

Belinda smiled at this from a corner of the kitchen where she was sorting silverware. Her eyes met mine, and I gave her a thumbs-up. She pushed her glasses up on her nose and grinned back at me, and I was struck by how attractive she was, how she had blossomed as a woman in love. I wondered if she and Doug would get married, or if now at least she would tell him that she loved him, too . . .

"Lena?" Sam said. "Are you ready?"

"What? Oh, sure. We have two cars; how are we dividing passengers?"

Carl donned a serious expression. "I have to stay for a while. My mom and dad have a whole checklist of things to do before we leave the property. Locks and alarms, and making sure things are unplugged and stuff. I need to go through the whole checklist." It dawned on me, as I made a quick trip to the little country-style bathroom in the corner of the dining room, that Carl seemed like just the person to put in charge of a detailed list.

When I returned to the kitchen, Belinda was hugging her brother and kissing his cheek. "You come right back after you do that. No side trips. And call me when you get back to Stafford. Now that I know you're so close, we can meet all the time. Meanwhile, Doug said he'll look into the whole Luis thing."

Carl nodded. "Thanks. I think Luis needs us."

We made our way back outside. I stole a glance over my shoulder and saw that Carl was in the doorway, just as he had been when we arrived, and his face was once again inscrutable. I called, "The food was delicious, Carl!" His smile, genuine and boyish, remained on his face as we drove away.

· 5 ·

One learns her personal vocabulary not so much from schooling as from books. Every book we read provides endless lessons in syntax, diction, and style. I would tell young people today who wish to become writers: read great books. You will reap untold rewards, the greatest of which will be a wonderful story.

—From the notebooks of Camilla Graham

THE JOURNEY HOME was happy and hilarious; we were all still riding a huge wave of relief. Belinda sat in the backseat, tucked firmly into Doug's arms, and I sat up front with Sam, laughing at the badinage between Doug and Sam and catching up on my correspondence via text message. I wrote to my father, filling him in on some of the plans for Camilla's birthday. He and Tabitha weren't able to make it, as her children were visiting, but they were going to send what he called "a giant bouquet," to her on the morning of her birthday.

I had received a new picture of Athena Lazos, the daughter of Sam's ex-wife. The baby was now a little more than a year old, and she was beautiful. Normally Athena was full of laughter, but this time Victoria had selected a serious photo in which the baby stared at the camera with a pensive expression, her large dark eyes wide and concerned. She had a full head of dark curls, which contrasted dramatically with her red velvet dress. Victoria had written, *Athena says hi to Aunt Lena and Uncle Sam, and that you should visit us in New York before the snow comes.*

With a little frisson of horror, I remembered once again the man who had held Victoria against her will, a man she had thought she loved. Nikon Lazos was in jail now, convicted of kidnapping his own child and being an accomplice to murder. I recalled the house in Blue Lake that had become his lair—a pretty, unassuming façade across the street from my friend Allison's house—in which three of the people now sitting in this car had almost died . . .

I texted back, *That sounds fun. I doubt Athena will remember us, but she is unforgettable. She may have dark hair, Victoria, but she is starting to look like you.*

Victoria sent back an emoji of a bouquet of roses.

I turned to Sam. "I have received an updated picture of Athena for our vast Athena photo library. Victoria called you 'Uncle Sam.'"

Sam pointed at me and said, "Uncle Sam wants *you*."

Doug tore his gaze away from Belinda long enough to say, "Nice. I give that the award for Best Double Entendre of the day."

"The day is young," Sam said.

I laughed and went back to my phone. I had a photo from Allison showing me an autumn display on her front porch, which included pumpkins with the names of all her friends on them. *For us to carve!* she had written. I showed this to the people assembled, and they nodded. Belinda said, "Allison is like our Blue Lake cruise director."

"She is!" Sam agreed with a laugh.

I took the risk of calling Adam, since he wasn't a fan of texting. His phone rang about four times, and then he answered. "Hello?" It was Adam's voice, but it sounded younger, more vibrant.

"Adam? It's Lena. Am I interrupting you?"

He laughed for no apparent reason. "Oh, I think I can spare some time for my coconspirator. I found a perfect present for Camilla out here in Moore County."

"Great! I just wanted to mention that I think I'll want to start decorating at about nine in the morning on her birthday. But you said that we have the restaurant all day, right?"

"We do. I've notified people of the closing on our website, on the marquee out front, and on a printed slip inside menus. It should be clear to everyone in town."

"Okay. I'm getting a little apprehensive. I want everything to go just right. I want Camilla to be pleased."

"She will be, dear. She will love it all. No matter how the party goes, she will know the effort we put in, and that's what she'll like."

With a burst of curiosity, I said, "How are you able to talk so freely? Isn't she there?"

He laughed again. "She's out breathing the fall air. I was just about to join her. I had to call in to the restaurant."

"Well, go have fun."

"Thank you, Lena. You, too," he said with his Adam-like civility.

I ended the call and sent an urgent look around the

car. "Something is up with Adam. He sounds weird. Different. I don't know, I can't put my finger on it."

Sam pursed his lips. "No more mysteries, please."

Doug leaned forward. "We still have one. This guy Luis. I'm actually getting a pretty bad feeling about it. When we get back I'm going to have Cliff get started on some inquiries."

Belinda sighed happily. "Yes, I know you'll get to the bottom of it. Meanwhile, we have the rest of the drive to enjoy ourselves. Who wants to play a word game?"

"I'll play whatever game you want," Doug said, kissing her hair. "I'm so relieved that things ended this way. Lena, Sam, thanks for being my moral support. I dragged you away from whatever you had planned . . ."

"We were making wedding plans," I said. "We can take those on the road. But I do have to get back and check on Camilla's dogs."

Sam turned slightly to look at Doug. "You can actually help us out with one plan. Lena and I are talking about a fairly small wedding, and that includes a small wedding party." I tapped his arm and pointed out the windshield, and he turned back to put his eyes on the road. "I asked Cliff to be my best man, but I wondered if you'd be a groomsman, too. Adam calls us the Three Amigos, and I guess I see us that way, too."

Sam was still looking at the road when he finished this speech, so only Belinda and I saw Doug's reaction, which was surprised, and then gratified. "I would be honored, Sam," he said.

I leaned toward them. "And we thought you could stand up with Belinda, if Belinda is willing to be my second bridesmaid. Allison is my maid of honor."

Belinda turned pink and pushed up her glasses so that she could wipe at her tear ducts with her pointer finger. "I—yes. I would like it. Thank you, Lena."

"Thank *you*." I smiled at her, then lifted my hand for a high five, and Sam slapped it. "One important wedding plan made. Bridal party in place."

"What about Camilla?" Doug asked.

I laughed. "Camilla would be horrified at the thought of being called a matron of honor. But Sam and I will find some special way to make her a part of the cere- mony." I turned, settling back into my seat and gazing at the autumn scenery flashing past. The trees were much lovelier now that we weren't fearful. I took a notebook out of my purse and flipped it open; it was my "Ideas to share with Camilla" page. I wrote, "Heroine's mood is reflected by the landscape—very Gothic."

Sam sent me a smile. "Having authorly inspirations?"

"Always. So many more than in my grad school days, now that Camilla and I bounce ideas off of each other."

"You two have that weird psychic connection," Doug said. "I swear you could collaborate on one of your books without even talking."

I smirked at him over my shoulder. Belinda said, "What are you writing now?"

"We have to think of a new project. Actually, I had two ideas I wanted to run past Camilla . . ."

"Well, get going," Doug said. "I've read six Camilla Graham novels now, and at some point I'm going to run out of them. Keep that train on track."

I laughed. "You've got a lot of good reading ahead of you. Meanwhile, you've got your own mystery to solve."

Doug's face grew serious. "Yeah, the more I think

about it, the less I like this setup. But beyond going to his house and his workplace, I don't know what more we can do if the wife's not reporting him missing."

"She's not, but Carl is," Belinda said. "So can't Carl file a report?"

"We'll be using that as the basis for our inquiry," Doug said. "We'll see how far it goes."

I thought about what Carl had said. "Even if you were angry with your husband, wouldn't you be concerned that he hadn't been to work or in touch with his friends?"

"Yeah, it's weird. Assuming Carl hasn't misunderstood the situation." He looked at Belinda. "Is that possible?"

She shrugged. "Carl is pretty smart. And as you saw, he's not super social, but he's loyal to his friends. If he thinks there's a problem, then there's a problem."

"Huh." Doug looked out the window as he thought about this.

I tried to recall the man in our book club. Had it been the same Luis? He had shown up as a new member (the group was always changing), so I didn't recall much about him except that he had smiled often and that he had worn blue jeans and a Notre Dame sweatshirt. And—my memory dredged up something else—he had spoken to me. What had he said? The discussion had ended and we were all filing toward the door, and he had commented on my charm bracelet, something Sam had commissioned a local artisan to make for me.

"That's so pretty," the man had said. *"Where did you get it? My wife loves stuff like that."*

I had told him my fiancé had it specially made, and he'd said he'd love to get the name of the jewelry maker. *"Maybe a gift like that will get me back in her good graces,"* he had said, making it sound like a joke. Was I creating a story around him, or had his eyes really looked sad?

"I think his marriage was unhappy," I said to the group in the car.

"What?" Doug asked, surprised.

I told them what I remembered. Belinda sat up straight. "I think he said something to me, too. About how he wanted his wife to come to check out the book club with him, but he couldn't get her out on dates anymore because she was always busy with her job. I think I was a little annoyed, thinking he was trying to turn our book discussion into marriage counseling. The poor guy probably just wanted to talk." Belinda looked sad. "I never would have given it another thought—it's funny how you can look backward and suddenly see details you hadn't seen before."

Sam saw that we were all starting to brood. "Hey!" he said loudly. "Did I tell you guys my latest Geronimo story?"

Geronimo was one of Sam's two cats. He'd adopted Geronimo and his sister Arabella as stray kittens in July, and now they were in that awkward stage in which their heads and paws were large but their bodies were still catching up. Geronimo was clearly going to be a big animal. Sam's tales of the cat's exploits had become famous in our little circle. The stories were mostly true, but sometimes Sam liked to embellish them for humorous reasons.

"No, tell us!" Belinda said.

"Well, Geronimo likes to bring presents, especially to Lena. His favorite delivery port is her shoe."

Belinda giggled, and I nodded. "It's true. He hasn't

put a dead mouse in there, thank God, but I've gotten all sorts of interesting things, from a Super Ball to an old pine frond from last year's Christmas tree."

Sam said, "Arabella doesn't get involved in the caper, but she tattles to Lena. She jumps up and swats Lena's arm, and then jumps down and stands by the shoe. That's how Lena knows to check."

"This morning I found a rubber band," I said. "He is especially fond of those. I don't know where he finds them all."

Doug laughed. "Everyone in this town has pets. I think Belinda and I need to shop around."

I turned in my seat. "Really? Isabelle told me they have some animals for adoption at the vet's office. That's where she got her Saint Bernard, right when she got to town. Have you guys met Barkley? He's just adorable. I see her walking him all the time." I was warming to the idea of helping Doug and Belinda find a pet.

Sam said, "What sort of animal do you want?" and Belinda began listing all her possible dream pets while Doug watched her, amused.

I smiled out the windshield, happy to be with my friends. As we approached Blue Lake, Doug leaned forward. "Sam, take the first exit. That way we'll have to drive past that Plasti-Source construction. I want to take a look at it."

"Oh, blech," Belinda said.

"Just for a minute," Doug insisted.

Sam took the exit, and for a time we drove past mysterious autumn woods and then some gold, open fields. Then, looming on the horizon like an Imperial Walker, Plasti-Source appeared—or the shell of what was going to become a Plasti-Source facility. It grew larger and uglier as we drove closer; finally we were in front of the framed construction, and Sam pulled onto the shoulder of the road. Two men stood near a sign pounded into the ground near the highway; they looked up as we parked, their faces unfriendly. They bent their heads close together as they said what seemed to be words of farewell, and then they both headed toward their own cars, parked right on the property. Doug hopped out of the car and said, "Excuse me? Can I ask you gentlemen—"

They ignored him and kept walking.

Sam stiffened beside me. "Does that guy in the blue flannel shirt look familiar to you?" he asked.

"I don't know," I said.

The men seemed by mutual consent to have decided not to talk to Doug. They got into their vehicles without another glance at any of us; one of them paused briefly, holding up his phone. Was he looking for a signal? Taking a photograph? I wasn't sure, but a moment later they drove away with such rapidity that their tires spun dirt and dust into the cold air. Doug stared after the departing cars for a moment, then looked at us and shrugged. He walked around, taking some pictures on his own phone. The sign the men had been standing in front of assured us that Plasti-Source was "Built proudly by Anemone Construction."

"Anemone," I said. "I've never heard of them."

"Me, either," said Sam. "You'd think we would have, if they're a Blue Lake company."

"I'm going to look into them," Belinda said, jotting a little note on a pad.

"My notes are for Camilla and yours are for Carl," I said. "We follow our loyalties."

Belinda nodded and tucked away her notebook. "Doug's right. Everything feels weird about this place."

Sam sighed. "We might just be projecting that feeling because we don't want an ugly hulking factory ruining the scenery. Cliff wasn't kidding. This thing will be a blot on the landscape, and it will block the sky."

We sat and looked out the car window while Doug took his photos, texted something, and then finally made a call. He paced around while he talked, looking disheveled and handsome. When he returned to the car, he tucked away his phone and blew into his hands. "It got colder," he said. "Feels like at least ten degrees, since we left. There must be something blowing in—rain or snow or something."

We all felt it now; he had brought the chill into the car when he opened the door, and as Sam pulled back into traffic, we were cold and rather somber, despite the happy ride we had taken with the newly reclaimed Belinda.

·⟨· 6 ·⟩·

My temptation has always been to make my characters happy, to let them live their lives in peaceful quietude. But I know that readers want them to earn that happiness, and so I must first make my protagonists miserable. Over the years, I've put my characters through some devastating events—but in the end I provide them with something delightful. That's for the characters and the readers alike—the gift of a happy ending.

—From the notebooks of Camilla Graham

SAM DROPPED OFF our companions at Belinda's, and then we returned to Graham House. "Do you want dog duty or dinner duty?" I asked.

"I need some exercise. I'll run these guys down the hill and back," he said, bending to pet the ecstatic Heathcliff and Rochester.

I picked up Lestrade, who had strolled in to greet us in his more subdued cat way. "Okay. I'll scrounge around for something to eat and we can keep the animals company for a while. We can even stay overnight here, if you want."

"Might be fun." He sent me a suggestive smile, and my blood felt warmer.

"Yeah. But first things first. Go take them for a walk;

if I'm not here when you get back I'll be upstairs making some notes."

"Got it." Sam found the dogs' leashes and clipped them on. "See you in about twenty minutes," he said.

They went out onto the porch. The dogs seemed bent on dragging Sam down the road, so he spoke sternly to them and they slowed their pace. They could be gentlemen when reminded. I smiled after them, then went to the kitchen and found a frozen pizza and some spinach that I could toss into a salad. "Easy," I said. I jogged upstairs and sat at the desk I had come to think of as mine. I ran my hand over its mahogany smoothness and flipped on the little light that someone had long ago installed to illuminate the surface. I opened my laptop, then took out my notebook so that I could transcribe my notes for Camilla. I wrote:

1. *We can try to capture, in the new book, more of the idea of the setting reflecting the heroine's mood or her fear (tell Camilla about landscape to and from Allegan County). You've done this before, of course, especially in* The Thorny Path *and* Sapphire Sea, *but I think it would be fun to go back to this Gothic staple and let the landscape suggest the mood.*

2. *I know you said you'd like to brainstorm about the new work, now that* Death at Delphi *is out of our hands (I miss our baby!). I had an idea in the car today, two ideas, actually . . .*

I paused here and glanced at my phone. It would be so much easier to talk to her. It was so strange not to have

Camilla here, within hail, so that I could tell her my every whim or idea. How spoiled I was, really, to live in her house, and eat her food, and drink in her view. How lucky I was to be in her life at all.

I felt on the verge of absurd tears at the thought. I pulled my phone over and sent a quick text:

Do you have time for a quick phone call? If not, I will go away and wait until you return, I promise.

Moments later I had a response:

Do call, Lena dear. We are resting, and Adam is enjoying a football game.

Relieved, I dialed her phone.

"Hello," I said in response to her greeting. "It's silly that I can't leave you alone for one day, but I already have a lot to tell you. I was writing it down, but then I thought . . ."

"I'm glad to hear your voice, as always," she said, sounding calm and rested and—young. The way Adam had sounded.

"Is there some kind of special autumn cider out there?" I joked. "Because you and Adam both sound great."

She laughed. "Fresh air, I suppose. What are these wonderful ideas bubbling within you? I must admit I am curious now."

"Well, first of all, I wondered if the new book could be set in one of the little towns that you and I visited on our book tour. Remember when we were driving to a second signing, and our driver was just racing down those country lanes in the dark? Those high cornstalks and the minimal moonlight? I thought it was quite sinister, actually."

"Oh yes, indeed. And I know the area well."

"What was that town?"

"We were just outside Debenham, I believe."

"Oh, Camilla. *Danger in Debenham*, or something like that."

"I'm assuming you had an idea for a story."

"Yes. We were driving, looking for Belinda, and I was worried about her. I was just thinking, 'lost girl.' And then Sam drove past some train tracks. And I thought—what if a young woman takes a train to meet her aunt or some distant family member. She's not exactly sure what this person looks like. So she arrives at the station in the dark, and she's picked up by the wrong people."

Camilla made a contented sound. "And when she finds out, she's unable to contact the aunt. She's already embroiled in a terrible scenario. I wonder what that is?" she asked, laughing.

"Yes, it would have to—"

"Lena! Do the people pick her up accidentally, thinking she is their own distant relation? Or do they go to the train station *on purpose*, looking for someone to abduct? Or even looking for *her*?"

"Those last two are quite ominous. So of course we have to choose one of them," I said cheerfully.

"Wonderful. You had me at the country lane. That was a harrowing ride, wasn't it?"

"It was. Okay, before I let you go, I want to ask how you're enjoying your trip."

"We are both enjoying it immensely. We needed to get away, but we'll also be happy to return. We'll see you tomorrow evening, I believe. Or the following morning. I'll let you know when my chauffeur fills me in."

"All right. Meanwhile we're back at your place, and the dogs are fine."

"Good—thank you, dear. I suppose I should also mention that I heard from Michelle, my editor. The publisher is strongly urging me to write some sort of memoir or writer's advice sort of book."

"That's amazing! Do you know how many people would devour a book like that? How they would treasure it? If I had never met you, and I heard that you were writing a book about writing, or about your life, I would preorder just the idea of it!"

She laughed in my ear. "Dear Lena, how I do love your endless enthusiasm. Perhaps you can talk me through it when I return. What form it would take, and what the benefits would be, and why I should consider it at all."

"Oh, I will! I'll have a whole page of notes for you!"

"All right, then. Adam is rustling in his chair. It must be halftime, at which point we were going to step out for some dinner."

"You do that. I promise no more intrusions from me. Except maybe a text."

Amused, she said, "I love your texts. Have a good evening with Sam. Kiss the dogs for me. And my friend Lestrade."

"Thank you, and I will. Good-bye, Camilla."

I ended the call and smiled down at my notebook. I wrote:

Camilla's memoir/writing notebook

1. This could be a combination of both biography and writer's advice manual, with tidbits from Camilla's life, but not a chronological life story, since

Camilla is so private. Perhaps each chapter could begin with an anecdote, but then it could lead into a different kind of practical writing advice.

I heard a door slam downstairs, and the prancing of excited dogs. Sam's voice, promising them dinner. I closed my notebook and went to the door; Lestrade was just strolling in. "Time for a nap, buddy?"

As if in response, he jumped up on my bed and began to groom his fluffy tail.

"I'll leave you to it, then," I said. I gave him a quick kiss on the head and a scratch behind the ears, then jogged out the door and down the stairs. Sam had just set down bowls of food and was filling up the dogs' water bowl.

"How was your run?"

"Invigorating. How was your writing?"

"Same."

He set the water on the floor, then walked to me and took me in his arms. His hands were very warm, despite his trip outside. "We should think of other invigorating activities."

I laughed, amused but also excited. "This really is your day for double entendre."

My phone buzzed on the counter; I walked over and picked it up to find a text from Belinda. It said, *Look at this!* Attached was an article she had found in our local newspaper with the headline "Local Man Wins Trivia Contest." I clicked on the article, which was about some contest sponsored by a Chicago radio station. People could take the trivia contest online, and the winner had received a book of trivia and a thousand dollars. It wouldn't have been news anywhere else, but in little Blue Lake it was a notable achievement. There was a picture of the winner, and a caption that read, "Blue Lake resident Luis Castellan was the big winner of a Chicago trivia contest sponsored by WTRX radio."

I stared at the photo and texted Belinda: *That's him. The man from book club. Is it Carl's friend?*

She wrote, *Yes! Doug's going to visit the wife today, and then he and Cliff are going to Plasti-Source.*

Good. I'll tell Sam, I texted. I turned to Sam and handed him the phone. "Read this text chain."

Sam bent his head and began to read; I waited until I saw his eyebrows rise. "Luis Castellan," he murmured. "We probably walked past this man more than once. It's a small town."

"You think something bad has happened to him. You talk like he's dead," I said, half-fearful, half-accusing.

Sam handed me my phone, his face concerned. "I do have a bad feeling. The same way that I felt Belinda was fine, I feel this guy is not. I hope I'm wrong."

"I hope so, too. I keep remembering little things about him from that book club meeting. Not everyone likes Dickens, but he really seemed to get the satire and to genuinely enjoy the novel. Some people were complaining that the words were too difficult or the characters were too odd. Luis loved it all."

Sam shrugged. "Doug and Cliff will do what they can." He glanced around the room. "Do we have a dinner plan?"

I laughed and began my preparations for pizza and salad. Moments later I stood at Camilla's sink, washing greens, gazing at the waves undulating on Blue Lake, and remembering the ugly shell of a building that was to become another Plasti-Source. How much plastic did the world need?

Perhaps there was no place on earth that wasn't somehow tainted by industry, but I had believed that Blue Lake was somehow untouchable, an Eden preserved for those who liked a quieter way of life. Now, after Luis's disappearance and the vision of the black monstrosity against the sky, both seemed like bad omens for our beloved town.

— ◆ · 7 · ◆ —

Those dreaded middle chapters! The ones between the exciting beginning and the breathtaking ending? Why, those chapters are the hard work, while the beginning and the ending are the fun.
— From the notebooks of Camilla Graham

IN THE MORNING, tucked into the warmth of my bed with a slightly snoring Sam, I studied the nuanced color of a leaf that the wind had pasted to my window. Autumn was truly the loveliest time, especially in Blue Lake, and I wanted to savor every bright color, every woody aroma, every howl of wind.

I closed my eyes briefly, then turned to look at Sam, who was no longer sleeping, but studying me through sleepy blue eyes. "Good morning," I said.

"Mmm. How do you already look so alert? You have that Lena London perpetual freshness about you."

"I wake up with ideas. That's invigorating."

"Yes, I suppose." He pulled me closer and I wiggled in protest.

"Ugh, Sam, I haven't brushed my teeth."

"Just a quick kiss," he said. I complied, enjoying a

moment of closeness with a warm and affectionate boyfriend.

Alerted by our voices, Camilla's dogs had bounded up the stairs, and now they came bursting into my room.

"Oh shoot. I guess I didn't latch the door all the way," I said, laughing, as two long dog snouts snuffled at the edges of our covers. "They'll want to go out, darn it."

Sam stretched and yawned, then jumped out of bed. "I'll take them out. I need to check on my two little tigers. I'll run these guys, tie them up outside my house for a minute so I can feed the kittens, and then we'll come back for some breakfast."

"You are the best boyfriend ever. I'm going to steal five more minutes of cover time, then take a shower and start on breakfast. Maybe an omelet or something?"

"Sounds good. I guess I'll take a quick army shower myself." He jogged into the bathroom, and moments later I heard the water go on. To Sam, "army shower" meant one that lasted only a couple of minutes, and sure enough, he was out looking clean, refreshed, and fully dressed within about six minutes.

"I don't know how you do that," I said from my lazy vantage point. "But I admire it."

"Okay, we're out of here, guys," he said to the dogs, who stood regarding him with hopeful expressions, their tails wagging. "Lena, we'll catch you in half an hour."

"Love you!" I called after them.

Lestrade appeared, looking casual, and leaped up on the bed. I scratched his ears and he purred at great volume. "You sit over there, bud. I want to check my texts." Lestrade, vaguely indignant, moved to Sam's spot and began to wash his paws.

I grabbed my phone from my bedside table and clicked it on. I had five messages. The first from my father, sending an emoji of a man blowing kisses. I sent a big heart back.

The second was from Adam, informing me that I should expect our packages today and to keep an eye open for the delivery. This brought me great excitement. One of our big surprises for Camilla's birthday was that Adam, Sam, and I had pitched in to buy canvas reproductions of all of her book covers, which we were going to put on easels all along the perimeter of the Wheat Grass dining room. It was going to look wonderful—a tribute to Camilla's accomplishments and a stunning gallery of truly good cover art. "Oh goodie!" I said to Lestrade.

He squinted at me briefly, his back paw stuck out like a pot handle, then returned to his grooming.

The third text was from Belinda. *Carl says that once he and Luis went to a gaming store called Blue Lake Games. Do you want to go there with me and see if anyone knows Luis? Doug and Cliff are going to be busy checking out his family and his workplace.*

Yes, I wrote back. *Having breakfast with Sam and plotting out our day; I'll get back to you.*

Doug had sent the fourth text to a group chat including Sam, Cliff, Belinda, and me. *Elena Castellan is sticking to her story. She and her husband were recently estranged; she doesn't expect him to return because they fought. I asked if he had taken his things with him or if his clothes were still at home. She did not want to answer the question. We'll put that on hold for now; we're heading to Plasti-Source this morning.*

I turned to my cat. "I have faith in Doug. He gets to the

bottom of things." I paused, thinking of Doug and Belinda, playing like children in the leaves outside the cabin. "He truly loves Belinda. I hope she has said it back to him."

Lestrade yawned hugely.

"Fine. Cats don't care about romance. But Lena does."

I scrolled to my final message, from Camilla. *My knightly companion assures me that we'll be home by this evening. You can shower me with all of your notes and ideas over a late dinner, perhaps.*

I can't wait, I typed. *We have a bit of a mystery for you. I already told you that Belinda's brother is searching for his friend. Have you ever heard of Luis Castellan?*

I waited, looking at my phone. After a minute, I read her response: *I think I have. For one thing, there's an Elena Castellan who runs the coffee shop. Not Blue Lake Coffee, but the one called Coffee Dreams, on Violet Street.*

I rarely had reason to go to Violet Street, although I had recently purchased some expensive clothing at Sasha's. Now I tried to picture a coffee shop near that location, and I thought I recalled seeing one near a florist on the corner of Violet and Braidwood.

Thanks, Camilla! I wrote. *See you tonight.*

I put my phone on the table and jogged to the bathroom for my own "army shower." I was clean, dressed, and waiting for Sam when he and the dogs came tumbling back into the kitchen.

"Change of plans," I said. "We're having breakfast at Coffee Dreams on Violet Street."

"That's very specific," said Sam, amused. "Is there a reason we are going there?"

"Camilla says it's run by Elena Castellan."

"Ah. We are planning to spy?"

I shrugged. "I guess so. The illusion of action, at least. That way we can tell Belinda that we did something to help Carl."

"I'm kind of glad you didn't make breakfast. All of a sudden I have no appetite," Sam said, and in the same instant, I noticed how pale his skin looked.

I moved forward to put my palm on his forehead. "Sam! You're burning up! Let me find Camilla's thermometer."

I darted to a kitchen drawer and retrieved the little glass tube, then rushed back to slip it under Sam's tongue. "Do you have any other symptoms? Did you feel strange last night? Are you low on energy?" I asked.

With an ironic expression, Sam pointed at the thermometer in his mouth.

"Well, you can answer in a minute," I said.

Moments later, we determined that Sam had a temperature of one hundred and three.

"Oh my gosh! That's terrible. You're going back to bed. Climb up there now and I'll bring you some ibuprofen and water. We need to keep you hydrated."

He shivered suddenly. "Oh man. Now I'm cold. I swear, I felt fine when I woke up. This just hit me out of nowhere."

"Go up and get under the covers. I'll be right there."

Sam trudged up the stairs; from the back, one might have thought he was an old man.

I found a bottle of Advil, filled a glass with water from Camilla's tap (Blue Lake water, the best in the world, Doug always said), and ran upstairs. Sam had put an extra afghan on the bed and now lay shivering under three blankets. I helped him sit up so that he could take the pills. "Thanks," he said, and flopped back down on the pillow.

I tucked the covers around him. "I'll stay right here," I said.

He shook his head. "No, I think I'm going to sleep for a couple of hours. You go ahead to the coffee shop. Let me know what happens."

"Sam, I can't leave you here alone!" I did like the idea of going to the drugstore to get some medicine, though.

He gestured sideways with his head. "Just leave my phone on the table there. If I need anything I'll call or text."

"Well—all right. I want to go to Sullivan's Drugs and see if they have anything for fever. But if you need anything, I'll race right home."

He nodded, his eyes closed. "It's fine. You'd just pace around down there waiting for me to be better."

That was true. I leaned forward to kiss his forehead. "I'm so sorry that you feel bad. You got a flu shot, didn't you?"

"Yeah. Let's hope this is one of those twenty-four-hour things."

"Yes. All right, you go to sleep, and I'll be right back."

I tucked him in again and he managed a smile. When I reached the doorway and turned back, he had already burrowed more deeply into the covers, curled into himself in an instinctive bid for warmth.

I fed the dogs their breakfast and then ran to my car. I dialed Allison's cell and her bright voice answered. "Hey, Lena!" I could see her in my mind's eye, her pink hospital scrubs, her blond ponytail, her clip-on ID that said, "Emergency Department, Allison Branch, RN."

"Allie, Sam is sick."

"Oh, poor guy. Does he have a cold?"

"No—a really high fever! Is there something going around?"

"There's *always* something going around. But there is a virus right now that people are getting. Fever is the main symptom, but also weariness, achy joints, exhaustion."

"How long does it last?"

"He might be down for two or three days. Maybe less. It all depends on his constitution."

"I'm just worried it might be something else. Something terrible."

"Take a deep breath, kiddo."

"Allie, are you on your way to work?"

"Yeah, I'm in my car."

"Do you think you could check on him tonight? Just see if it looks like that virus you were talking about?"

"Of course I can. As soon as my shift ends. Meanwhile, keep him hydrated and just let him rest. It's what his body needs."

"I hate it. I've never seen him sick."

"He'll be okay, Lena. He's a strong, healthy man who just caught a bug."

"I know, I just—I feel anxious."

"He'll be fine. Go take a walk by the lake and then come back to a nice cup of tea."

"Yeah, I'm running out for medicine and some coffee. I'll fill you in tonight about something else that's going on. It has to do with Belinda's brother."

I heard traffic sounds and a horn honking. "Darn Blue Lake drivers," Allison murmured. "Okay, that's intriguing. We should talk about Camilla's party, too. I need that list of music Camilla likes."

"Oh right; I started writing one when I was upstairs. I can finish it while I keep an eye on Sam. I'll have it tonight."

"Good, see you then. Lena? Don't worry."

I PURCHASED A variety of medicines, not sure what Sam would need, and an amused pharmacist suggested that I might start my own infirmary. I managed a smile and turned to find a gray-haired man with a pleasant face and a basket full of camping supplies, including a kerosene lamp, a gallon of kerosene, some plastic dishware, and a couple of bungee cords. The pharmacy, like every other store in Blue Lake, had unexpected wares, and Sullivan's had a whole camping aisle. I pointed to the man's basket. "Ready to escape?" I joked.

He grinned. "At least for a couple of days. Before it gets too cold to camp."

"It got too cold for me about three weeks ago, but I'm not much of an outdoorsman," I said.

"Don't knock it till you've tried it," he said. "A good night in the elements brings clarity. Helps you make life decisions." His eyes grew sad when he said that.

"I get the same effect from eating a pint of ice cream in a dim room," I joked, and his face lit up again.

"I'll have to try it," he said. "But not this trip."

I waved and walked toward the door; the pharmacist said, "That's a lot of kerosene for one camping trip," in a jovial tone, and the gray-haired man said something that I couldn't hear; then they both laughed.

I returned to the bracing air outside and went to my car. I was only a block from Coffee Dreams; it would be silly to drive that short distance. I stowed Sam's medicine under the driver's seat (Doug had assured me that people stole bags from cars on a regular basis, especially if they believed pills were inside those bags) and walked down the leaf-strewn sidewalk to the shop that Camilla said was managed by Luis Castellan's wife.

I wasn't sure exactly what I thought I would accomplish, but the moment I entered the small, attractive space, fragrant with coffee beans and cooked food, I knew that I would at least be dining there. Under the windows was a long, low bookshelf that said, "Take a book, bring some back next time you visit!" I bent down to study some titles and spied two Camilla Graham novels on the shelf. I picked up *For the Love of Jane* and sat down in a corner where I had a view of Violet Street and of the entire restaurant. A young woman appeared at my table; she was tall and thin with an abundance of blond hair worn in a messy bun on top of her head. This casually chic touch went with the trendy feeling of the restaurant itself, which had that same careless-yet-stylish feel to it.

She leaned toward me with a practiced smile. "Hi, I'm Jada. What can I get for you today? We have a flavor of the week called Blue Lake French Roast Blend. It's delicious."

"That sounds great. I'll have a cup of that." I consulted the little menu that I had barely had time to read and added, "And a cheddar and tomato omelet."

"With toast or potatoes?"

"Toast, please."

She pointed at the novel. "That's a great book! You gonna read it?"

"I already have. Many times."

She leaned in. "I'll tell you a secret. That author lives here in town."

Normally I would just tell her that I was Camilla's assistant, but today I was lying low. "Really?"

"Yeah. She's like the one celebrity of Blue Lake. She's been here for years. That book is great! So exciting. It's about this guy who disappears—oh wait! You said you read it."

"Yes. But I might reread it. As you said, it's great."

"You got it. I'll take your menu, and I'll be right back with that coffee, hon," she said. She strolled away, checking in on a couple of other tables before she reached the entrance. I glanced at my phone; no texts from Sam or anyone. A *Blue Lake Banner* lay on the table next to mine; I picked it up and glanced at the headlines, which told me of a shake-up on the school board and of protesters at a town council meeting. The name "Plasti-Source" jumped out at me, and I read the whole article, entitled "Blue Lake Locals Protest New Factory at Council Meeting."

More than fifty Blue Lake residents spoke out at a town council meeting with concerns about a plastics plant to be built on Route 14. Plasti-Source, a relatively new company with locations in four states, has been ordered to halt construction while the council investigates claims that the company does not follow EPA regulations in its waste disposal practices. Edward Grange, company president, assured residents that the company met "a rigorous environmental checklist" and that locals should not be concerned. Philip Enderby, the vice president of Plasti-Source, passed out pamphlets explaining their quality control and the careful process they used in disposing of any potentially harmful chemicals combined with polymers to create their trademarked plastic products.

Grange agreed that they did occasionally use toxic chemicals in the production of their unique plastic products. "But many plants throughout the world use toxic substances," he said. "It is merely a matter of remaining responsible and adhering to federal guidelines."

Enderby and Grange remained on hand after the council had adjourned, speaking personally to concerned residents. Randolph Brett, a thirty-year Blue Lake resident, said that his fears had been assuaged by Grange and Enderby. "They said that this plant will meet all safety procedures, that it will be open to public tours, and that they will be happy to address citizen concerns at any time."

The Blue Lake Plasti-Source plant is expected to resume construction in early November.

I set the paper aside, wondering if Doug and Cliff had been at that meeting. The doorbell jangled; a young man in a dark jacket entered wearing a hopeful expression. He spoke to Jada in a low voice and she called, "Elena? Your interview is here."

I sat up straighter at the name but made sure to keep my eyes down when Elena Castellan came from the back room and introduced herself, shaking the young man's hand. "Let's sit at a table and talk," she told him. "You can fill out the form there."

They chose a booth two tables away from me, but there was no one in between us, so I could hear relatively well. I had looked up while they were settling into their seats to determine that Elena was young—perhaps late twenties or early thirties—and that she had shoulder-length dark hair and large dark eyes. She wasn't thin, like Jada, but curvy and attractive. She wore a wedding and engagement ring on her left hand.

At first Elena asked job-related questions. When are you available to work? Do you have another part-time job? Do you have any experience in the restaurant industry? Are you a coffee lover?

Then, apparently while he was filling out his application, she spoke more generally, telling him that the store had opened in 2015 and that she was the second owner. That they had some competition in Blue Lake, but they also had a loyal clientele. "Our coffee is the best," she said. "Word spreads. We're doing better than ever before, which is why we need more help."

She cleared her throat; Jada came by to pour them both some coffee. She waited while he took a sip. "What do you think, Kevin?" Elena asked.

Kevin knew his role. "It's amazing," he said. "Worth the price."

Elena laughed. "I happen to agree. Okay, I'll take that form when you're finished. Do you need some more time?"

"I'm just about done." Kevin scrawled something on the page. I picked up my phone and began to scroll through Instagram, trying to look busy. Jada had brought my coffee, and I sipped it with an absorbed expression. I was starting to think that my visit had been pointless, and I was itching to return to Sam, but then Kevin spoke again.

"I happen to know your husband," he said, in the tone of one trying to ingratiate.

Her tone was cool. "Oh?"

"Yeah. I guess he and my brother went to college together. They lived in the same dorm and everything. You'll have to ask him if he remembers David Spellman."

"Isn't that something? What a small world. I will certainly ask him that."

"Dave says he'd love to get together with him, talk about old times. I can give you his cell number to pass on."

"Sure, sure." She seemed to be hesitating—determining her next move? "My husband and I aren't actually cohabitating right now," she finally said. "Some disagreements."

This was a blow to Kevin, who clearly thought he had this job in the bag. "Oh wow. I'm sorry to hear that."

I glanced up as she lifted her shoulders in a dismissive shrug. "What can you do? These things happen. Especially when your husband cheats on you with someone from his work."

"Oh man," Kevin said, clearly regretting his choice of conversational topics. "I can't believe Luis would do that. Kevin always said he was such a straight arrow of a guy."

Elena's sadness sounded forced. "I always thought so. That's why I married him. Anyway, water under the bridge." She paused. "Thanks for coming in, Kevin. I'll give you a call this week after I do a couple other interviews."

Kevin seemed to deflate. This wasn't a good sign. "Yeah, great. Thanks, Elena."

She stood up and went to the back with her sheaf of papers. Jada brought my food, and I tore into it, suddenly ravenous.

Ten minutes later I was finished eating; I left a tip for Jada on my table and paid my bill at the register with Elena herself. "Everything okay?" she asked.

I was retrieving my credit card from my wallet; I looked up to find her dark eyes studying me. "Everything was delicious. I couldn't help but overhear that you might be hiring? I have a friend who's looking."

Her eyes had a flat look. "Oh? Well, have them come in, fill out an application."

"Thanks! I'll pass that on to them."

"What's the name? I'll be listening for it."

I paused only a fraction of a second, then said, "Kurt Saylor." My ex-boyfriend, safely in the past and out of Blue Lake, seemed a safe choice.

"I'll be on the lookout for Kurt." She didn't smile, but she gave a sort of nod. "Be sure to return to Coffee Dreams. Have a good day." She paused for a moment, then added, "Miss London."

Of course. My name was on my credit card.

"Thank you," I told her. She smiled then, but only with her mouth. Her coffee-colored eyes retained a lackluster and watchful quality, and I was sure they were still gazing at me as I turned and walked toward the door.

I CALLED DOUG from my car.

"Doug Heller."

"I just had breakfast at Coffee Dreams. Elena Castellan runs the place."

"Okay. And?"

"I'm not sure what I thought I'd find. On the one hand, she just seemed like a regular person. She was interviewing someone, and I sat there eavesdropping for nebulous reasons."

"Just naturally nosy, pretty much," Doug joked.

"I guess. She did tell him that her husband didn't live with her because he cheated on her with a woman from his work. From Plasti-Source, I guess."

"That's not what she told me this morning," Doug said. "She said they had a fight."

"Huh. I mean, I guess she could have been embarrassed to say it to you. She did say they had been fighting, right? But why would she say it to a total stranger, then? He said his brother was college friend of her husband and he wanted to get together with him. Maybe she felt obligated to say that she couldn't arrange that. We need to ask Carl if this matches what he knows."

"Hmm. Interesting."

"I will say—" I hesitated. It was hard to put my finger on what bothered me about Elena Castellan.

"Yeah? I've been waiting for your 'on the other hand.'"

"She gave me a weird vibe. I felt uncomfortable. She's hiding something."

"Okay. Your instincts tend to be good. I'll find a way to visit her again, ask some more questions."

"Hey, there was a newspaper in there. Did you know about some town council meeting about Plasti-Source?"

Doug cleared his throat. "Yeah. Rusty was there." Rusty was the police chief.

"They said some people were concerned about them getting toxins into the environment. I don't know what form that would take. Would they dump it into the soil? Into the lake?" Either possibility was upsetting.

Some static buzzed on the line, so Doug's voice was harder to hear when he said, "I don't know. I'll try to find out."

"Okay. Anyway, I just thought I'd mention the whole Elena thing. Maybe Luis isn't who Carl thought he was."

"Maybe, maybe not. Thanks, Lena. I hear you and Belinda are doing some sleuthing later. Is Sam joining you?"

"No—he's suddenly sick. He has a terrible fever. I'm going to check on him now and bring him a tiny pharmacy."

Doug paused. "That's weird. He was fine yesterday."

"I know. But these viruses appear when they appear, right?"

"Tell him I said to get well soon."

"I will. Thanks. Let us know if you find Luis."

Even as I said it I felt a sense of doom. The pendulum Sam had spoken of in the car, that Blue Lake pendulum that perpetually swung between sadness and celebration, loss and gain, had swung back to the negative side. Life felt oddly disjointed without Camilla in town, Sam was inexplicably sick, and poor Luis had disappeared from his own life.

Uncertain of my emotions, I started the car and made my way back to Green Glass Highway, where I would be able to glimpse the lake, a sight that always managed to restore my equanimity.

8

She wondered, years after the event at Debenham, if she could have avoided her fate simply by taking an earlier train.

—From *Danger at Debenham Station,*
a work in progress

SAM WAS ASLEEP when I got back, but now his fever was making him feel hot; he had flung off all of his covers and his face was flushed. I rushed to the bathroom and dampened a cloth with cool water, then came back to Sam and placed the cloth on his head. He opened his eyes and said, "Yuck. I'm boiling."

"Keep this on; I want to bring this fever down. Let me take these socks off, too." I went to the foot of the bed and began tugging at his running shoes and sport socks.

"Find anything good at the coffee place?" he asked, his eyes closed.

"Not really. I brought you some medicine."

"I'll take it later," he murmured. He was falling back asleep.

"Do you need anything?"

"Geronimo," he murmured. "Arabella."

"You want me to feed them?"

"Bring them over. They're lonely."

Those sweet words made me want to yank him into a sitting position and hug him tightly. Instead, I sat beside him and stroked his hair. "Okay, I'll get them. Let me freshen your water." I took his glass and walked to the bathroom, where I refilled it from the tap. I returned to Sam and said, "Drink a little bit. Allison says I need to keep you hydrated."

I pulled on his arms until he was sitting upright, then held the glass while he drank a few sips of water. He fell back on the pillow and closed his eyes. "Thanks," he said.

"Keep those covers off. When you wake up, I'll take your temperature again and give you some more pills. Okay? Just rest for now."

"Hmm." He was already halfway out.

"I love you," I murmured.

Sam snored slightly.

I backed out of the room and went down the stairs, where I found the dogs waiting. I let them into the backyard and prepared an early lunch for them, then texted Belinda. *Sam is sick, but I guess I can sneak out for an hour or so. Come pick me up at around two.*

She sent back a thumbs-up emoji, and I set down the phone. I put the dogs' food on the floor and let them back in; they bounded to their bowls with puppyish enthusiasm but proceeded to eat with a delicacy that always surprised me.

I scanned the room for Lestrade, who was in one of his favorite spots, the kitchen windowsill, from which he would keep track of all manner of birds, insects, and sunbeams. He turned to give me a bored but affectionate glance.

I pointed at him. "Listen, you're going to be a little bit mad at me, but I have to bring some other felines in the house. I think Sam is going to stay here until he's better, and he misses his little guys. So you're going to be locked out of the blue bedroom for a while, and they'll be locked in, and they shouldn't affect your routine at all. Okay?"

He twitched a whisker at me and then turned back to his view.

I nodded, grabbed the keys, and went out the front door, locking it behind me. I marched down Camilla's pebbled driveway and turned left onto the bluff road, walking downward until I got to the next driveway—the one belonging to Sam West's house. I walked up to his door, flooded by memories of the various times I had stood in front of his house, for reasons good and bad.

On the porch I picked up a couple of packages on his stoop, then unlocked the door and went in. Two playful kittens, one orange and one black-and-white, came tumbling down the hallway. They weren't tiny anymore, but they were still young and adorable. I moved swiftly into Sam's kitchen and set the packages on his island. I went back to the door to retrieve his mail from the box, and I brought that to his island, too. He could sort it when he felt better. Then I turned to the cats, who had followed me to the kitchen, then to the door, and back to the kitchen.

I bent down to scoop them up and kiss their fuzzy ears. "I missed you, too. Sam's not the only one who loves little Geronimo and AB." They purred loudly, and I laughed. "Let's get you a little taste of food, and while you're crunching I'll grab your litter box and your travel case."

The cats seemed amenable to this plan, and ten minutes later they were stowed in one kitty travel bag (they both fit inside, which allowed them to nestle together). I picked up their little litter pan in one hand and the bag in the other, went outside, set down my burdens, locked Sam's door, picked them up again, and started toward Graham House. "Whew. Just two little kitties, and look at all the arrangements we have to make!" I said to them, peering through the mesh in the bag. They seemed less afraid than curious, and they looked out with wide eyes.

At Graham House, I went once again through the process of setting down, unlocking, and picking up, and then we marched up the stairs to my room, where Sam was still asleep. I set down the kitten bag, stowed the litter pan in a corner by the window, and shut the door of the room before Lestrade could barge in. Then I opened the bag and let the kittens wander out, which they did almost immediately, driven by their curiosity. They found the windowsill first and stared out at the leaves of the tree just beyond the glass, and at the rippling waves on the lake. Arabella jumped down on the floor, padded around for a bit, and then leaped on the bed, where she discovered Sam. She strolled up to his head and sniffed his hair, then tucked against his side and closed her eyes. "Good, Arabella. You help me watch him," I said.

Geronimo looked out the window for a while longer, then joined Arabella on the bed. He always had to one-up his sister, so he sat directly on Sam's stomach, curling into a ball and looking like a little golden cinnamon roll. I laughed but scooted him off. "I'm trying to cool him off, not put a furry little cat body on him," I said. "Just guard him, the way your sister is doing."

Geronimo glared at me with leonine disdain; he relocated to a spot between Sam's feet and curled up once again.

I paused for a moment, enjoying the sight of Sam with his beloved kittens, both of whom he had rescued from hunger and homelessness. He didn't like to be away from them for very long, a fact that added another layer to my deepening love for him.

Sam was still asleep, and the cloth I had placed on his head before visiting his house had now lost its coolness. I removed the washrag and felt his forehead. A bit better, but still feverish. I went to the bathroom, rinsed the rag and made it cold again, then brought it back and put it once again on his heated skin; I ran my cool, damp hands through his hair.

The doorbell rang; I left the room, carefully shutting the door behind me, and ran to the front door. I could see a delivery truck through the window, and I realized this meant that Camilla's covers had arrived. I opened the door and greeted the woman in khaki garb. "Sign here," she said.

I did, feeling excited, and the woman helped me bring in the various boxes, which we set in the living room. I knew they would make Camilla curious, but they were too big to hide, and I figured Adam could come up with some kind of story for her.

I thanked the woman, who moved swiftly back to her truck and drove away. I closed and locked the door, then jogged back up to Sam, who was in the same position, sleeping, still guarded by his little cats.

For about twenty minutes, I sat beside him, worrying over his weakened state. His biggest ally, I knew, was sleep, and that was something he could give to himself. I stood up, restless, and arranged the items on the bedside table so that everything was within his reach: phone, water, notepad, pen. On the pad I had written, "I'm meeting briefly with Belinda. Text me if you need anything! Back soon."

I backed out of the room, making sure once again that the cats stayed in place and Lestrade did not come in. The latter was actually nowhere to be seen; I was surprised he hadn't sniffed out the new occupants of his room by now.

By the time I got downstairs, I had received a text from Belinda: *I'm out front.*

⚜ · 9 · ⚜

In the car, Celia studied the back of her aunt's head
and realized that her hair was naturally blond.
And in that instant a snatch of dialogue came back
to her, years old, in which her mother had told her
how, as a girl, she had envied her sister's black
hair, dark as a raven's wing . . . for the first time,
Celia's stomach clenched with fear.
— From *Danger at Debenham Station,*
a work in progress

IN THE CAR, I felt relief on many levels. First, because I
had been with Sam and felt so connected to his illness, I
had begun to feel almost feverish myself, and the brisk
fall air felt good against my skin. Second, because Belinda's car, so ominous-looking the day before in her
driveway, now reclaimed its positive connotations, especially with Belinda's smiling face behind the wheel.
Third, without Camilla in the house I had been longing
for someone to talk to—someone who wasn't Sam but
who would be willing to listen to my blissful ramblings
about Sam. Belinda was willing to do this as long as I
gave equal time to her ruminations about Doug.

I studied Belinda's profile as she pulled out of the

driveway. "Thanks for picking me up. I am going stir-crazy without Camilla."

"How's Sam?"

"Feverish and sleeping. I think he's going to need a few days to get over this, but I am very impatient for him to be well. I'm not good with illness; I don't know how Allison does it."

"We all have our strengths," Belinda said with a wise expression.

I laughed. "You crack me up. How's the research coming?"

She frowned, thoughtful now, and left the bluff road, turning left on Wentworth Street. "Plasti-Source has been investigated more than once by the EPA. I haven't yet found all of the complaints or rulings, but in at least two cases, one in Michigan and one in Ohio, they had to make alterations to their plant procedures before they were allowed to open for production again. I also found something about a lawsuit, but it seems that some sort of settlement was reached and the results were sealed. Since the Blue Lake building has been stalled, I'm wondering if they're currently being investigated, or maybe sued again. I'll ask Doug what he found out when he went to the Stafford plant today. Carl said that the plant makes some noxious fumes when they're in production mode. But I don't know if that just means it smells bad, or if he thinks it's truly detrimental to the health of employees, or maybe the whole community. The company has locations throughout the Midwest, but they haven't been around that long. They opened their first plant in 2011."

"Hmm. I can't tell you how sad I am to think they're

opening that big ugly thing here. I hope Doug finds some terrible violation and the mayor persuades them to move to some other place."

"Yes." Belinda looked thoughtful. "Anyway, Carl is back in Stafford and back on his meds." She darted a look at me. "I'm sorry again about the whole thing."

I reached out to touch her shoulder. "It was nice meeting him. Really. He's adorable."

She beamed at me. "He's always been my little boy. I mothered him, I guess because there were five years between us. And he's the youngest, so you know how that goes."

"Not really. I'm the oldest and the youngest. And the middle, if that's possible."

She laughed. "A family unto yourself."

"It seems fitting that Sam and I would get together; we're like the two orphans of Blue Lake."

"Except you have a perfectly fine dad."

"True. He is wonderful. Hey, I think that's it on the left," I said, pointing at an awning on the corner of Wentworth and Bookman Drive. The lettering said, "Blue Lake Games—Come In and Play!"

"Right. I'll park here, but we'll have to cross the street," Belinda said, tucking into a space in front of a home goods store, to which she pointed. "And I might need to go in there and buy a pasta strainer."

"Hey, before we go into the game store, there's something you should know," I said. I told her about my visit to Elena's coffee shop, and what Elena had said.

Belinda's blonde eyebrows rose high. "I'm going to call Carl about that. See if it matches what she told him."

"Good. A part of me thinks this is all some big misunderstanding and we'll feel like we were doing this for nothing. Then another part of me feels like there's something . . . insidious at work."

"Ooh, that is writer language."

"Yeah, I guess. But let's scope out the situation in Blue Lake Games; then we can see if there's anything else to ask Carl."

Belinda parked the car and paid the meter, and we crossed the street together to enter Blue Lake Games. There were fewer than ten people in the place, but it still felt crowded, with bodies, machines, and large cardboard advertisements for games yet to come. One of these cut-outs was called "Blood World," and the letters of the title were written in a dark, dripping red.

"Yuck," I said.

A young man approached us. Everyone in the store was a young man except for a middle-aged woman who was murmuring something to the manager about a game her son wanted for his birthday. The person who stood before us was probably about twenty; he had longish brown hair and the ambition of a mustache, which sported about twelve hairs. "Can I help you ladies find something?"

Belinda shrugged. "We're just kind of looking around. I want to get a game for my brother, but I'm not sure where to start. He's been in here before; his name is Carl."

"Carl Frailey?" asked the man. "Sure, I know him. He comes in with Luis."

"Yes, that's them. Is Luis around? He can probably tell me what Carl would like."

The man shook his head. "Naw, I haven't seen Luis for a few days. Which is weird, because he reserved a game to buy on the day it came out. *Blood World*—see the sign? It came out yesterday, and I thought for sure Luis would be here first thing after work. He must have had something with his job or his family or something." He scratched his jaw and shrugged.

Belinda glanced at me, then said, "That's too bad. Does Carl like any games in particular? Or has he had his eye on one?"

"Come back here," he said. He led us to the back wall, where a sign said, "New Releases." All sorts of video game covers demonstrated various exciting scenarios: knights in battle, wizards making magic, lions fighting men in a coliseum, athletes playing basketball, cowboys riding a dusty trail with guns held over their laps. "Carl usually shops here. I know for sure he's got some of these already, or Luis does. They kind of share each other's games so it's less expensive."

"Sure, sure," Belinda said.

I shook my head. "I can't believe Luis wouldn't have come in for that game. That's not like him."

The young man turned to me. "You know Luis?"

"We're in a book club together."

Now he scratched his arm. I wondered if he scratched parts of himself when he felt uncomfortable, just for something to do. "Yeah, it's surprising. He's a regular in here. Although he was kind of weird the last time we saw him."

The hair on my arms stood up slightly. Something wasn't right . . .

Another person had joined us. This guy was a bit older—perhaps in his late twenties, so around my age or a little older. He had disheveled blond hair and a goatee. His Blue Lake Games polo had come untucked from his khaki trousers. "You guys talking about Luis?"

"Yes, Luis Castellan. He and my brother Carl come in here a lot, I'm told," Belinda said.

"Oh yeah, we know Luis and Carl." He stuck out his hand. "I'm Alan. I'm the manager here."

"Nice to meet you, Alan," I said, shaking his hand. Belinda did the same.

A burst of noise behind us made me jump. Some players were looking at a demo of *Blood World* and shouting with excitement at some detail of the game.

"This is a great place," Belinda said, pretending to scan the game covers. Or perhaps she was really scanning them, if she wanted a gift for Carl.

"Yeah, we're doing pretty well," Alan said. "We've been here seven years."

"This gentleman," I said, gesturing to the younger man, "was telling us that Luis was sort of strange last time he was here." I peered at the boy's name tag and added, "Perry was telling us, I mean."

Alan nodded, exchanging a glance with Perry. "Yeah, he was kind of odd that night. What I would call restless."

"Isn't he usually restless? Especially surrounded by video games?" Belinda asked.

Perry shook his head. "No, Luis is super laid-back. Like really Zen. But last—what was it? Thursday?—he came in after work and was kind of pacing around like a tiger in a cage."

"Did he say why?" I asked, picking up a game called *Gemma's Odyssey* and staring at the beautiful cartoon woman on the cover.

Alan straightened some boxes on a nearby table. They seemed to be plastic toy figures of popular video game characters. "He didn't say why. He was being all weird and mysterious. I think—oh yeah, he asked Perry if he had ever felt disillusioned."

"Yeah. I had to look up that word later," Perry admitted with a grin. "Luis said he was disillusioned."

Alan laughed. "Yeah, he said that, but then suddenly he was talking classic rock with me. Asked me if I knew Uriah Heep. I said yeah, man, one of the best bands to come out of London in the sixties. Then we got to talking about Pink Floyd, the Clash, Queen. Or I guess I brought them up. Once I get started on British rock, man, I can talk all night."

"So he was talking about disillusionment and music?" I asked. I noted that Belinda was gripping a video box cover but staring at us with wide eyes.

Alan shrugged. "Yeah, I guess so. He was even mumbling about how he needed to quit his job. At the time, I just figured he was tired, you know. Everyone's busy at work these days, and then they come in tired at night. That's why we stay open until nine, so people can come after work."

Belinda held up two boxes. "Which of these would Carl like better?"

Perry and Alan laughed. Belinda blinked at them, not getting the joke. Finally, Perry took pity on her. "He hates those Space Origins games. He thinks they're a total rip-off, which they are, man. He does like *Captain of the Storm*, though." He pointed to a second box, which sported a cover with a bold-looking warrior standing at a ship's wheel in a thunderstorm; one of his giant hands was on the wheel, and the other held a magic wand, sparking out green stars.

She nodded. "Does he have this one?"

Perry shook his head. "I don't think so. He's only bought a couple in the last few months, and they were both in the Vicious Viking series."

"Okay. I'll take it. His birthday is next month; don't let him buy his own copy," she said with a sudden smile that clearly dazzled both men.

"No problem," Alan said. "I can ring you up at the front." She followed him to the cash register, and I was left standing with Perry, who was still looking at Belinda.

"I didn't know Carl had a sister," he said in a wistful tone.

"She's spoken for," I said, feeling mischievous.

Perry turned red. "Oh, I mean—I just didn't know— but I guess she's dating someone, huh? She would have been a good person for Alan to ask out. He just broke up with his girlfriend."

"She's dating Doug Heller," I said. I loved dropping Doug's name because he was a bit of a celebrity in Blue Lake since he had arrested Nikon Lazos.

Sure enough, Perry brightened. "That cop? The one that was on TV? Wow, that's really cool."

I sighed. "I wish you guys knew where I could reach Luis. I wanted to ask him something about book club."

"Well—like—isn't he at home?" Perry asked.

"No. He hasn't been there for days."

"That's weird. I know Carl said once he has a cabin somewhere. Maybe Luis—"

I shook my head. "We were at the cabin yesterday. He wasn't there."

"Wow, so he's kind of—missing?" Perry looked concerned about this, but he was also distracted by a group of gamers who had formed around a demo of *Blood World*; he looked like he wanted to join them.

"I don't know. But thanks for the information. If we see him, we'll tell him you've got his game."

"Cool. Nice to meet you," Perry said, and then he drifted toward the gamers, leaning in to see what they found so alluring on the demo screen.

Belinda met me at the counter, holding a blue bag. Alan was waiting on someone else; he held up a hand in a wave and said, "Come back soon."

We went out into the cold air; the day had gone gray, and the streetlights were coming on. "Nothing super specific," I said. "But more negative vibes."

Belinda nodded. "That 'tiger in a cage' thing gave me the chills. What in the world was going on with him? And how does it affect Carl?" Her tone was worried.

"It probably doesn't affect Carl at all, especially if Luis was just bummed out about a fight he had with his wife. She said he cheated; that would be enough, right?"

"Except if you're the cheater, *you're* not the one who's disillusioned, are you?"

"No." I felt disillusioned, too, on the gray street, faced with a missing man, a worried Carl, an absent Camilla, a sick Sam. "I have to get back. Sam will be looking for me. Let's run and get your pasta strainer and hurry to Graham House."

Belinda tucked her arm in mine, sensing my anxiety. "He'll be better soon." We waited for a lull in traffic and strolled across the road. "I love the fact that Camilla's house has a name. And now Sam's does, too, right?"

"Well, we jokingly call it Sam House."

"Yeah. I want my house to have a name. Allison's is Branch House. What would mine be?"

"Book House?"

"Hmm. Sounds nice, but that's more a name for the library."

I thought of Belinda's home, full of light and books and pretty things. "How about Warm House? Or Sanctuary House?"

We reached her car, and she gave me a spontaneous hug. "Warm House. I love it. Thanks, Lena. I'm going to put that on my next party invitation."

Belinda ran into the store to get her strainer, and I got into her car to check my texts. Nothing from Sam, which meant he was probably sleeping. One picture from Camilla, of some beautiful autumn scenery out the car window, taken past Adam's noble profile as he sat at the wheel. He was smiling and looking at Camilla out of the corner of his eye. *The captain*, she had written.

I smiled and clicked out. No other texts waiting. This should have been a good thing, but it made me feel nervous. Belinda came out with another bag, and she stowed both of her purchases in the backseat before climbing in beside me. Then she turned to me. "I asked the girl at the counter if they supply to any shops around here. She said sure, lots of the restaurants and shops buy from them. I asked about coffee shops, and she said both proprietors run in now and then for filters or place mats or things like that."

"Okay."

"I guess that's just interesting because it means Luis and Elena are both well-known in this town. It's not like they can be anonymous and have some private fight. People know and recognize them both."

She started the motor and pulled into traffic, and I thought about what she'd said. It was true—when Carl first mentioned Luis, I had thought of him as an anonymous man. But more and more he was taking shape as a vibrant Blue Lake resident, a life that blended in with all our lives. "I have to think about that some more," I said.

When we got to Graham House, Belinda pulled up in front of the porch, but she was looking away, toward the rutted bluff road we had just left. "That was weird."

"What?" I followed her gaze but saw nothing aside from the colorful, rustling trees.

"There was this black car behind us. I was joking around in my head that it looked like every car that has ever followed someone in the movies. But it did stay behind us, all the way down Wentworth Street, and even onto the bluff road. And then I turned, and it kept going."

"Up *there*?" I said, pointing at the area beyond Camilla's house. "I guess they could be going to the overlook. So few people go there, though, and there's really no parking to speak of, just that sort of turnaround."

As I said it, a dark car passed Camilla's driveway and drove down the bluff. Belinda looked at me. "Should we be paranoid?"

Something twisted in my stomach. "We need to take note of it, for sure. Keep an eye out for dark cars. Black, I'm pretty sure. Maybe dark blue."

She sighed. "I like solving mysteries of research. It's not quite as fun when we're out in the world with unanswered questions."

"Do you want to come in?" I asked.

She shook her blond head. "It's my day off, and I have chores to do. *Warm House* is kind of a *hot mess* right now," she joked.

"Well, go work on that. I'll talk to you soon."

"Take care of Sam. Text me about his condition."

"I will, thanks. You'll fill in Doug, right?"

"Yeah, right now."

I blew her a kiss and climbed out of the car. She drove down the pebbled drive, and I climbed the steps and unlocked Camilla's door. The boxes still sat in the living room, waiting for Adam and me to open them. The dogs swarmed me seconds later, and I let them into the backyard for some frolicking time.

I tidied up the kitchen, let the dogs back in, and went to check on Sam. He was still asleep. I felt his forehead; still hot.

He rustled a bit in bed, and I sat on the edge of his mattress. "How are you?" I said softly.

"I've been better," he croaked. "Can I have some water?"

I grabbed the cup and helped Sam drink a substantial amount of water. I pulled out some of the pills I had bought him and persuaded him to take those, too. "Allison's going to make a house call and check you out with her nurse expertise."

"Good. So many pretty girls feeling my forehead."

"But only one is going to kiss you," I said, leaning in to kiss his cheek.

He smiled wanly. "Only one girl I *want* to kiss me," he said, his eyes closed.

Geronimo climbed up Sam's body and sniffed his chin. Sam smiled. "You brought them. Thanks."

"They were glad to see you." I looked around for Arabella, who was no longer on the bed. I didn't see her anywhere, and I was starting to panic, but I peeked into the bathroom, where a giant heat vent was placed at floor level. Sam had tossed a sweatshirt in the corner, and Arabella lay curled on this, directly in front of the flow of warm air. "Smart girl," I murmured.

I went back into my room. "I brought the thermometer," I told Sam. "Let me take your temperature."

He submitted with a shrug, and I slid the glass tube under his tongue, brushing his hair back from his face, then leaving my cold hand on his warm forehead. When I finally checked his temperature, I was troubled to see that it was still high—102.5.

"You still have a fever."

"Yeah. It's knocking me out."

"Do you want some more water?"

"Just a sip. Then I'll sleep some more."

I helped him drink some water and then tucked his covers loosely around him—he would probably fling them off soon anyway. "I'll be just downstairs if you need me. I'll prop your phone on the headboard here, see? So you won't even have to reach for it if you need me."

"Okay." I got as far as the door, and he said, "Lena."

"Yes?"

"I love you."

Something bloomed inside me, quietly. "I love you, too."

I ducked out of the room; this time I found Lestrade in the hall, looking very curious. He tried to dart past me into the room, but I scooped him up. "Not just now, my friend. Sam doesn't need to hear squalling cats while he's trying to get better. Let's go see what the dogs are doing, hmm?"

Lestrade, always adaptable, began purring in my arms, and when we reached the main floor, I went into Camilla's office, where I was able to persuade him to curl up in my purple chair for an autumn nap.

I returned to the front hall and looked out the window. No sign of a dark car now, but the day had turned gray and twilight was near. It would be hard to see things lurking in the dark . . .

My mind swarmed with anxious thoughts. What if someone *had* followed us? What was their intention? Did someone, somehow, know that we were looking into the disappearance of Luis Castellan? A new thought came to mind unbidden: had someone, somehow, poisoned Sam? He had become sick so suddenly . . .

I shook my head and clapped my hands together once. I would not be going down the road of paranoia. Thanks to some prescription medicine, I had spent the latter part of the summer viewing the behaviors of others with suspicion, but also second-guessing myself.

I knew that my worries were probably ridiculous, but they also would have grown worse if Allison had not pulled up in the driveway and emerged like a ray of sunshine. I flew out the door and down the steps to meet her, and she gave me a hug. "How's the patient?" she asked.

We started walking up the steps. "He's mostly been sleeping. Is it weird that this just came out of nowhere? He woke up fine, and half an hour later he had a fever."

"He didn't wake up fine, he just looked fine. If he has a virus, that infection started before the fever did."

"What do you mean *if* he has a virus? What else could

it be?" I opened the door and ushered her in, and she put her hands on my shoulders.

"First things first. Let's take a peek at Sam. Is he in your room?"

"Yes."

She moved to the stairs and started marching upward. "Why don't you get some tea or something? You can meet me up here in a few."

"Okay." I went to the kitchen, filled the kettle with water, and put it on the stove to boil. Outside in the dimness Blue Lake was beginning to twinkle with reflected light. The dogs milled up to me and snuffled against my legs, so I gave them their dinner. Lestrade had not yet left the purple chair, so I jumped when another creature wandered into the kitchen. It was Geronimo, Sam's orange kitten, taking careful steps and peering around with wide eyes.

"Oh shoot, Allison let you out," I said to him. The kettle wasn't yet whistling, so I scooped him up and ran upstairs, scanning for Arabella as I went. I needn't have worried. In my room Allison sat on the edge of Sam's bed and Arabella sat on his chest. He petted his little cat absently while he spoke to Allison. I had never seen him look so groggy and disheveled.

I set Geronimo on the bed. "We have to keep these guys locked in here with Sam for the time being."

Allison nodded. "Sorry about that. He darted out before I could shut the door."

"He's an explorer," Sam croaked.

I moved forward to feel Sam's forehead, which was still hot. I frowned and turned to Allison. "Why won't this fever break?"

She shrugged. "It can take two or three days sometimes. Right now he's at one-oh-two and a half, and he said it peaked at one-oh-three, true?"

I nodded.

"If it goes above that at any point, I want you to bring him to the ER. Otherwise, everything looks okay. You're strong, Sam, and you don't have any other symptoms that would suggest this is something other than a virus. Lena is a worrier and always has been, but I think you'll be fine. Just keep drinking that water and getting tons of rest. Your body won't let you do anything else."

Sam nodded, rubbing Arabella's supersoft ears.

Allison put a comforting hand on one of his covered feet. "You've been through a lot in the last year and kept up your defenses. Your body is probably relaxing into a less guarded state, and that's how this virus wormed its way in there."

"Great," he said. Arabella leaned into his hand, trying to get the maximum massage, and we all laughed.

"Would you like some tea?" I asked. "Are you hot or cold right now?"

"Getting the chills again, so tea would be nice," Sam said.

Allison stood up. "I'll help Lena get it together, and then I have to run. John is barbecuing tonight. Take care, Sam. I'll come again tomorrow night to see how things are going."

Sam thanked her and waved as we left the room carefully, keeping our eyes on the kittens to make sure they stayed on the bed.

When we reached the kitchen, Allison said, "I can see that you're on anxiety overdrive. Take care of yourself, or you won't be able to help Sam."

"Okay."

"Do some deep breathing," she insisted, looking into my eyes with her big blue ones.

"I'm fine. I think I'm just on edge because of this Luis Castellan thing."

"What's that?" she asked.

I filled her in while I made Sam's tea, starting with the missing Belinda and ending with our visit to the game store.

She shook her head in disbelief. "Is it this *house*? Is it because Camilla has written suspense novels for forty years? Because it is *relentless*, the intrigue and the—just—craziness of the connections . . ."

"I don't know. Sam said there's a pendulum effect in Blue Lake. From extreme conflict to extreme happiness, back and forth."

"Maybe." She nodded. "Maybe that's just life. I see terrible things every day, so I don't know why I'm surprised that we experience them as well. Hopefully this will have a happy ending, right? This Luis could be okay."

"Yeah." For some reason I pictured Carl—his thin body and the vulnerability of his eyes. "I hope so."

She gave me a quick hug and patted my cheek. "I've got to fly. John's cooking, but we have a guest coming—do you know Jane Varney?"

"I think you've mentioned her."

"She's the real estate agent trying to sell Nikon Lazos's house. Trying and failing, of course. She thought people would be drawn to the weird factor, but I guess ultimately they don't want to live in the house of a criminal."

My insides turned cold at the mention of Nikon Lazos, the man who had hidden in plain sight and done any number of terrible things to Sam, Victoria, me, and even his own daughter. "Good—I wouldn't expect anyone to want to live there. I can't even look at it when I come to visit you."

She sniffed her agreement. "Anyway, poor Jane has been out there doing so many open houses that we have gotten to know her pretty well."

"Friendships formed by crime," I joked.

She laughed and kissed my cheek. "I'm just a phone call away. Let Sam rest, and his body will fight its inner battle. Okay? Meanwhile I think you should have some chocolate."

I laughed. "Yeah, that might be a good idea."

I walked her to the door and waved as she drove away. I returned to the kitchen and put Sam's tea on a tray with a few mild biscuits and a banana. I moved carefully up the stairs and brought it to his bedside table. Arabella and Geronimo were asleep now, huddled together near Sam's elbow.

Sam was almost asleep, too, but I persuaded him to take a few sips of tea.

"Thanks," he said, and then, "I'm cold."

I tucked his covers around him and he murmured his thanks.

He was out before I left the room.

10

My marriage was an inspiration to me, from beginning to end.
　　　　　—From the notebooks of Camilla Graham

ALLISON HAD CORRECTLY identified me as "a worrier," but I had reached a state of calm an hour later. Ultimately, Luis Castellan's disappearance had nothing to do with me. Doug Heller was on it, which meant that Cliff Blake was on it, too, and I could back away. Belinda would update me, whatever happened. Carl would be all right, because his sister was just a quick drive away.

I drank my own cup of tea and did the deep breathing that Allison had advised. When Rochester started growling, I thought at first that he was just in an argument with his brother; moments later Heathcliff growled, too, and both dogs moved swiftly out of the room, heading toward the front window, where they planted their paws on the sill and stared into the darkness, their hackles raised. The growling grew more menacing; their teeth shone white in the dark room.

"What's going on, guys?" I asked, walking up behind them and peering out.

No sign of Adam and Camilla, and Sam was sick upstairs. What had I done with my phone?

I leaned forward, my hand on Rochester's back. Normally I would have seen nothing, but the dogs' hyperalertness had me peering hard into the dark driveway. Was that movement I saw near the back of my car?

A sudden burst of light, and headlights appeared on the dark driveway. A car pulled up next to mine, and I kept my slightly shaking hand on Rochester's back until Adam had turned on the car's interior light so that Camilla could gather her things from the front seat. They were talking, smiling in the pale light, a little planet of companionship in the darkness.

I rushed to the front door and flung it open, and the dogs flowed out, bounding to greet the travelers. I followed, almost bounding myself, meeting Camilla at her open door. "Welcome back! Can I help you carry anything?"

She stood into my embrace and made a chuckling sound in my ear. I was probably squeezing her too tightly, but I realized just before she let go that she had been holding me tightly, too. "I'm so glad you're back," I said. "I know it's only been a couple of days, but—"

"She missed you, too, Lena," Adam said in a wry tone, coming around the car to give me a hug. "And, yes, you can help. I'll get the bags if you'll grab that little cooler there."

"Of course!" I picked it up and started for the porch at Camilla's side. The dogs were making joyful circles around her, and she paused to pat their big heads and say soothing things to them.

"Yes, yes, Rochester, I see that bone you're carrying. It's splendid. Yes, Heathcliff, he is a show-off, isn't he?"

We climbed the porch and went inside; Camilla looked around and said, "What are all these boxes?"

"Oh, that's just something Adam and I ordered." Adam stood in the doorway, holding suitcases, and I pointed at the boxes containing Camilla's book covers. He looked pleased, and he winked at me.

Camilla wore a droll expression. "I won't ask, then."

I patted her arm. "Have you had dinner?"

"Oh yes, Adam has kept me well fed for our entire journey. I'm sure I've gained five pounds."

"Well, you look gorgeous." She did: her hair, soft and slightly windblown, framed her fine-boned face, bright now with the cold, and her aura was relaxed, rested, happy.

"Thank you, dear." She studied me for a moment with an affectionate expression, then said, "I wonder if we should have some tea? You are clearly bursting to tell me things."

"I am, yes."

"Come in the kitchen, then. Oh, Adam, you don't have to march those up right away! Just leave them by the stairs. Come have tea with Lena and me."

Adam, with a shrewd glance at us, said, "I've been sitting too long. I think I'll take the boys for a quick walk." In seconds, he had found the leashes and clipped them onto the dogs' collars.

I said, "Adam—the dogs were growling just before you arrived. I had halfway convinced myself that I saw someone prowling around out there. Maybe you shouldn't go."

My words had the opposite effect of what I intended. Adam looked almost eager to go now. "We didn't see anyone when we pulled in. But all three of us will be vigilant." His eyes were bright with the idea of a challenge. "You ladies do your catching up, and I'll be back for the cookies."

We waved, and he was gone.

I turned back to Camilla. "I love him," I said.

"I'm glad."

"He's so brave. I still think of it all the time, Camilla—the way he confronted a murderer and rescued me."

She nodded. "With his *gun*. I've tried to talk him out of keeping it, although I realize it was perhaps—necessary in that situation. And I know you and I have faced down malevolent people with weapons in the past year, and that's why Adam wants to have it around. I can't quite decide how I feel about it. What with this violent world."

"I see the dilemma." I patted her arm. "We have plenty of time to talk it through."

"Yes." She took off her coat, hung it on a rack near the door, and sighed contentedly.

"Let me boil the water. I just did this an hour ago for Sam. You should know he's upstairs in my bed, sick with a fever."

"Oh, poor boy!"

"Yes. I asked Allison to come and inspect him, and she says I shouldn't worry, that it's just a virus. But with everything else, I've been nervous."

"I think I'll go say hello. Just check on him," she said. I followed her up the stairs and into my room. She saw the kittens first; they sat curled together on the windowsill, probably looking at nocturnal creatures. She whispered, "We have visitors!"

The room was dim, for I had left on only one corner

lamp. Camilla strode to the bed and felt Sam's forehead. "Hmm," she said.

Sam rustled and looked up at her. "Welcome back," he murmured. Then he closed his eyes again.

"Sam? Do you need water? Or something to eat?" I asked.

He shook his head. "Just sleep is fine."

Camilla murmured, "He's hot, still feverish, but not alarmingly so. Let him sleep, and with luck it will break by morning."

She stroked his hair with a doting expression, then walked toward the door. I straightened Sam's covers and followed her. In the hall she said, "How nice that his kittens are with him. He would worry about them in his house all alone."

"Yes. I'm not sure how Lestrade will feel about being turned out."

Camilla giggled. "We'll give him lots of attention. Where is he, anyway?"

"I think he might be in your office. He's been lurking there."

"Ah." We had reached the bottom of the stairs, and by unspoken consent we went into the kitchen and sat down at the table. She smiled at me and said, "Home again."

"Yes, thank goodness."

Camilla stretched out her jean-clad legs. "Now. Earlier you said that with 'everything else' you've been nervous. So now I need to hear about the 'everything else.' Of course, I know about this boy Carl who absconded with Belinda. He is, you tell me, her unpredictable yet sweet-natured brother."

"Yes. Carl is worried—so worried he forgot to take

his medication, which made him erratic. Because of the friend who has disappeared."

"The Castellan man?"

"Yes. And I did visit his wife's shop, after you mentioned her."

"Ah?" Her eyes glittered a bit. "And how did that go?"

I told her about my clandestine excursion, and about Elena's claim that Luis had cheated on her. About Elena's dead-looking eyes. About my visit, with Belinda, to the game shop, where we heard Luis had been "disillusioned" about something at work. About our stop at the Plasti-Source site on the way home from Michigan, and about Belinda's research regarding their possible lawsuits. About Carl's face when he talked about his friend, and about the strangeness of people not acknowledging that a man was missing. Then, because I told her everything, I mentioned the dark car that had followed us (perhaps) up the rutted bluff road.

"That's why I felt so nervous when the dogs growled," I said.

"Hmm," she said.

I got up to make the tea, and when I sat back down she said, "This all comes down to one thing for me, Lena. The boy, his friend, the wife, the car, the new plant in Blue Lake. It's all Plasti-Source. That's the reason Carl and Luis met. It's the thing that links Blue Lake to Stafford. It's the thing, apparently, that had Luis agitated before he disappeared and stopped communicating with Carl."

"That makes sense. You always seem to—" I paused, arrested by something glittering on her left hand. "Camilla."

I lifted her hand and studied the diamond ring. "Oh

my gosh, this explains it all! Why Adam sounded so happy on the phone, and why you and he look so peaceful and mellow. You got engaged!"

Camilla shook her head at me; I was still clutching her wrist. "We didn't get engaged, my dear girl."

For some reason this disappointed me. "Oh."

"We got married," Camilla said.

I opened my mouth, but nothing came out. I stood up, then sat back down again.

A huge smile bloomed on her face, and I felt an answering smile on my own. "Married?"

"Yes. We certainly didn't want to take attention away from your impending nuptials with Sam, but we did think it was time. So we drove out to Hanover and had an engagement dinner, then had a simple little wedding this morning, and then we celebrated all day long. It was quiet and perfect."

"Oh, Camilla! But—you didn't want anyone to—be a witness, or—?"

"They had someone there, at the chapel. It was the loveliest church, Lena. Perched on a bluff, surrounded by trees. They took pictures for us; I'll share them with you."

"Camilla. I knew you loved Adam, but you never actually said those words out loud, and—"

"How lucky am I, really, to have loved two such wonderful men in one lifetime? Each one kind, and good, and dedicated to my happiness. Yes, I love him, and I've married him. So now we'll have to weave him into our Graham House life."

"Of course! He was already there. It's just a matter of changing his title," I said. "You'll probably want me to move out—"

"I want no such thing. Adam knows that you and I are rather joined at the hip these days, and he understands."

"So does Sam."

"Good."

I pulled her out of her chair and gave her a hearty hug. "Congratulations! You are a beautiful bride."

"Thank you, dear."

"We have to have a party! A huge, giant—"

She put a hand on my arm. "That's why we did things quietly, Lena. To avoid fuss."

I sighed. "Well—can I at least call some people? Maybe arrange a little gathering of friends?"

"Of course. That sounds best."

"I'm going to call Doug first because he goes back the furthest with you, doesn't he? Your first Blue Lake son."

Camilla looked surprised, then pleased. "Yes, I suppose so!"

I grabbed my phone from the counter and pressed a button.

"Doug Heller."

"Doug! I have some amazing—"

Doug sounded harried. "Lena, I can't talk right now, but listen. I just got off the phone with Blueville PD and then with Belinda, so I should probably tell you, too."

"What?" My face and hands were suddenly numb.

"They found Luis Castellan's car in a ditch off Route 47. He wasn't inside, but there was blood. It doesn't look good."

11

*They reached a dark, shadowy structure and
pulled into an unwelcoming driveway. The woman
who was not her aunt turned to smile at her, and
Celia realized, in one nightmarish epiphany, that
she was a prisoner.*

—From *Danger at Debenham Station,*
a work in progress

CAMILLA WAS QUIET after I gave her this news. Adam,
who had encountered no intruders and had finished un-
packing the car, joined us in time to hear about poor Luis.

"I'll root around and make us a snack," he said. "Food
is comfort."

I was going to protest, since we were removed from
the circle of potential grievers, but the reality was that
Camilla and I *were* both sad, not only because a young
man might have been killed, but also because it would
hurt Belinda's brother to know it, and by association that
would hurt Belinda.

Adam rustled around behind us, looking through Camilla's fridge, and she tapped her fingers together. I was
on the verge of asking her what was wrong, but then she
looked up at me with her brilliant violet eyes.

"Uriah Heep," she said.

"What?"

"That's the clue. Uriah Heep. He said that to the young men at the game store, yes?"

"Yes. The guy said they were talking about classic rock, and—"

"Were they? If there is a band named Uriah Heep, then that band takes its name from the Dickens character from *David Copperfield*. And Luis Castellan loved the classics. Isn't that what you said? That your library book group read and discussed the classics."

"Yes."

"Did your group read *Copperfield*?"

"No, we read *Great Expectations*. But he said something, I think, about how he had read all of the Dickens novels."

"All right." She sat up in her chair. "So let's review some things about Uriah. He is a horrible toady, a slimy sycophant."

"Yes. And a corrupt embezzler."

We locked eyes. I folded and unfolded my hands, thinking. "Luis came straight from work to the game store, said he was disillusioned, and asked if anyone knew of Uriah Heep."

Camilla took up my line of thought. "The clerk at the store misunderstood and took the conversation in another direction. Luis accepted this but was distracted and, what did you say? 'Pacing like a tiger.'"

A chill ran through me. "He found something out at Plasti-Source. And they killed him for it."

Adam set little sandwiches and potato chips down in

front of us, then pulled out a third chair. "I know you two have amazing instincts, but I wouldn't rush right into an accusation of murder in the absence of a body."

I smiled, slightly embarrassed. "You'll keep us grounded, Adam. And this tiny sandwich looks amazing. I should have thought to have made something for *you*."

"I like making things, and I really did need to stretch my legs," he said. "It was a long ride, but it seemed to fly by since I was seated beside my bride."

His face, as he pulled off a piece of his sandwich, held love and devotion. I leaped up and moved behind his chair so that I could hug him around the neck. "I haven't said congratulations to you, dear Adam. I'm so happy for you both."

"Thank you, Lena. Oh my goodness," he said, as I planted sloppy kisses on his cheek.

Camilla laughed. "Perhaps Lena is initiating you into our club."

Adam shook his head. "I don't meet the criteria for membership. But I can be your mascot. And sometime chef."

"Lovely," Camilla said. She reached toward him, and he clasped her hand in his. A small gesture, but an intimate one. I felt like a voyeur, but I couldn't look away. They were beautiful.

The spell was broken a moment later, and Adam took a bite of his sandwich with a placid expression. Camilla picked up a potato chip and studied it. "Here is my question, though. If someone at work wanted Luis out of the way, it would explain why they made up the whole 'Luis is unreliable, we don't expect him back,' story. But why would his *wife* say the same thing?"

We ruminated about this while we ate. Adam's sandwiches were delicious despite the minimal ingredients he had found in our refrigerator. Finally, I said, "Let's consider the possibilities. One—that Luis really was an unreliable husband, that he really had cheated on his wife, as she told the man in the coffee shop, and therefore she was telling the police the truth."

Camilla nodded.

"Two, Luis is a good husband, but they had a fight about something else and she told him not to come back. Which would mean she was still sort of telling the truth."

Adam said, "But if the police came to your door, no matter how upset you were with your husband, wouldn't you want to work with them to find him? Maybe offer up some places that he could be?"

"Yes, that's the part I can't get over," I said. "So then there's three. For reasons unknown, Luis's wife knows that he is in danger, even that he might be dead. She tells the police that he's terrible and probably won't return because he's a bad husband, because—why? She's hoping they won't investigate? She's hoping they'll take her word for it that he simply ran off but is fine?"

Camilla, finished eating, pushed her plate away and leaned back in her chair. "How would she know he was in danger? Unless she put him there? Maybe we're barking up the wrong tree. Maybe he wasn't 'disillusioned' about work. Maybe it was about his wife. Maybe he went home that night, got into a fight with her, and she killed him."

Adam held up a finger. "Doug didn't mention a body, did he?"

Camilla and I viewed him with slight disapproval. He was putting a wrench into our theories.

I pointed my finger at his finger. "Let's say that, *hypothetically*, Luis has been murdered. But Doug said they found his car off Route 47, and I assume they'll find it's his blood inside. That means Luis was in the car, and alive when he was shot or stabbed, right? Doug said it didn't look good. He implied it looked like a crime scene."

"Oh dear," Camilla said.

"And if Elena had killed him in their house, she would have blood evidence to deal with. If it was a bloodless murder—let's say she poisoned him or hit him over the head—then his blood couldn't be in the car. Plus, how would she transfer the body? She's not a big woman."

"Good questions," Adam said.

Camilla tapped the table with a fingernail. "On the other hand, Elena could have talked him into a drive, had him pull over for one thing or another, and killed him or shot him to take the suspicion off her. To make it look like a random assault, perhaps."

"I'm sure Doug can tell whether he was shot in the car or put there later. We can ask him."

"Except that it's not Doug's case. It would be a case for the Blueville PD," Camilla said.

I pondered this. "But Luis is from Blue Lake. Surely they'll work together, right? To find Luis or his—body?"

Adam said, "Hopefully Luis himself. There's always the possibility that someone tried to attack him, but it went wrong, and he ran away."

"For Carl's sake, I hope there are possibilities other than murder," I said.

There was a moment of quiet, a peaceful lull, during which Adam cleared our plates and rustled around at the sink. I looked over to see him gazing out at Blue Lake through Camilla's kitchen window. I had stared dreamily at the same view many times. I wondered what was going through his mind; he had loved Camilla for more than forty years, and now he was married to her. Judging by the look on his face, it must have felt as though a star had fallen from the heavens into his hands.

My gaze moved furtively to Camilla, and I saw that she was watching him, too.

I was about to leave, to give them their privacy and check on Sam, when the doorbell rang. I looked at my watch; it was eight o'clock.

"I'll get it," I said, darting down the main hall to the front door. I opened it to find Belinda and Carl, the latter of whom looked particularly distressed. "Hi," I said, uncertain. "Carl, I'm so sorry about your friend."

"Oh—you know?" Belinda said.

"I called Doug to tell him something and he said he couldn't talk because—he was busy. And that he had told you."

"Is this a bad time?" Belinda asked, looking past me. "I told Carl we should come tomorrow, but—"

"We had to come now," Carl said. He looked sad, but not agitated as he had at the cabin. His eyes were calm when they met mine, but they glinted with determination. "I have to talk to her."

I heard Camilla coming down the hall behind me. Carl looked at her and said, "Are you Camilla Graham? The mystery writer?"

Belinda looked chagrined. "Camilla, I'm so sorry to burst in on you like this."

Camilla came forward and held out her hand. "You must be Carl Frailey. Lena told me she met you yesterday."

Carl shook her hand and nodded, his face grave. "Yes. She said she knew you, and I realized tonight that you were the person I had to talk to. The police didn't do anything to help Luis, and now it might be too late." Carl's chin jutted out in a fierce attempt to cover his grief. "I need someone smart to figure out what happened. I need you to solve the mystery, like you do in your books, before the killer gets away."

Belinda, her blond hair slightly tousled, looked at her brother with concern. She touched his shoulder. "Carl, you know that Doug is doing his best."

He shook his head; the vulnerable, boy-like look was back on his face. "I need someone who knows about mysteries. Not just cases."

Camilla held out her hand. "Carl, would you like some tea? Why don't you come into the kitchen back here, and we'll talk about Luis? I'm so very sorry to hear about your friend. And what a good friend you are to him, to seek justice with such passion on his behalf. I'm sure he would be grateful."

Carl took her proffered hand; he seemed to be grasping it tightly. "Thank you," he said. His eyes were wet, but he maintained a dignified demeanor as he followed her into the kitchen.

I held Belinda back. "Is he okay?"

She nodded. "He took the news hard, but he was calm. He's just so determined! He wouldn't let up about me bringing him out here, and I finally gave in. I hope Camilla doesn't mind. I know she probably just got back." Her green eyes were worried.

"She did. But she wanted to meet Carl anyway, and I think she admires him for being so devoted to Luis. It will be fine." I put an affectionate arm around her, then patted her hair back in place. "Listen, there's something you should know. It's why I was calling Doug in the first place, because he and Camilla go way back."

Her eyes widened. "Is something wrong? Is she all right?"

"She's great. She and Adam got married on their trip. A super-private wedding, just them, in a church on a bluff in the woods."

Belinda beamed. "Married!"

"I still can't totally believe it, I never had a clue. Never heard either of them making arrangements or saw them exchanging secret glances or leaving documents lying around. But I guess I've been distracted with my own wedding plans . . ."

"This is wonderful," Belinda said. "They're perfect together. Oh, this is such good news! What did Doug say?"

"I didn't tell him yet. He was—I think he had just heard about Luis's car. So my news—Camilla's news, really—had to go on the back burner."

"Yes, well. Hopefully you or Camilla can tell him soon. I'll keep quiet about it."

"We can tell him together. I haven't told Sam yet, either, because he's in no shape to hear anything."

"Still feverish?" she asked as I led her toward the kitchen.

"Yes. I'm hoping he'll be better tomorrow."

"I'm sure he will be," Belinda offered, ever loyal.

We reached the kitchen and sat down at the table. Adam and Camilla were ministering to Carl, who sat across from us like a dispirited scarecrow. Camilla set a cup of tea in front of him, and Adam had retrieved the tin of cookies and set some on one of Camilla's serving plates.

Carl thanked them politely, and Camilla sat down across from him. "Tell me what you think I should know," she said in a soothing voice. She looked perfect, just as she looked on the jackets of her books: authoritative, gray-haired and wise, intelligent, curious, and somehow forgiving.

Carl leaned toward her as a plant does to light.

12

When in doubt, write in a stranger.
—From the notebooks of Camilla Graham

"First of all, he never would have left home," Carl said. "That's just not true."

"Did Belinda tell you what his wife said in the coffee shop?" I asked.

Belinda, who had sat down next to Carl, shook her head. "No, I didn't see Carl until later, and then we got distracted with some—family things."

Carl turned his thoughtful green eyes on me. "What did she say?"

"That her husband had been kicked out for cheating on her."

"No." Carl didn't even bother to get upset. "That's not true. The last time I saw him, he was going on about what a good wife she was. He bought her some kind of little bracelet."

A little bracelet. He had asked me about mine, the one Sam had designed with such love . . . "A charm bracelet?" I said.

"Yeah. With tiny figures and stuff on it. He was excited to give it to her. And it wasn't a guilty cheating gift. He just liked to bring her things."

"So if Elena lied, there are a few possibilities," I said. "She could have just been lying to save face. If Luis walked out on her and she didn't want to admit that, for example. Then she might say she threw him out, or she might manufacture the cheating story."

Carl shook his head. "He didn't walk out on her."

Camilla said, "Then there must be some other reason why Elena lied. Why she was so certain that he wouldn't come home."

We sat there, contemplating the dark possibilities. Carl took a bite of his cookie, rather absently, then said, "Almond extract. But also cinnamon, and cloves. And nutmeg."

Adam, leaning against the counter, grew alert. He said, "That's spot on! You have a discerning palate."

Belinda said, "Carl is a chef. He is so, so talented with food and making food."

"Is that right?" Adam was ever the businessman, and he dearly loved his restaurant, Wheat Grass. "I happen to be looking for a new sous chef. My Andre can't function well without a couple of them, and one has just given us her two weeks' notice." He looked at Carl. "Do you have restaurant experience?"

Carl looked surprised, and Belinda said, "Carl, Mr. Rayburn is the owner of Wheat Grass."

Carl's eyes grew huge. "Wheat Grass? That's one of my favorite restaurants! My mom would always take me there on my birthday!" He looked at his sister, then at Adam. "I can't believe I'm meeting two famous people!"

Adam grinned. "Hardly famous, but thanks for the compliment. So—do you have experience?"

Carl shrugged. "I worked at a place in California for a while, but it was just a diner. I got good reviews, though. I can show you. And I cooked for my mom and dad."

"I see." Adam's enthusiasm waned slightly.

Carl sat up. "I can make something for you now. To show you what I can do."

Adam looked at Camilla; clearly he wanted to see Carl at work. She waved her hand. "Go ahead, dear. We don't have much on hand, but make use of whatever you can find. We can talk while you work."

"If it works out, I would love to work for you and tell Plasti-Source where they can go," Carl said, standing up and moving to Camilla's refrigerator.

Camilla and I exchanged a glance. "We'll want you to stay at Plasti-Source for at least a little longer," she said. "To get some information. Our man on the inside."

"Like in the movies," Carl said, digging around now in the mixing bowls under her sink.

"Yes, I suppose."

In moments, Carl had assembled an array of bowls, some milk, cream, eggs, various cheeses and spices, and some bacon. "I'll make a quiche," he said. "Is that okay?"

"Fine." Adam's reticence was rapidly being replaced by fascination. As I had seen in the cabin, Carl's various gestures in a kitchen were compelling, like a food ballet. He had already passed into a zone that made him seemingly oblivious to the rest of us. He moved back and forth, pouring, measuring, whipping, all with deft, sure movements. His work had a machinelike regularity, but his natural grace saved him from looking robotic.

Adam moved back to the table, pulling a chair up next to Camilla's, and murmured, "What have we here?"

Belinda leaned in and whispered, "I think cooking is good therapy for him. He's so upset, but he finds it really soothing to make things."

By the time Carl had poured his quiche into two pie pans and eased them into the oven, Adam whispered, "I *must* have him. Andre will be beside himself with joy. He told me he longs for a protégé, and I think I just found him." Carl was still busy, this time with cleaning up. He was singing softly to himself; I thought I recognized the tune.

"Is that song—a million years old?" I asked.

"Not a million," Camilla said, her brows furrowed in a faux frown.

"Really," Adam agreed, also feigning disapproval. "It's called a torch song. And the one Carl is crooning is one of my favorites. It's called 'I'll Be Seeing You.'"

"Oh yes. So romantic," Camilla added, touching Adam's hand.

I stared at her. "What have you done with Camilla?"

She sniffed. "You have read my books, haven't you, Lena? I'm a romantic at heart." She smiled at me, then turned to Belinda. "Why does young Carl like the music of a bygone era?"

Belinda had found a stray napkin and was folding it into an accordion shape. "My parents had a CD with all the great ones. Carl's been listening to them since he was a baby. It's his favorite music."

Carl seemed to be finished tidying; he stopped singing and turned to us with a mildly surprised expression.

"Did that take long? It didn't feel that long."

It had been about half an hour, but Adam said, "No, it was perfect. You are adept in the kitchen."

"I learned a lot from the cooking shows," Carl said. "I'm self-taught, but I've read a lot of books."

"Come back and sit with us while your quiche bakes," Camilla said. "Lena and Belinda have to tell you about their visit to the game store. Or did you already tell him?" Camilla asked Belinda.

Belinda shook her head. "No, I haven't yet. Carl, we talked to the two guys at Blue Lake Games. What were their names, Lena?"

"Uh—Perry and Adam. No, Perry and Alan."

"Yeah, I know those guys," Carl said.

Belinda looked at me, so I took up the story. "They said Luis came in after work a few nights ago. I'm guessing it was the night he—disappeared."

Carl's lips thinned. We feared we knew what had happened to Luis that night.

"Anyway, they said that Luis had been agitated and 'disillusioned,' and he mentioned Uriah Heep—"

"Who?" asked Carl.

"He's a character from a Dickens novel called *David Copperfield*. There's also a British band named that, and Alan thought Luis was talking about the band. But Camilla thinks he was referencing Heep in the novel. He pretended to be humble and good while secretly stealing from his employer."

"What?" Carl sat up straight.

Camilla said, "I know it will be hard to go to work knowing about Luis. But I'm assuming they'll be told tomorrow, and I would love for you to tell us whatever reactions you note. See what you can see. That's all."

Carl nodded. Belinda was studying his face with a concerned expression. His green eyes did seem to have hardened and aged in the few minutes of conversation.

Adam said, "My Lord, something smells good."

"You're right," I said. "Carl, can we taste these when they're finished?"

"Of course," he said, looking slightly distracted. "I made them for you. It's Mrs. Graham's food."

I darted a look at Adam, whose cheeks reddened ever so slightly. Camilla said, "I do go by the name Mrs. Graham, in honor of my past, but I am also Mrs. Adam Rayburn."

Belinda got up and rushed around the table to give Camilla a hug. "Oh, congratulations, Camilla. And you, too, Adam. You two are perfect together. I hope you'll be very happy."

"We are," they said in unison, and they laughed as they gazed at each other.

I said, "Camilla—in terms of your novels—I mean, going forward—"

Adam held up a hand. "Camilla the writer will always be Camilla Graham. She's mostly Camilla Rayburn on paper. That's fine with me. She's wearing my ring, and that's all I really need."

"You talk like a lovesick boy," Camilla joked.

"I have felt like one for the past several years," Adam said. Camilla kissed him on the cheek, and he looked pleased as a cat on a heat vent.

Carl got up to check on his quiche, then sat back down. "Ten more minutes," he said.

It was disappointing, the thought of waiting for the delectable quiches, but soon enough he had taken them out and put them on the counter to cool. Adam had opened a window above the sink about an hour earlier to let in some fresh fall air. Now it almost felt like sensory overload to smell the buttery, bacony quiche along with the scent of the trees and someone's distant wood-burning fireplace, and to see the glimmer of starlight in the darkness outside the window as a contrast to our unlikely little group of late-night-snack companions, sitting together under the bright kitchen chandelier.

Carl finally cut up his quiche and served it on some of Camilla's good china (he assured her he would wash the dishes).

I divided my attention between my own plate and Adam's face. He poked at the quiche first, checking its consistency, and made a pleased little grunting sound. Then he forked up a sizable bite and put it in his mouth. By then we were all watching him chew, waiting for his verdict.

He swallowed and turned to Carl. "Is this from a recipe? Something you have memorized?"

Carl shrugged. "No. I just like to improvise. I've seen lots of different chefs make stuff, but then I get my own ideas about what to add or subtract."

"It's delicious. Amazing, really. If you want a job at Wheat Grass, you have it."

"Oh man!" Carl jumped out of his seat, spun around, clapped his hands, and sat back down.

Belinda giggled. "Oh, Carl—the perfect job! And you can stay with me at the house!"

Carl looked at her, his green eyes solemn. "I would like to, until I find an apartment. I can save up some money that way."

"Your old room is basically the same; I haven't done much refinishing in there," she said.

"That's good," he said. "Thanks to all of you."

He offered up one of his rare and beautiful smiles. We were all still eating, and I was hoping for a second piece, as I had hoped for more of Carl's caramel apples. Belinda said, "Carl, what was that song you were singing earlier? Adam and Camilla liked it."

In a surprising response, Carl started to sing it for us, in a sweet, clear voice. He crooned about an unnamed person who was no longer there, and how the speaker of the song would see that person everywhere. It was exquisite, heartbreaking. Perhaps we were all thinking of someone we had lost, and by the time his voice tapered off, we all had tears in our eyes, including Carl.

Camilla wiped at her ducts with a tissue. "Oh, sometimes a sad song can be so satisfying, can't it?"

Belinda stiffened beside me, and then she screamed.

I looked up in time to see the face at the open window, white in the darkness and eerily familiar, and I screamed, too.

"A man," Belinda said, pointing.

Adam was up in an instant. "Which way did he go?"

"Toward the east lawn," I said.

Carl leaped up and grabbed a rolling pin. "I'll come with you," he said.

"Good lad," Adam told him, and they raced out of the room. Seconds later, we heard the front door open and close.

Camilla looked at me with her dark purple eyes. "Did you recognize him?"

"I think I did. But I'm not sure. He was only there for a second—"

"Like a nightmare face!" Belinda said, her arms wrapped around herself in a defensive posture.

We sat in tense silence; the breeze from the open window seemed cold now, not invigorating but invasive. I stood, moved swiftly to the sink, and cranked the window shut.

Five minutes later the men were back, their faces bright from the cold. "We saw him running," Carl said. "He got into a dark car and it drove away."

"A dark car," Belinda said, looking at me.

I felt my first inner shiver then.

I studied her face. "A car was waiting. So . . . two people at least. And one waited while the other, what? Was sent to look in our window?"

"Something odd about it all," Camilla said, frowning. "We need to call Doug."

"Taking care of it," said Adam, his phone already out. He marched into the hallway to speak to Doug away from the group.

I turned to Belinda. "Your boyfriend to the rescue," I said. "How many times have we called the Blue Lake police in the past year? I certainly didn't expect that, when I came to this quiet house on the bluff."

Belinda nodded. "Doug needs to know all of this. He's got to have all the puzzle pieces."

"As does Camilla," I said. "They can exchange notes."

Adam's voice drifted down the hall. "Doug! I'm glad I caught you."

Belinda and I smiled at each other. "And speaking of boyfriends," I said. "I'm going to go up and check on mine."

13

Celia wondered if she could count on the man who had danced with her. Hadn't she seen real concern on his face? But he had been a stranger. She felt that somehow, some way, her brother would realize she was in trouble and find a way to help. Somehow, Richard would come for her. As time went by, though, she realized the truth: she would need to save herself.

—From *Danger at Debenham Station,*
a work in progress

SAM HAD ONCE again thrown off his covers. I put my hand on his forehead; it was warm, but perhaps not hot. Hope sparked within me. "Sam?" I whispered. At the sound of my voice, Geronimo and Arabella stirred in the nest they had made near Sam's shoulder.

His eyes opened and focused on me. "Hmm?"

"How do you feel? Would you like some water?"

He took a deep breath and squinted around the room. "What time is it?"

"It's close to ten now, I think."

He sat up a bit and I helped him drink a few sips out of his cup. "I have a little bit of energy," he said. "That's good, right?"

"Very good. Does anything hurt? Allison said there can be body aches with this virus."

"Not too bad, no. Just a crick in my back from sleeping in a weird position. Do I hear voices downstairs?"

"Yes, we have a houseful. Camilla and Adam have returned, and Belinda and Carl showed up."

His brows rose as he took another sip of water. "Why is that?"

I frowned. "A lot has happened. Do you really want to hear all this now?"

He smiled, and I saw that my Sam was at least halfway back to his normal self. "Yes."

"Okay." I sat on the edge of his bed. "First of all, Camilla and Adam got married."

"What?"

I nodded.

"Well, that's great! Adam, you romantic old devil."

"He must be, because he's really bringing out the romantic in Camilla. She's—playful. Young at heart."

"That's great," he repeated. He smoothed his covers. "So get to the bad stuff."

"How do you know there's bad stuff?"

"Your face gives you away."

"Okay." I sighed. "They found Luis's car in a ditch in Blueville. There was blood. It doesn't look good."

"Oh no. How's Carl taking it?"

"He's angry, and he came here to basically beg Camilla to look into it because she's a famous mystery novelist. But then Adam heard Carl is a good cook, and he said that he needs someone at Wheat Grass, so Carl kind of auditioned for the job by making quiche, which is the delightful aroma that has floated up the stairs."

Sam stretched. "Is there any left?"

I studied him. "Do you think you can eat?"

"I don't know, but I do feel hungry."

"Well, that's a good sign."

He nodded, picking up Geronimo and rubbing his fuzzy little head. "Okay, back to the story."

"The quiche was delicious, and—well, you saw how Carl works."

"Adam was impressed?"

"So much so that he gave Carl the job."

"Wow!" Sam set Geronimo down and the kitten returned to his sister and started to bathe her ears with his tongue. "I did miss a lot."

"Then, while we were all feeling a little better and celebrating, a man's face appeared in the kitchen window, and Belinda and I both saw him and screamed."

"I heard that! I thought it was in my dream. I was trying to help you . . ."

"Adam and Carl ran outside and saw the guy get into a dark car. Which is weird because when Belinda and I came back from talking to some people at Blue Lake Games, Belinda saw a dark car behind us. It kept going, up to the overlook."

"That's weird. No one drives up there."

"Exactly. Anyway, Adam called Doug, and he's going to be coming over. We need to tell him all this and more."

"There's more?"

"Just some theories we've been batting around. They can wait."

He sat up. "I want to go to the washroom. Maybe splash some cold water on my face." I helped him get out of bed, and he padded slowly over to the little bathroom in the corner of my room. He shut the door, and I tidied his bed, careful to leave the kittens where they were. They were both purring with their eyes closed.

Sam returned and climbed back into bed. His skin was pale. "I just used up my energy walking across the room," he said with a wan smile.

"A night of sleep will do wonders." I tucked him back in. "I hate seeing you like this. You've never been sick a day."

His blue eyes were solemn. "I was sick, about a year ago. Before you came to town. It was some crazy virus like this. I was living up here on the bluff all alone, hiding away from other human beings, and I felt terrible." He scratched Geronimo's head. "I was sick, and I felt— alone."

"Oh, *Sam*!" I said, lunging forward to hug him. "I'm so sorry." I kissed his cheek, then leaned back to look at him. "You do know you'll never be alone like that again, right?"

We heard feet pounding loudly up the stairs, and Cliff poked his head into the room, verifying my last comment. "Someone told me my little brother was sick."

Sam shrugged; he couldn't help grinning. "Just a virus."

Cliff marched into the room, and as usual he seemed to take up a good deal of space. He looked around and nodded. "I've never been in Lena's chamber before. Very nice. A little writer's retreat, huh?"

"Yes. I've done zero writing in the last few days, though. Just some planning with Camilla. As soon as Sam is better I need to get on the ball."

Cliff edged forward and poked Sam's foot. "Yeah, what's your problem?"

"I don't know. Weak antibodies?"

"Figures. I thought my manly strength was in my genes, but . . ." He shrugged, feigning disappointment.

Sam laughed. "Shut up."

This cheered Cliff. "Well, you don't sound that sick."

"He needs more rest and sleep," I said. "But I think the kittens have done wonders for his morale. How are *your* kittens, Cliff?"

He had adopted two of the cats he and Sam had found—two gray brothers that he'd named Jeeves and Wooster. "They're good. Running my house, walking all over me, literally and figuratively. They're pretty awesome, though. I never had cats before, and we get along really well."

"I suppose Isabelle comes over to check on them now and then?" I asked, unable to resist.

Cliff's eyes darted away from mine. "No, not yet."

"What? Cliff, you did call her after I told you she liked you, didn't you? Back in July?"

He shrugged. "I got busy. And then I didn't see her anywhere and I guess I—chickened out."

Arabella woke up and jumped off Sam's bed in search of her food bowl. Sam sat up slightly and scowled at his brother. "You didn't call her? What's *your* problem?"

Cliff put his hands on his hips. "You."

"She's gorgeous, she likes you, she lives in town. What's to stop you from asking her out?"

"I don't know. It hasn't come up. I can't just go wandering into the vet's office with some fake story about my cats. That would look obvious. And I don't want to call her on the phone like I'm in seventh grade. It has to happen naturally."

"Oh, like reuniting with your brother? That only took you, what, seventeen years? Isabelle will be close to fifty by then, but I'm sure she'll still be attractive," I said.

"You can both lay off," Cliff said. "I came up here to check on Sam, not face the Spanish Inquisition."

"Fine." I pursed my lips. If Cliff wasn't going to arrange a meeting, I would.

He turned to me. "Don't get any ideas, either, London."

"Okay."

He nodded, then pointed backward, toward the stairs. "What's the kid doing here?"

"Carl? He wanted to talk to Camilla. As a professional. He figures she can work some miracle of detection and find out what happened to poor Luis. Carl was really upset when he got here, but luckily Adam distracted him with restaurant talk."

"Why would that distract him?" He blinked at me.

"Oh, because he's a really good cook. It seems innate with him. Adam is excited, and so is Carl. But he's also determined to find out more about Luis. There was a look on his face, when we told him what the guys at the game store said. It made me nervous. Did you hear all about that?"

He nodded again. "Belinda told Doug, and Doug told me."

Sam had settled back against his pillow. "Why are you here, anyway?"

Cliff didn't take offense. "I was driving Doug home when he got Adam's call. And I need to go downstairs and find out what I can about this intruder."

"Don't let Lena go anywhere until you guys catch him, okay?" Sam pointed weakly at me. "She tends to wander into dangerous situations."

I opened my mouth to protest, but I realized he was right.

Cliff darted forward to feel Sam's head, a quick concerned gesture that belied all of his posturing and name-calling. For a moment, their resemblance was very strong: Cliff's dark head bent over Sam's, both of them with one subtle gray stripe in their bangs, both with a noble jaw, square and slightly cleft at the chin. "Not that bad," Cliff said. "I'll check in on you tomorrow, maybe challenge you to some racquetball or something."

Sam grinned, but his eyes were closed.

I kissed his cheek again and said, "Go to sleep. I'll come back in a while."

"Mmm," he said.

"Cliff, I'll walk you down. Don't let the kittens out."

Cliff scooped up Arabella, who had marched with queenly grace to the door and was waiting to depart with us. "No, you don't, pretty girl," he said. "You can sit on this windowsill and scan for bats."

Arabella's eyes widened as she stared out into the darkness. I smiled and followed Cliff out the door.

On the stairs he said, "How long has he been sick?"

"Just today. He woke up okay, but then it hit him like a hammer about half an hour later."

"Huh. He always struck me as too sturdy to get sick. I guess because when I was recovering from my bullet wound he always looked so young and strong and fit by comparison."

"He still does," I joked, and Cliff gave me an approving nod.

"Anyway, I'm on duty tomorrow, but text me with a health update, okay?"

"Sure. I've been watching him pretty obsessively."

We had reached the bottom of the stairs and stood together in Camilla's foyer. He pulled me against him in a half hug. "I'm glad he has you," Cliff said. "You're a good kid."

I looked up at him. "Seriously, though, why haven't you called Isabelle? You knew in July that she liked you, and here it is October already."

"Yeah, I know." He shrugged. "I don't—I'm not good at—getting started. You know? I need some kind of plan, or I'll lose my nerve."

"You don't need nerve. You're a great guy, you're tall and handsome, and wear a uniform, and risked your life to save someone else's. You love your cats and built them a special cat tree from scratch. No pun intended. Do you know how many of those things would be in the average woman's 'dream man' scenario?"

"Uh, *no*. I don't know anything about women, Lena. That's the point. I've gotten pretty good at being alone. Besides . . ."

I narrowed my eyes at him. "Besides what?"

"Back in August I saw her with some guy at the grocery store."

"Oh." I had seen Isabelle fairly regularly since she had arrived in town, but she hadn't mentioned anything about a boyfriend. "Well, I'll look into that."

"Good. I'd appreciate it."

I grabbed his hand and pulled him toward the kitchen. "Let's see what they're up to in here. Did you know that Camilla and Adam got married?"

"*What?* That's awesome."

"Yeah. I called Doug to tell him first, since he and

Camilla go way back, but it was right after he heard from Blueville. So he doesn't know, I don't think."

We reached the kitchen door and found Doug at the table, listening gravely to the testimony of Belinda, Carl, Adam, and Camilla, who all seemed to be talking at once.

Cliff and I pulled up a couple more chairs and joined the group. Carl stood up and put a piece of quiche on a plate for Cliff; Doug, I saw, had already devoured one. Carl retrieved Doug's plate and carried it to Camilla's sink, where he washed it. Truly the boy was a wonder.

Belinda was saying, "And Adam said the man was picked up by a dark car. I understand that at night every car looks dark, and that 'dark' is not much to go on, but just to be clear—Lena and I had an encounter with a dark car, too."

Doug's blue eyes darted to mine for a moment. "When was this?"

"Belinda and I were coming back from our visit to Blue Lake Games. I didn't see anything on the way up, but Belinda said there was a black car behind us. And that it went up the bluff road. Later we both saw a dark car coming down."

Cliff frowned. "Even if that had anything to do with the disappearance of Luis, why would someone think to follow the two of you? You were just two women going shopping, right? Did anyone in the game shop even seem to be interested in the questions you were asking?"

Belinda and I exchanged a glance and shook our heads. "No, I don't think so," she said.

Doug sighed. "Did anyone happen to recognize this man in the window?"

I held up my hand. "I did, I think. But I can't remember where I remember him from. I mean, when I saw him I realized I'd seen him before, but then he was gone so quickly . . ."

"Think hard on it, Lena. It's the only clue we've got."

I closed my eyes and tried to picture the man's face again. I tuned out the conversation around me and brought his features back into my mind's eye: dark hair, thin mouth, eyes narrowed in suspicion or dislike . . . "I know who it was!" I cried, disrupting a conversation between Adam and Doug.

"What? Who was he?"

I looked at Belinda. "Wasn't he one of the guys that we saw in front of Plasti-Source, when Sam pulled over on the shoulder, coming back into town? There were two men, and they didn't talk to us—"

Belinda sat up straighter. "Yes—*yes*! It was him. Because at the time I thought he looked like a cartoon villain. And that's how he looked peering in the window. Almost impossible to be real—more like a bad guy on the cover of a Nancy Drew book."

Adam, concerned, pushed aside his coffee cup and leaned closer. "If that is the case, and if these men had even an instant to study the car you were driving, perhaps to look at the license plate number . . ."

"Or to take a picture of it," Doug said. "That would only take a second."

I shook my head. "But when the dark car followed us, we were in Belinda's car. Not mine."

Cliff looked at his place mat, his brows furrowed in concentration. "Let's say that from the time that you pulled over on the side of the road, these people were interested in knowing who you were. Assuming they didn't recognize Doug from his press conferences, they would have only the license plate to go on."

"But that would mean they'd need some connection to run the plate," Doug said. "Someone in our department."

"They might have other means," Cliff said. "Some unscrupulous source on the Internet. We know they're out there. Anyway, let's say they got Lena's location from her plate, and they started following her." He turned to me. "Where did you go before you met with Belinda?"

"Coffee Dreams. On Violet Street. Luis's wife works there."

"And then you and Belinda went to the game store—a place Luis frequented. So if this person was worried about you looking into the whole Luis thing, these two visits would not necessarily make him feel good."

Doug nodded. "That's interesting. And that might make him take a risk. Might make him leave the safety of the car, walk past a driveway full of cars to see what the people inside were doing—or to hear what they were saying." We all looked at the window, now closed, that had been bringing in fresh fall air. "And who knows how much he heard, if anything at all."

Camilla's eyes glowed purple in the kitchen light. "You do see what this means."

We all looked at her. "It means that Luis's disappearance was in fact linked to Plasti-Source. Carl is right. The boy was targeted because of his job. The man looking in this window was standing at a Plasti-Source construction site. Luis told someone at Blue Lake Games that he had been disillusioned at work. He hinted at corruption via the allusion to Uriah Heep. I don't think Doug or Cliff need look farther than the Plasti-Source in Stafford."

Doug tipped his chair backward slightly, his lips pursed in thought. "We were there this morning," he said. "Before we got the call about Luis's car. Everyone on the factory floor was super polite, wore expressions of concern, said they hoped we found Luis. Said he was a good worker, a good person, a nice colleague. In the second-floor offices, the story was different. He was unreliable, and they couldn't afford to have someone like that on the staff. They hoped all was well, but it wasn't their job to hunt him down."

"And everyone upstairs said words kind of similar to everyone else's," Cliff said. "The president, the vice president, the plant manager. They were all there for a meeting, so we chatted with them. Apparently, the president, Edward Grange, has been out of town. His wife had been ill and she died, and he was off at her funeral. So his underlings have been running things for a while. Like I said, they all basically told the same story—Luis was a deadbeat, and he'd probably turn up, but they had a business to run."

"Toeing the party line?" Adam asked.

Belinda looked shocked. "But only *one* of them is guilty! This isn't some Agatha Christie novel where every person is a part of the denouement. So you have to assume that much of that testimony is true. That those people really did consider Luis good and loyal."

Something was bothering me, and Doug saw it. "What is it, Lena?"

"Well . . . Carl said that initially some boss there said he didn't expect Luis to return because he had been repeatedly late or absent or something. That's why they weren't concerned when he didn't show up. But that doesn't seem to jibe with what you just said."

Doug gave me an approving glance. "You're right. I asked about that today, and the big bosses had changed their story. Said initially they weren't concerned about his absence because they heard a *rumor* that Luis was unreliable. Word had been going around the office that Luis was on the outs with his wife and that he may have left town. The bosses weren't basing their decision to dismiss on his actual performance—they were basing it on hearsay. Essentially, they believed the worst and were ready to fire him when he returned. That was from the big boss, Edward Grange. And his VP, Phil Enderby, seconded him. They didn't impress me as good people, but they were probably just thinking of their business."

"Maybe, maybe not," said Camilla.

Carl had been silent through this whole conversation, taking people's dishes and washing them. Camilla's counter gleamed, and there was no evidence that Carl had made a meal at all except for a plate with a few last pieces of quiche. I got up and went to the counter while Doug and Cliff interrogated Adam about what he had seen outside.

"Carl, that quiche truly was delicious. You are such a talented cook," I said.

"Thanks," he said. He wasn't smiling, and I thought I knew why.

"Will you put aside one of those pieces for Sam? He's sick upstairs, but he asked me to save him one."

"Sure. I'll wrap them all up for him." He opened the cabinet where Camilla had plastic wrap and tin foil and removed some Reynolds Wrap.

"How did you know where that was?" I asked. It had taken me a full week to figure out the layout of Camilla's kitchen.

He shrugged. "I memorized everything while I was cooking. It's pretty organized."

"You Fraileys have really detail-oriented brains," I said.

This earned a smile. "Yeah, I guess we do."

I studied him until he looked at me. His green eyes held pain and something else—something hard and determined. "Are you okay, Carl?"

His expression reminded me of the cowboy in every Western who realizes that he will have to fight alone in order to save the town. It made me nervous. "I'm fine," he said. "But I have to get going. I have work in the morning. I'm going to give notice."

"Good. That's good. Luis wouldn't want you there anymore, would he?"

He finished wrapping the food and turned to put it in the refrigerator. His back was to me when he said, "I think I know what Luis would want."

14

The night sky outside her window brought her a paradox of hope and despair. Hope, a scattering of light and beauty in the speckling of stars, and despair in the vastness of it all, suggesting that she was an infinitesimal thing, never to be found in a universe of the lost.

—From *Danger at Debenham Station*,
a work in progress

EVERYONE LEFT A few minutes later. Belinda was taking Carl home with her, and he paused in front of Doug and Cliff on the way out the door. "Are you guys going to come back to Plasti-Source now? To talk to the big bosses again?"

Doug thought about this, nodding. "I do want to go back. Keep the pressure on, see if anyone says something different. So, yeah, we'll be there bright and early."

Carl smiled. His expression was almost serene, and definitely secretive. "Good," he said. "I'll be on the lookout for you."

They moved out the door, still talking, and Camilla shut it after them. "Oh my," she said. "What an evening."

The unexpected events did not seem to have exhausted

her; Camilla found any sort of mystery invigorating, and now her mind was clearly working out the possibilities. A glance at Adam told me that he understood this, too. "My dear wife," he said, bending to kiss her. "I think that you and Lena will want to talk about this turn of events. I'm going to deal with the dogs and then head up to bed. You know I'm an early riser."

"I do, dear. I'll be up soon." She smiled after him and then turned to me. "Oh, Lena, what have you stumbled upon this time?"

"What?"

"Luis. This poor young man. I fear that this is going to be a case of wrong place and wrong time."

"Why?" We were still standing in the front foyer as she gestured to her right, and we moved into her living room and sat on the couch.

She sighed. "Because this Luis, who was not known to any of us and yet was our neighbor—who did in fact take part in a book club with you and Belinda—was just a nice young man. I think Doug will find he didn't have dark secrets, wasn't in some drug deal or dastardly plot, wasn't cheating on his wife."

"He just made the mistake of working at Plasti-Source, that's what you're saying."

She leaned back into the cushions. "That is what I'm saying."

"You've said that from the start. And it's the only thing that makes sense. But why? This is a respected company with many locations. Well, sort of respected. John had mentioned in our text chain that the one in Chicago had an unsavory reputation, at least among the locals. And Belinda said there was some evidence of law-suits, things suppressed . . ."

"We'll want to find out what was suppressed," Camilla said.

"Meanwhile, I guess it's all in the hands of our local police."

"Yes, I suppose so."

She looked disappointed, and I laughed. "Speaking of Nancy Drew. But you are far more sophisticated. You're not Miss Marple, either, because you actually hate knitting."

With a shrug, she said, "I don't hate it. I just wish I liked it more. It's such an attractive hobby, and I do wish I could make things. Big mufflers for Adam, or pretty gloves for you."

"You can buy those on Etsy. But no one has your particular creative skill. The *New York Times* said that you were 'unmatched' as a suspense novelist."

"Leave it to Lena to memorize my blurbs." She stifled a yawn, and I stood up.

"I have to go check on Sam, and you probably want to go off to bed, too. But I'll be ready bright and early to talk about our new mystery and about your writer's book. Part memoir, part writer's manual, is that right? I had some ideas about how you could combine the two." I held out my hand to help her off the couch, which was so absorbent and comfortable it was sometimes hard to extricate one's limbs.

"I'm glad. Yes, morning tea and toast and teamwork."

"There's the name of the book," I joked.

Camilla giggled again. Her dogs came trotting in and we petted their big heads; their ears were cold from their recent visit outside. Adam had turned out the kitchen lights, and the distant Blue Lake glimmered outside Camilla's kitchen window. How irresistible it was, that lake, the backdrop of all life in this town.

Camilla said good night and went upstairs, the dogs at her heels.

I moved closer to the window, lured as always by the vision of the sky and water beyond the casement. The serenity I normally felt in contemplating the view was marred by the memory of the face we had seen only briefly, but which brought a sinister reality and a jarring encroachment on our privacy. Whoever had stood there, in Camilla's autumn flower bed, had not been there for friendly reasons. And how long had he been outside? Had I in fact seen him moving around hours before he appeared in the window just before Adam and Camilla arrived, when Heathcliff and Rochester had growled into the darkness? If so, what had he been doing out there in the dark?

I shivered and turned away from the window. Doug had told us, before he left, that he would have patrols driving up the bluff road for the rest of the night, just to be sure all was quiet.

I went to the hallway and turned off the last remaining light, then used the light on my cell phone to illuminate the stairs to my room. I was afraid I would have to turn poor Lestrade away at the door to keep him from the kittens, but he wasn't anywhere in the hall. Camilla had confided that she feared Lestrade had cornered a mouse somewhere because she had seen him move furtively down the basement stairs. "Enjoy your mouse pursuits," I whispered, and I entered my room, shutting the door carefully.

Sam stirred in the bed. "Lena?"

"Hi. Let me just get in pajamas, and I'll join you." I

went into my little bathroom, brushed my teeth, washed my face, and changed into my flannel night attire.

Sam was only half-conscious when I climbed under the covers. "You shouldn't be here," he said groggily. "You could catch something from me."

"It will be fine," I said, feeling his forehead. Warm and a bit clammy. "Like I told you. You're never going to be alone again."

"That's my worst fear," he said sleepily. "Being alone. Being utterly alone." Then he was asleep, snoring slightly. I stroked his hair and then flopped back on my pillow, consumed by a sudden sadness.

How impossible, really, to learn that your entire family has died, as Sam had learned when he was nineteen years old; to learn that not just one beloved person, but three, had perished, and that the unit you had been a part of for almost twenty years had been destroyed? How unmoored, how lonely, would that feel? And how would one recover?

This was what Sam West had faced in the still-formative years of his life, and he had survived, learned strength, kept his goodness. He had not hardened into a cynic or a misanthrope; he was a man of great sensitivity. A man who had proposed to me in the most beautiful way possible. A man who had saved kittens from homelessness and now worried over their welfare. A man so devoted to his brother that he called him every day.

I slung an arm over him and hugged him against me.

Allison was right, I was a worrier, and my mind kept working over the idea that Sam had become sick very suddenly. It wasn't likely that someone had poisoned him, but the idea of poison was frightening. What if someone's food or drink were poisoned? Generally, people trust those who serve them food. We eat what we're given, drink what we're offered. We would never consider the idea that someone might have put something noxious within, something that could attack our organs or our cells, some substance that, once consumed, could not be removed or expunged. Something that would bring a terrible death.

I sat up and rubbed my face. Why did I make myself think these things? Sam was already getting better. I ran my hand lightly over his shoulder, his arm, his hand. Then I lay back down and did some deep breathing. Why did I even think of poison? I realized in an instant that it was Plasti-Source, and my fears, conscious or unconscious, that they were poisoning the water we all drank. It wasn't really about Sam at all, but I did have a fear of poison.

Before I drifted into sleep, I recalled what Sam had said about the pendulum of Blue Lake and its momentous movement back and forth. At one extreme, the dreaded swing brought suffering and heartache; at the other, it brought extreme happiness. Was this really a phenomenon of this magical little town? Or was it just a reality of life, the yin and yang of existence? Did it somehow change with the ebbing and flowing of the waves?

I thought I could hear the waves now, splashing against the shore at the foot of Camilla's long back stairway, the red stairs built into the rocky bluff.

Instead of counting sheep, I imagined that I was moving down those red stairs, closer and closer to the sound of the water, one step after another, descending into darkness and uncertainty . . .

My eyes opened wide. The intruder at the window

probably hadn't come through the front yard at all; that way he would risk detection. Perhaps, after alerting the dogs earlier in the evening, he had darted away, or been picked up by his friend in the dark car and made his way back to Wentworth Street and the sandy beach of Blue Lake. From there it was far more likely that he had climbed the stairs behind Camilla's house. He could have feigned a walk along the beach and then darted up the stairs and straight to the kitchen window. His accomplice would have been instructed to wait in front again in case the person had to make a quick departure. The stairs wouldn't work, because people from the house could give chase and eventually catch him on the beach. No, he needed that getaway car to be at the ready.

Which meant that at least two people were concerned about what was said inside Camilla Graham's house—and mine.

15

It's almost impossible to write a suspense novel without a scene in which someone follows some-one else. We are ever dogged by the footsteps of The Other.

—From the notebooks of Camilla Graham

THE FOLLOWING MORNING I woke up to find Sam gone. I sat up, shocked, and saw him sitting in a chair across from the bed and petting Lestrade, who sat peacefully in his lap.

"Sam! What—why is Lestrade in here?"

Sam shrugged. "He was mewing out in the hall. I opened the door and he strolled in, discovered the two visitors, jumped about four feet in the air, then ran to the windowsill. Eventually he came down and sniffed them, and now they're friends."

"Wow. Okay—and why are you out of bed?"

He stretched his legs, and Lestrade stayed in place, buoyant as a passenger on a boat. "I woke up and had some energy. I took a shower, snuck downstairs, and said hi to Camilla; she gave me some coffee and a sweet roll and a piece of Carl's quiche." He pointed at his coffee and a crumb-covered plate sitting on the table beside him. "Then I came back up and watched you sleep. You were having a dream, and it was making you jump sometimes."

A hazy memory returned to me. "Someone was chasing me. I was thinking about those stairs last night—how the visitor probably came up that way. The image was in my brain, I guess."

He grinned at me. "Your hair is all messy. I think you were doing a lot of tossing and turning."

"I'll bet I look great," I said drily.

"You do." He reached out to reclaim his coffee cup. "I feel about eighty percent today—well enough to go home and get some work done—but I was ordered by a no-nonsense Camilla to remain here for another day of recovery."

"I agree with her wholeheartedly."

"I bow to the wisdom of the two most important women in my life." He took a sip of coffee. "So I guess I'll be lying low, playing with the cats, helping you and Camilla with whatever you need."

"That's wonderful. It will be fun, all of us together in the house like a patchwork family. Camilla and Adam and you and me."

His blue eyes met mine. "There's another reason I'm glad to be staying close, obviously. If anyone lurks around again, I want to be here and ready to act."

"Good. Although I'm guessing that Doug and Cliff will find out a lot at Plasti-Source today, don't you think?"

"One can hope."

"Camilla called it from the start. Every element ties back to that company. I remembered that the man I saw in the window looked like one of the men we saw on the side of the road when we came back to town. Remember those two guys?"

"You mean the ones we saw going into the woods?"

I had forgotten them. "No—we saw them before we even picked up Doug. Although I still wonder—"

"Oh, you mean Furtive and Unfriendly, outside the Plasti-Source skeleton! Yeah, I recall them. It seemed like one of them took a picture before they left. And that gives me a really bad feeling. They looked like people trying out for the role of Hoodlum Number One."

The cats took this moment to do some reorganizing. Lestrade jumped off Sam's lap and leaped up on the bed to demand my allegiance. I petted the ruff of his neck, and he purred.

Geronimo, who had been invisible up until now, emerged from beneath the bed to find the bottom of Sam's jeans, which he tested with his claws. "Where's Arabella?" I asked.

"She's in the bathroom, in front of the heat vent. It is pretty chilly out there today. I checked the thermometer downstairs and it said forty-six."

"Oooh. That means a sweater." I gave Lestrade one last pat and climbed out of bed. "And a hot shower." I bent to kiss Sam's cheek, and then I felt his forehead. "You feel good; I'm so glad. I was irrationally worried about your fever."

"It didn't feel great, but I'm glad it only lasted a day. It could have been way worse."

"I know."

He slid an arm around my waist. "You made it all bearable. Another reason why I'm marrying you."

"To have a permanent caretaker?"

"To have you in my life."

The expression in his blue eyes was somewhere between grateful and yearning.

"Me, too." It was an inadequate response, but Sam knew the emotion behind it.

"Take your shower, then. I'll see you downstairs."

I looked dubiously at the kittens. "Do you think we should let them out? Now that Lestrade has accepted them?"

"Why not?" he said. "Let them explore. I think you've learned you can trust the barking beasts to be accepting."

"Okay, go ahead."

Sam went to the door and opened it. "They'll follow me, I'm sure." He went out into the hall and proceeded to the stairway. The kittens stared after him for a time from their respective places. Then, as if by agreement, they started creeping toward the door, their bodies crouched low. On the verge of escape, they paused to sniff the door frame; then they went prowling out into the hall.

Lestrade had assumed an extremely relaxed position against one of my pillows. He'd seen the rest of the house. It was time now to reclaim the territory of my bedroom, and he seemed smug about being able to do just that. He looked at me through slitted eyes and purred his approval.

"Oh, Lestrade. I remember when you were the new cat, and I was the visitor to this place. There was no Sam, no anyone except Camilla, and I found her rather— strange, at first. Look how far we've come."

Now his eyes were fully closed.

I laughed and moved toward my shower and the start of the day.

* * *

CAMILLA AND I had settled in her office: I sat in my beloved purple chair; she sat behind her desk. Sam was in the sunroom, reading a book he'd found on Camilla's shelf and drinking tea. Adam had gone to work, excited at the prospect of telling his chef about Carl.

"Before we get back to our Debenham idea," Camilla said, playing with a silver pen on her desk, "tell me your ideas for the writing manual."

"Oh yes. Well, I approached it from the perspective of a Camilla Graham fan. Which I am, as you know."

Camilla smirked. She hated it when I fawned over her, but she had grown used to it. "And what would my fan want to see in this book?"

"I would definitely want biographical information. But, as a writer, I would also want writing advice. In order to market this to a vast audience, though, you'd want to suggest that everyone has a story in them."

She raised her eyebrows. "Everyone has a story—I like that. Hmm." She poked her blotter with the pen. It was a smooth, silver-plated instrument, a gift from her publisher, inscribed with the words *To Camilla Graham, in appreciation of our forty years together.*

"So you could start each chapter with a real anecdote about your life. Let's say that you introduce a theme or technique in each chapter, and then you demonstrate that with your biographical story."

"Hmm. But if it's biography, then I'm not really using narrative techniques."

"Or are you?"

"Hmm," she said for a third time. I loved earning

"hmms" from Camilla because it meant she found an idea worth considering.

Emboldened, I said, "What if you started with that story you told me about your childhood—about how your grandfather would invite you into his lap under the apple tree in your backyard, and you would eat a fresh, ripe apple while he read you a fairy tale."

Her eyes gentled with the memory. Camilla had loved that particular grandfather the best. "Lena, that is a perfect idea. So let's say I began with that anecdote, and explained that it may well have been the foundation for my love of a good story. Then, in a passage afterward that encourages readers to write, I might ask them, 'What is the story of your beginning? What might be the origin of your special talent? And if you were going to write this story down for your descendants, what is the inevitable starting point?'"

I clapped. "You see? And then the more stories you tell, the more specific you could become with technique. One memory could focus on tone. You could ask the reader, 'Did you become anxious when you read that tale about my youth? Did the fact that a man followed my friend and me to school make you worried for us? Now consider how my word choice may have led you to have those reactions.'"

She nodded slowly. "My concern in writing this book was that I wasn't interested in relating one long linear tale of my life. I fear it's not as interesting as people might imagine, and frankly I'm too private a person. But carefully curated memories—really good stories—that would be far more fun. You are brilliant, Lena."

"I'm so glad you like the idea. And I can't tell you how much I will enjoy reading this one."

"I'll have pages ready for you this week. I'll need to work on that one in the background as we do our other tasks. *Death at Delphi* is ready to send in, after we give it one last glance. Oh, and I forgot to tell you!"

She put down her pen and rifled through a little stack of correspondence. "I printed this e-mail for you, Lena. It's from Michelle."

I took the paper and read the brief note from Camilla's editor—a note that contained five exclamation points. "*Death on the Danube* is going to be a bestseller?"

"It will be on the list next week, landing at number three."

I stood up and danced around. Camilla laughed.

"You dance with me," I said, pointing at her. To my vast surprise, she stood up, came around her desk, and began to sway gently with my conga-line chanting: "We made the bestseller *list*, we made the bestseller *list*!"

Sam appeared in the doorway, holding a blue mug. "You ladies make writing look fun."

Camilla and I burst into giggles and hugged each other. Sometimes our brainstorming sessions did have a slumber-party tone to them.

Camilla leaned on her desk, slightly winded, and said, "What can we get for you, Sam? Would you like to take your kittens upstairs to join you in a nap?"

"Maybe later." He smiled. "I still have some energy, so I was thinking I might take a walk. Just to the bottom of the bluff and back."

The dogs had heard the word "walk" and appeared almost stealthily in the room, their giant ears at attention.

Sam frowned. "I wasn't going to take them this time."

Camilla studied his face with her shrewd eyes, then

nodded. "Star should be coming for them any minute, so you're off the hook." Star Kelly walked the dogs for Camilla three times a week.

"How is Star?" I asked. "I haven't talked to her lately."

"She's doing well. She and her father are planning a little fall getaway, too. They're flying to New York to see some Broadway shows. Star is very excited."

I was pleased to hear that Star, a nice girl who had gotten into some trouble back in the summer, partly due to her father's emotional neglect, was now in a better situation.

A knock at the door alerted us to Star's arrival. Sam went to let her in, and for a moment there was a chaos of reunion in the hallway. The dogs loved Star, and they did some barking and jumping to remind her.

Camilla moved swiftly to the door. "Boys, be good," she said, and the dogs went quiet.

I followed her to the doorway and waved at Star, who looked casually pretty in jeans and a red sweatshirt. Her dark hair was pulled back in a ponytail and her blue eyes were bright. "Hi, Star."

"Hi, Lena! Okay, I'd better take these guys because they seem really peppy today!"

Camilla thanked her as she found the leashes that Camilla kept on a nail near the door and hooked them on the shepherds. As she and the dogs went barreling out, Carl Frailey appeared in the doorway. I had not seen or heard a car, so his appearance was rather startling.

"Oh!" Camilla said. "Carl, where did you come from? And you're pale as a ghost. Come inside, and we'll make you some tea."

"Thanks," Carl said, moving stiffly toward us. He

wore a polo shirt and khaki pants that looked like semi-professional office wear.

Sam waved and mouthed the words, "I'll be back." Then he disappeared out the front door.

"Shouldn't you be at work?" I asked Carl.

He looked at me with his uncanny green eyes. "I should, but I got fired. They told me to leave the building and to not even get my things out of my desk. Just to go."

"Oh, Carl! I don't think they can do that, can they?" I cried.

Camilla was studying his face, as she had just done to Sam's. She put a hand on his shoulder and said, "Come in the kitchen. Your favorite place in every house, right?"

Carl nodded with a brief smile.

We went into the kitchen to find Geronimo in the center of the table, his legs tucked under him, making him look like a little marmalade-colored box. "Not okay, mister," I said, scooping him up and putting him on the windowsill. I scanned for Arabella, who was never far from her brother, and saw that she was curled in front of the refrigerator.

"Cute cats," Carl said, unsmiling. He sat in a kitchen chair. "Sorry I came here, but Belinda is at work and her boyfriend is at work. So I didn't know where to go or who to tell."

Camilla turned on the flame beneath the kettle and then sat across from Carl. "I'm wondering," she said, "what you did, Carl. Because you've only been at work a few hours, and I assume you either just gave your two weeks' notice or didn't even have time to do it yet?"

He shook his head. "I didn't. But when they said I was fired, I said I was going to give notice today, anyway.

They said on my record it would show I was fired. But I don't care. I have a new job."

"Yes, you do." Camilla was calm, soothing. "So what did you do?"

Carl shrugged. "I hacked into some computers. Of guys I work with."

I gasped.

Carl looked unapologetic. "One of them, I didn't even have to try, because his e-mail was open on his screen. And the other one I just tried some stuff until I got in."

I stared, openmouthed. "That's illegal, Carl. Isn't it?" I turned to Camilla.

"It's a fireable offense. I don't know if you can get arrested for it." Her eyes went back to Carl. "Why did you hack into their e-mail?"

"To see what they were hiding about Luis." He said this as though we should have figured it out on our own.

I wondered in that moment if Carl was emotionally stable. "That's a job for the police, Carl. Now Plasti-Source can press charges against you, I think."

He lifted his chin. "They won't, though. They should be afraid of me."

An icy feeling began to inch its way up my arms. "Why is that?"

"Because I know they had him killed, that's why. And now they'll want to kill me, too."

Camilla's dark eyes were fixed on him, fascinated. She shook herself slightly. "We have to call the police," she said. "But first, Carl—tell us what the e-mails said. You must tell us while you remember and before they get here."

"Why?" Carl and I asked in unison.

"Because the information was illegally obtained. Doug and Cliff can't use it to arrest anyone. But they can certainly take the advice of some friends who heard things and made rational deductions."

Carl nodded. "Okay, fine."

"How much do you think you can remember?" I asked, grabbing a paper and pen from the sideboard. "I can take notes."

Once again, his luminous green eyes met mine. "I remember every word. I have an eidetic memory."

"What's that?"

Camilla was pleased. She lifted Arabella, who was biting her shoe, and looked into her tiny face. "It means Carl has a photographic memory, and that means we may as well have been right there reading over his shoulder."

16

In order to make suspense grow, one must escalate the conflict: with escalation comes discomfort. I want my readers to be very uncomfortable, indeed.
—From the notebooks of Camilla Graham

CARL'S FACE WAS calm, but his fingers were busy, pulling at one another in agitated motion. "You did this because you knew Doug and Cliff were coming," I said. "You figured your bosses would be distracted."

"Yeah." Carl shrugged. "There are two guys whose e-mail I read, but I was also looking at e-mail sent to them by other people in the building. So I can tell you things about five people who work there."

We sat around the kitchen table, leaning inward, a conspiratorial circle.

Camilla had given Carl a pad and a pencil, and he jotted things down as he talked. "There's Edward Grange. He's the president of the company. I've never met him, but I know he's come to our plant a few times this year, and he talked to the police when they came the other day.

Then there's Phil Enderby, the vice president. He's in and out of our plant. I don't talk to him much because I'm in IT and no one talks to us unless they have a computer problem. We're sort of invisible."

"I read about both of those men in the article at Coffee Dreams. They are the guys who presided over that community meeting."

"Yeah, that's them," Carl said, studying his pencil.

I touched his elbow. "Carl, why do we care about those two? Is it their e-mail you hacked?"

He shook his head. "No, but they both wrote e-mails to the people I was looking at. One was Joe Piper, who is our plant manager. And the other one was Gino Perucci, our quality control manager."

"And why did you want to look at their e-mail in particular?" Camilla asked.

"Because they're the ones who acted like Luis didn't exist. But they both saw him every day, and they knew he was a good person and a loyal employee, so there's something wrong. And now I know for sure."

Camilla pointed at Carl's pad and at mine with one sweeping gesture. "Get it all down, one of you. What was the first e-mail that bothered you?"

Carl said, "Lena can start; I can't write and talk at the same time. I'll write it down when I'm finished." He sighed and put his elbows on the table, leaning forward slightly. "I was reading Gino's e-mail. He's the one who just left it open on his desk. I knew he and Joe were both at a meeting with the police. Doug said so yesterday, and I waited until I saw Doug and another guy come in. Then I went to Gino's office. He had an e-mail from Edward

Grange, telling Gino that he wanted to know what had been going on while he was gone, and to be sure to sign off on the contract from Crandall Construction."

"Crandall?" I said. "I thought they were working with Anemone Construction. That's what it said on the sign outside the new plant."

Carl shrugged. "It was weird, because the e-mail implied that Gino had not been on board for signing it, or approving it, or whatever he had to do, so Grange was telling him to sign off. He was being a jerk about it."

"Interesting," Camilla said, her eyes on the window. A gold tree rustled just outside, providing an alluring visual while her mind did its brilliant work.

"Yeah. And there were some e-mails back and forth between Gino and Joe, kind of arguing about it. I only got to skim those, because by then I heard them coming."

"And the other computer? The one belonging to Joe Piper?"

Carl nodded. "I looked at his first. I pretended I was fixing something in his office. No one cared, because people were always calling me in to look at their computers. That wasn't even my job, but it sort of was, if you know what I mean."

"I doubt they were paying you enough, Carl," I said.

"They definitely weren't," he agreed. "I looked up IT salaries online. It's a big joke, what they paid me. Adam said they'd pay me much more at Wheat Grass."

I touched his sleeve. "I'm so glad you got that job!"

He smiled, his green eyes crinkling momentarily. "Me, too."

"Back to business," Camilla said. "We have to call Doug soon."

"Right," Carl said. "Joe Piper was also getting e-mails from both Grange and Enderby. They were kind of urgent, saying things like 'We have a deadline' and 'Crandall has threatened to go public.'"

"Ah," Camilla said.

"And Joe got a lot of e-mails from someone called Elephant21, who talked about Luis. The first one said, 'I'm worried about our Luis cover story. Will they buy it? What do we do if they don't? Would it be better to say nothing?'"

"Who is Elephant21?" I asked, shocked.

"I don't know yet. I'll find out, though," Carl said, his jaw jutting out.

"Our *Luis cover story*," Camilla said, stunned.

"What else did Elephant21 say?"

"He said it put him in a weird position. That he couldn't keep covering, and he was getting worried."

"Covering what? What the heck is going on at that place?" I asked. "What did poor Luis find?"

"That's what I was trying to figure out. The closest I got was in an e-mail from Enderby. He was in charge for a long time because Edward Grange took personal leave. He told Joe Piper that 'we were recently spared some unpleasant public exposure of the project.'" Camilla and I gasped.

"Is that a reference to Luis being—put out of the way?"

Carl said nothing; his face said it all, and his quiet fury was unsettling.

"Carl, did he say what the project was?"

"No, but he mentioned that they had an EPA visit next week, both at the plant in Stafford and at the new place being built out here. They seemed to be linking the project to the EPA visit."

"If it's the EPA, it's not just a visit," Camilla said. "It's an investigation. They're being investigated for some environmental concern. Perhaps their 'project' was helping them cover something up."

I had been writing furiously, but now I stopped. "And perhaps Luis found that out," I said.

Now Carl took up where I left off, writing furiously on his pad. "I'm going to put it all down," he said.

Camilla lifted her cell phone. "You do that, dear. And I'm going to call the police."

"You did what?" Doug yelled. He was in the kitchen with Carl, and Cliff was standing nearby, hands on hips.

Carl sat at the table where we had left him, holding his pad full of information. "I did what I had to do."

Doug sighed and looked out the kitchen window. "Well, Carl, that information was illegally obtained. I cannot use one bit of it. Don't even show it to me."

"Okay," Carl said.

Doug stood glaring at him, clearly nonplussed by the whole situation.

Cliff moved toward the table. "Why did you do it if you didn't want to show it to Doug?"

Carl remained calm. "I did it because I knew they were hiding something about Luis. I was right. And another thing: how come they didn't call you right away and say that I stole confidential information? How come they didn't ask you to arrest me?"

Doug sat down in the chair Camilla had vacated. "Maybe they did. I haven't been back to the station since—"

"No, they didn't, and they won't, because they don't

want me talking to you or anyone. They don't know what I saw, but I'll bet they're afraid about it."

Now both cops looked curious, even yearning. "Well, like I said," Doug insisted weakly.

Camilla strolled back into the room, holding Geronimo. "Doug, I wonder if I, as a friend who has worked with you before, could just offer some advice about this case. Based not on anything in particular—just things I picked up here and there, and some thinking I've done about the disappearance and the situation of poor Luis."

Doug studied Camilla, then looked at Cliff, who nodded. "And the 'here and there' sources of information—they just accumulated over time?" His voice was dry.

"Yes. Over a short amount of time. But I think I've come up with some interesting theories. I wonder if you have a moment to discuss them."

Carl smiled, pleased at Camilla's workaround. "Would anyone like something to eat?" he asked. Apparently, he now felt comfortable enough in Camilla's kitchen to offer her food to others. Doug was still glaring, Cliff looked rather bemused, and I stood hesitantly in the doorway, feeling the urgency of the situation. Into this scene walked Rhonda, Camilla's cook, who had arrived to start making lunch.

Camilla turned and smiled. "Oh, Rhonda, dear, I have to introduce you to Carl Frailey. He's the brother of Belinda Frailey, from the library," she said, setting Geronimo down. He scuttled off into the hallway, where Arabella had been waiting to pounce on him. She did so now, and they tore into the living room together.

"Hello, Carl," Rhonda said, removing a rain hood from her caramel hair. "Oh, it's unpleasant out there."

Carl stared at her, uncertain. Camilla touched his arm. "Carl, Rhonda is my cook."

"Yeah? You have your own cook? That's pretty cool." He turned to Rhonda. "What were you going to make?"

Camilla saw Rhonda's surprise and said, "Carl is a connoisseur. He just got a job at Wheat Grass."

"Oh wow!" Rhonda said. She seemed to understand, in one instant, both Carl's slight oddness and his talent. "Well, I wouldn't mind some suggestions about my menu today," she said.

"Okay," Carl agreed. He followed her to the counter and they began to chat about salads.

I pointed at Doug and Cliff. "Could we talk in Camilla's office for a minute?"

"Good idea," Cliff said. He moved toward me, Doug on his heels, Camilla last of all. I waited until they all came through the door, then followed Camilla down the hall, to her office adjacent to the foyer. She moved to her desk and sat behind it. I pulled up some chairs for the visitors, reserving the purple chair for myself. Sam, who had returned before Doug and Cliff got there and had been sent up to my room to rest, now appeared in the doorway.

"What am I missing?" he said.

"Pull up a chair," Doug said with a roll of his eyes. "My girlfriend's brother has put us in a bit of a dilemma."

"Only because he was being loyal to his best friend," I said.

Doug sighed and looked out the window; he said nothing.

Sam, his color closer to normal, sat down between Cliff and me. "What's up?"

I told him, in low tones, what Carl had done and why, and that it had led to his dismissal.

Sam's eyes went to Camilla. "So—what's happening now?"

Camilla nodded. "I was just telling our friends on the police force that I have had some insights over the last couple of days that I believe they should investigate. Some of these are based on gossip, yes, but I'm an old woman with a lot of time on my hands, and I indulge in gossip sessions. You're not liable for how I got information, correct? I can simply tell you what I heard, and you can follow up on it."

"I suppose so," Doug said slowly.

"Listen, we need to do something. I'm afraid Carl is in real danger," I said. "These men—wait a minute!" I took out my phone and Googled "Plasti-Source, Edward Grange," then tapped on "Images." A few results popped up from the company's website and from various public events Grange had attended. He was predictably silver-haired and handsome. He looked mildly familiar—probably because I had seen his image in some Plasti-Source–related article. I did the same search with the other three names: Phil Enderby, Gino Perucci, and Joe Piper. "Darn," I said. "I was hoping one of these guys would be the man from the window. That would tie a lot of things together."

"Do any of them look familiar?" Camilla asked.

"Maybe Joe Piper, but I don't know why."

Doug cleared his throat. "Cliff and I are on duty."

Camilla nodded. "All right. Well, my theory is this. Plasti-Source is up to something illegal—potentially an environmental crime. I have reason to believe they're being investigated by the EPA."

"Okay," Doug said, stunned.

Cliff leaned in. "I assume there's more?"

"Yes. I suspect, based only on my old woman's whims—"

Doug snorted, and Cliff grinned.

"—that someone in the company, perhaps even the vice president, has been attempting to cover up evidence of whatever this environmental offense may be. He may be in cahoots with either Joe Piper or Gino Perucci. Although one of those latter two might be working against the illegality."

"Right," Doug said.

I had my phone out again, and I Googled "Crandall Construction." This took me to their main page; they were a firm out of Chicago. A button on their site called "Recent Projects" caught my eye. I clicked it, then scrolled down to read some of their projects, which included "a new restaurant, a city hall, and a pipeline."

"A pipeline project," I said.

"What?" Doug said. He had been interrogating Camilla, but now he looked at me.

"The website for Crandall Construction says they recently worked on a pipeline." I handed the phone to Sam, who studied the web page.

Doug stared. "Why should I care about Crandall Construction?"

Camilla snapped her fingers. "Do you know—I think I overheard somewhere that Plasti-Source worked with them as a subcontractor. That in fact Crandall is waiting for Plasti-Source to sign some sort of quality control document."

Doug took out his phone and began to type things into

his online notebook. "You sure have a lot of contacts at your coffee shops, Camilla."

"Yes." She beamed at Cliff and said, "My role as a mystery writer helps me to see and hear interesting things around me."

Cliff grunted. "Why exactly do you fear Carl is in danger?" He looked from Camilla to me.

"Well—it's just—we think Carl might have some of the same information that Camilla's contacts have. And that—people at Plasti-Source might know that he has it. You see? And they might be concerned. In the same way that they were concerned that Luis had information."

Doug turned a shade lighter at those words. "I need to get Carl underground."

Camilla nodded. "I think that would be a good idea. Perhaps the cabin again?"

Doug shook his head. "Traceable. And too isolated. He'd have nowhere to go if they showed up."

Sam raised a hand. "I might know of a place."

We all looked at him. He said, "When I was hiding away from humanity, I got myself a little apartment in Daleville. A nice spot above a bakery. Very private. No one knew who I was, nor did they care. I escaped there sometimes, when Blue Lake got oppressive. I still have the apartment; I rent it out once in a while, but it's uninhabited right now. Furnished, even stocked a little bit."

Sam had mentioned this to me once, long ago, but I had forgotten. "That sounds perfect," I said.

Doug nodded. "Can we move him in today? Right after this? We'll make sure no one is tailing us."

"I'll give you the key and directions. You can go in the back way, through a little-used alley."

"Good."

Cliff looked thoughtful. He had been studying the Crandall website on the phone in Sam's hand. "Meanwhile, I'm putting two things together: pipeline and EPA investigation." He looked around at all of us and pointed at himself. "Makes this guy suspicious about illegal dumping."

Camilla gasped, and I said, "Do you mean into Blue Lake?"

Blue Lake, our constant companion, soothing us to sleep at night, refreshing us throughout the bright summer, inviting us to brood on its gray-sky days. Glimmering in twilight, mysterious in moonlight, poetic in the rising sun. Blue Lake, fresh and cool, provided drinking water for all the towns around it, including ours. Blue Lake, pristine, pure, and innocent. Who would dare to dump anything into a pure water source?

I met Camilla's gaze; she seemed to have read my mind. Her mouth tightened in disapproval. Of course people polluted, all the time, and often without the public's knowledge. We had fallen into the trap of "but it won't happen to us."

"I could be wrong," Cliff said.

"I hope you are." My phone buzzed in my lap. I looked down and saw that it was Isabelle calling; I had meant to return an earlier call of hers and had forgotten to do so. I didn't want her to think I was avoiding her. "Excuse me for one minute," I said and walked into the hallway, sliding my finger across my phone screen to answer the call. "Isabelle?"

"Hi, Lena! I was starting to wonder how I offended you. Remember how we were supposed to get together last week?"

"Oh, Belle, I'm so sorry. We've had so much going on here, you wouldn't believe. First Belinda went missing—"

Isabelle gasped.

"No, it was—kind of a misunderstanding, but in the process we met her brother, and he had a problem with a friend of his, Luis Castellan, and—"

"Oh yes, I know Luis. Both Castellans. They bring their Siamese here all the time. She's quite the queenly feline. She—"

"You know the Castellans?"

"Sure. In fact, I think they're bringing Olympia in today. Just a basic physical, but—"

"What time? What time is she coming?"

She didn't answer for a moment. Then, "What's going on, Lena?"

I sighed. "I can't go into it all this instant, but Luis is missing, Belle."

"What—oh God!"

"So his wife probably won't even keep her appointment—"

"She just called. She's coming at three."

"What? Really?" Why would Elena go to the vet when her husband had likely been killed? Unless it didn't bother her very much. "Listen, could I call in a favor? Let's say I were to bring in one of Camilla's shepherds around the same time. Could I hang out in your waiting room with her? Could you maybe delay calling her in?"

"Why?"

"I don't know. It just seems like a good opportunity. Let me talk to some people and call you back, okay?"

She sighed. "I was hoping we could just make a lunch date. Geez."

"Hey—while we're on the subject of dates—are you seeing anyone?"

This surprised her. "Romantically? No. Why?"

"Um—someone said they saw you with some guy at the grocery store."

"Who would—that was probably Emilio. He does odd jobs at my apartment building, and I hired him one Saturday to carry a bunch of heavy bags of pet food and bird food and stuff. I didn't feel like hauling it all up my stairs."

"Okay. Could you do me a favor?"

"What?"

"Next time you see Cliff Blake, could you ask him out?"

Her voice was wry. "I kind of thought he was going to ask *me* out."

"I did, too. He obviously likes you. But sloths move faster than that man. I think he's just going to think about it for about a year."

She sighed. "I have to go, Lena. My noon appointment just got here."

"Okay. I'll call back about the other thing."

"You do that. See you." She hung up, and I returned to the room, where Doug and Cliff were murmuring about possible infractions that the EPA might want to investigate.

"Uh, guys? I was just talking to Isabelle, and she said the Castellans come to the vet all the time. They have a pampered cat."

"Who could imagine," Camilla said, smiling, as Lestrade jumped onto her desk and demanded affection.

"Yeah. The thing is—she said Elena is coming in today."

Doug's brows rose. "Her husband is missing, but she's going about her business as if nothing is wrong?"

"I asked Isabelle if I could go in there, maybe with

one of Camilla's dogs, just pretend to be a regular old client. Maybe chat with Elena, get some information."

To my surprise, Doug didn't immediately shut me down, but he did point at me. "It can't be you. She just saw you at her restaurant. She would know something was up."

"Would she really remember, though?" I asked.

Everyone in the room nodded. "You're young and pretty, Lena. And women notice other women," Camilla said.

"Well, then—you go, Doug. Wear undercover clothes."

Now Sam shook his head. "No, Doug's been too visible with his press conferences over the last few months. She'd recognize him."

Cliff agreed and pointed at Sam. "She'd recognize you, too. The notorious Sam West. Everyone knows your face by now, don't they?"

Camilla stroked Lestrade's silky ears. "Then it should be you, Cliff. You can take Rochester—he's better in overall behavior and deportment. You've been in the paper, too, but we can give you a pair of glasses, and you can comb your hair differently. You can bond over your indulged pets."

Cliff looked at Doug, who nodded. "What I'd like to get a sense of is her general state of mind. I mean, shouldn't she be worrying over her husband, one way or the other? Either she should be worried that she'll be caught for whatever she did, or that people are looking for him, right? Why is she taking the time to go to the vet?"

"A distraction?" I offered. "Maybe she needs to do everyday things so she doesn't go crazy."

"Makes sense," Sam said. "But there could be other reasons."

Doug sat up straight and slapped his knees. "I have to get going. I'll grab Carl, and Sam can tell me how to drive him out to his hideout. I'll have to call Belinda and tell her we're absconding with her brother. Meanwhile, Cliff, you can don your friendly neighbor clothes. What time did you say she'll be there, Lena?"

"Three o'clock."

"Great. Plenty of time to get Cliff and Rochester ready," Doug said, standing up and pressing a button on his phone. "I have to make a call."

Camilla sighed. "Well, I suppose I should break the news to Carl, eh? Although I think he'll be relieved. The boy was quite nervous when he got here."

I had been biting the inside of my cheek—an old anxious habit. I made myself stop. "I hope he doesn't have to stay underground for long."

"The apartment is stocked with dry goods," Sam said. "We can pack up some milk and eggs for him, stuff like that. He can lie low for days, making his recipes in peace."

Camilla nodded, then left the office to talk to Carl.

Cliff scratched his head and gazed out Camilla's office window. "I think one of you should come with me and stay in the car."

"Why?" I asked.

He shrugged. "This could lead to absolutely zero. But let's say it doesn't. Always prepare for the unexpected, right? If I end up following her, or even chasing her, then you need to take the dog. Plus, who knows what you'll see outside? Two sets of eyes."

"Three," Sam said.

I turned to him. "You're still sick." He was starting to look pale again; I felt his head and found it clammy.

"I'm well enough to sit in a car. And I don't want you in it alone." Sam folded his arms and looked at me with his determined face. Cliff put a hand on his shoulder, perhaps in solidarity.

"Okay, fine." I smiled at the two of them; they looked more like brothers every day. "We go to town, Doug hides Carl, and Camilla stays at home base with Rhonda."

Cliff sobered. "Right. Taking action is good; action can make things happen. Start those dominoes rolling."

"I guess so," I said. "But once the dominoes start falling, they keep falling—until the end."

Outside some orange leaves blew past on a gust of wind. I thought of the first day I had come to town, almost a year ago: it had been cold autumn, and a storm was coming in. When it came, it brought murder and chaos.

Somehow history seemed to be repeating itself.

17

*The unexpected: we all dread it, but we long for it
as well. It's the dichotomy of our existence.*
                    —From the notebooks of Camilla Graham

SAM SAT WITH his brother in the front of Cliff's car. Cliff
had changed into a pair of jeans and one of Sam's flannel
shirts, and he looked ruggedly handsome as he stared
solemnly out the front window, squinting through a pair
of cheaters that Adam had lent him.

Rochester sat beside me, tongue lolling, tail wagging
like mad if anyone even dared to look at him. He rarely
got rides in the car; I hoped that poor Heathcliff didn't
know what a perk his brother was getting while he sat
inside.

"Do you remember what to say?" I asked Cliff.

"His name is Rocky, and he's been limping on and
off," he said automatically. "I'm concerned he might
have a thorn."

"Okay, great. And while you're in the lobby with her,
ask about her cat. People love to talk about their—*ouch*,

Rochester, that is my *leg*! Cliff, see if they'll trim this guy's nails, too. He just stabbed me with three of them."

Rochester thrust his big face into mine; he did not look apologetic.

"You're lucky you're cute," I said, scratching his ears. He leaned in to sniff my neck.

Sam turned and said, "Hey! I've got some competition back there. Rochester is romancing Lena."

I giggled. "He's tickling me. Go over *there*. Now, stay on your side, you monster."

Rochester, looking pleased, turned his attention to the window and the passing traffic. Cliff was nearing the Blue Lake Animal Center, which took up two storefronts on Maxwell Street. He parked halfway down the block "so she doesn't see you two through the window." Then he stepped out of the car, opened the back door to retrieve a joyful Rochester, and sloped toward the entrance door with a casual stride.

"The crazy stunts we pull," Sam murmured, his eyes on his brother and the dog. From behind, Cliff looked like any other dog walker in Blue Lake. Halfway up the block he turned to his right, opened a door, and ushered Rochester in. I heard the dog bark once, happily, before they disappeared.

"I'm dying to text Isabelle, but she'll be too busy. But she does know that *Brock Cromwell* is coming in with his dog," I said, half laughing. "Where did he come up with that name, anyway?"

Sam turned to me, grinning. "He said it was his name when he played cowboys as a kid."

"Does every boy have a pretend cowboy name?"

He shrugged. "Probably."

"What was yours?"

His face was a bit sheepish. "Nate Champion."

I laughed. *"What?"*

"He was a real guy! A hero. A small rancher who stood up to corrupt cattlemen in 1890s Wyoming. Did you ever hear of the Johnson County War?"

"Can't say that I have, pardner. But then again, you've never heard of Daphne du Maurier, so we are at an impasse."

He studied me for a moment and said, "I'm sure a fun part of our marriage will be recommending books to each other."

"Sam!"

"What?"

"That's her." I pointed out the window at Elena Castellan, who was emerging from the passenger side of a dark blue car, holding a cat carrier. She waved vaguely to whoever was driving and moved swiftly into the vet's office.

"Okay. Here we go," Sam said. "Suddenly this feels silly, like an episode of a bad TV show."

"I know. What are we even here for? Did you happen to get the license number of that car?"

"No." He was still peering out the front window. "There were too many other cars in the way."

"Oh well. We can watch for it. I know it was a dark blue sedan—I think it was a Ford."

"Okay."

We sat together in companionable silence for several minutes, looking at traffic. At one point, Sam leaned against the headrest and relaxed in his seat. I thought he might be sleeping, but eventually I saw him rustle and look at his phone.

"Hey," I said.

He turned back to me. "What?"

"Another fun thing about being married?"

"Yeah?"

"We—" My phone buzzed in my hand and I jumped. I saw Belinda's name and answered it.

"Hey," I said.

"Do you know that Doug is putting my brother in some kind of safe house?" she asked, her voice breathless in my ear.

"Yeah—Sam offered an apartment he has in Daleville. Have you talked to Carl? Your brother has been up to some stuff."

She sighed. I thought she might be near tears. "He doesn't have good impulse control. He shouldn't have done that. Now I have to worry about someone hunting him down . . ."

"No, you don't," I said. "You know that. Doug will make sure he's safe."

I could almost feel the calming effect my voice had on her anxiety. "Well—it was nice of Sam to offer a place. Thank him for me."

"I will. Meanwhile we're sitting outside the vet's office on the off chance that Cliff might glean some clue from Elena Castellan."

Belinda sighed. "I've been looking into Plasti-Source here at the library. I can't find too much in print, but I did find one lawsuit that alleged their improper waste disposal practices put workers at risk."

"Waste disposal," I said. "What kind of waste does a plastics plant dispose of?"

"Their mixing process produces something that they

call 'toxic sludge' in one part of their plant, and this is what concerns people."

"Toxic?"

"Potentially harmful. I'm guessing that chemicals would be involved, right? So they would have to go through proper channels and inspections and such."

"They claim they are doing so. Did you see the article in the paper? And if they're not doing it legally—why aren't they? Is it expensive to go the legal route?"

"Yes, I suppose. They would have to hire a disposal company, which involves transportation, probably of barrels or something like that. And then an approved site for dropping off toxic waste. But it's also expensive in the long run to break the law, isn't it?"

"Good point." I felt a sudden wave of affection for Belinda. I pictured her in her back office in the library, poring over books or old files, her green eyes glowing with the love of research. Her hair tended to fall over her eyes while she worked, so generally she pulled it up into a shiny tail or librarian's bun. She couldn't keep her glasses contained in the same way, which is why she often had to push them up the bridge of her nose.

"Listen, I'm here with Sam, and—oh shoot!" I ducked down in my seat, but not before I made eye contact with Elena Castellan, who had walked past our car, texting, her cat carrier handle slung like a purse strap over her shoulder. She looked up just as I squirmed in my seat, and in that millisecond that we looked at each other, I saw recognition in her eyes.

"Gotta go," I said, ending my conversation.

Sam turned around. "Was that—?"

"Yes. And she saw me. Where is Cliff?"

We looked toward the entrance of BLAC, and Cliff came wandering out with Rochester, pausing to breathe in the fall air. He appeared to be a man with not a care in the world. I spun around for a view out the back window; Elena was tucking her cat into the backseat of the blue car. This time I took a surreptitious photograph. Elena climbed in the front passenger seat, and the car drove past us. I gasped.

I spun back toward Sam and said, "Hey—" just as Cliff and Rochester arrived. Cliff opened the back door and Rochester dove in, greeting me as he would a long-lost friend. "Bah. Rochester! No licking. Blech. Okay, I like you, too." I petted his big head and his soft ears, then scrubbed his tuxedo-white chest for a while. He looked nobly out the window, panting occasionally. Cliff climbed in the front and started the engine. "Okay, that was interesting."

"What happened?" Sam said.

"I did my act. Very handsome local man with very handsome dog, just headed to the vet for a checkup."

Sam snorted.

"Hey, they clipped his nails!" I said, studying Rochester's neat paws.

"Isabelle did. In about five seconds. She's great." I noticed that his face was particularly pleased when he mentioned her name.

"Anyway?" Sam prompted.

"Yeah. So I was in the lobby petting Rochester, and Elena came in. I acted like a lonely guy desperate for conversation."

"You *are* one of those," Sam said.

"She was quiet, sort of solemn, but friendly. I asked about her cat, and she started right in about how she got her, why she named her Sasha, stuff like that." He cleared his throat. "Then she got a phone call. I don't know who it was, but she told the person she was at the vet. She said, 'Yeah, I would have canceled, but Sasha was making weird choking noises. I wanted to make sure she was okay.' So I guess that explains why she's at the vet right after her husband potentially died. I didn't get any majorly weird vibes up front."

"But?" I said.

He turned to smile at me. "But I asked her if she had any other pictures of Sasha." He turned back to look at the road. "She didn't think twice—got out her phone to show me. But she had just used it to send an e-mail, and her send page was still open." He stopped at a red light and turned back to me. "Guess what her username is."

"Elephant21," I said.

Cliff's face fell. "How did you know that?"

"I wouldn't have, except about two minutes ago she climbed into a car with a guy I'm pretty sure was Joe Piper. They both looked at me, and they were both glaring." It gave me the chills, thinking about the look on their faces: a shared expression that bordered on hate.

Sam spun around. "What? Just now?"

"Yeah. Cliff can double-check, because this time I got the license number."

Cliff stared hard out the window. "So what does this mean? We can definitely link her to Plasti-Source, and to the disappearance of Luis."

"But why is Joe Piper driving her around town? Why is he picking her up at a vet appointment?" Sam mused. "It's a workday, right?"

"What if it's not Luis who was having an affair?" I

said. "What if it's Elena? What if she and Joe Piper were seeing each other behind Luis's back, and that's what they had a fight about?"

"If they had a fight at all," Cliff said. "Carl made it sound like nothing of the sort happened."

"Well, let's say Elena had an affair." I studied the back of Sam's head as I thought it through. "Carl said that the e-mail said that she acknowledged Luis was missing and didn't know what to do. She mentioned a "cover story." That meant she was asking Joe Piper about some sort of secret they shared related to Luis. That's suspicious."

"It is," Sam said. "As is the fact that she said it put her in an odd position, and she was worried."

We sat for a while; it seemed as though we were just gliding through the streets of Blue Lake, our thoughts acting as buffers that kept out sound and sight. Even Rochester seemed to be thinking as he sat arrow straight beside me.

Cliff said, "Let's give Elena the benefit of the doubt. Let's assume for a minute that she's not a horrible person. That she really was worried about Luis, but for some reason, as her e-mail suggested, she couldn't say so. What would prevent her from going to the police? And why would she be telling Joe Piper this?"

Sam said, "You have to interrogate both of them, obviously. I can't think of an innocent reason for what she's doing."

"Agreed. In fact, I need to get Doug on the horn. He should have Carl safely installed in your Daleville place by now."

Sam leaned closer to Cliff and studied him for a moment. "Why are you in such a good mood?"

Cliff shrugged. "Break in the case."

Now I was alert, too. Cliff had been sort of smiling since he had returned to the car. I had attributed it to the invigorating weather. "You asked her out!" I said.

He grinned at me via the rearview mirror. "I did."

"Tell me."

He smiled. "I took Rochester in first. She was cool about that—she didn't want to let Elena leave while I was in my 'appointment.' So she did a quick ear check and nail clip, and then she looked at me with those eyes. She has gorgeous dark eyes."

"And?"

"She said, 'How have you been, Cliff?' It was just us in that little room, and it just flowed out of me. I said, 'I've been kicking myself that I didn't ask you out three months ago when I wanted to. And feeling like a jerk ever since.'"

"Oh wow! What did she say?"

Cliff turned onto Wentworth Street. "She kissed me."

"What?" Sam yelled.

"She leaned in and kissed me on the mouth, and then she said, 'Why don't you just ask me out now?' So I did. We're having dinner Wednesday night."

I clapped. "Now, that is more *like* it, Cliff. She does have pretty eyes, doesn't she?"

"She does. I'm going to dream about that. I would never have thought it could be romantic, standing in an antiseptic room with a woman who has just clipped a German shepherd's nails. But it was really romantic."

Sam turned to make a face at me—a blend of pride, disdain, and amusement. He still looked pale, and I leaned forward to feel his forehead. He said, "I'm okay,

Lena. I'll take a quick nap when we get back, and tomorrow I'll probably be one hundred percent again."

"Okay." I studied him, feeling dubious, and my phone buzzed again. This time it was Adam.

"Lena, I'm at Wheat Grass. I've moved our boxes here, and I wonder if you could come by and help me go through them."

"Of course. I'm on the road now—I'll get Cliff to drop me off. See you soon."

Sam peered at me, surprised. I told my companions what Adam had said, and Cliff said, "Sure, I can drop you off and then take Sam home. Will Adam give you a ride?"

"I'm sure he will. He and I really need to get started on Camilla's party room. The event is in two weekends, you know. Barring any other crazy occurrences."

"Like Luis staggering in with bloodstained clothing?" Sam said, his expression dark.

"Oh God. That's like something out of a Poe story."

"Sorry. I need sleep."

"Turn here, Cliff. This road meets up with Green Glass Highway."

Cliff smirked at me in the rearview mirror. "I *know*, Lena. I've lived here for months now, and I'm a *cop*. We tend to learn all the byways."

"Sorry." I studied him in the mirror as his eyes returned to the road. "At your date tomorrow, make sure you invite Isabelle to Camilla's party as your date."

"Good idea." He turned into the driveway of Wheat Grass moments later, and, as always, I admired its driftwood façade and tasteful landscaping.

"Thanks, guys. Adam will get me home. Sam, you go to bed," I said.

"I will," Sam said. It was clear that his energy was ebbing again.

I leaned forward to kiss his cheek, and Cliff's. "See you later." I climbed out and waved as they drove away. Then I mounted the steps and opened the door, pushing through the elegant main room, where diners spoke in muted tones and made gentle clinking sounds with their silver and china, to the back hallway, which led to the kitchen and to Adam's office. I had never actually gone into the office before, but I assumed Adam would be there. I knocked on the door and he opened it almost immediately, thrusting his head out through a narrow opening. "Oh good. I was halfway afraid it was Camilla, coming by to check on me."

"No, I think she's fairly distracted right now. There have been some . . . developments."

"So I heard. She texted me earlier. Come in."

He opened the door wide and I saw a spacious room with a gray desk beneath the sole window, and a series of shelves on the opposite wall, holding all sorts of restaurant supplies. A couch sat against the south wall, and a Native American rug covered much of the floor. "Hey, it's nice in here!" I said. My mind was still half on Elena Castellan, and the look she had given me when she and Joe Piper drove past . . .

"Yes, I like it. A good place to get work done. Come here—I've got five out of the boxes, but I need some help."

The wall opposite the couch was lined with tall boxes and with the unpacked book covers he had mentioned. "Oh, Adam! The *colors* on this one!" I stroked the canvas reproduction of *The Lost Child*, my favorite Camilla novel. "Look at the light around the Eiffel Tower! Camilla is going to love this."

He handed me an X-Acto knife. "Work while you talk."

I laughed and walked up to a box. Carefully, I sliced away the tape holding the sides together, then opened the top and pulled out another canvas—this one for *On London Bridge.* "Ahhh," I said.

Adam laughed. "You might be too much of a fan to help with this."

"No, I'll be fast, I promise." I set the painting against the wall and went back to work. One by one, we pulled out covers that represented a lifetime of work. Each cover, with visuals tapping symbols that were important in the novel, provided a testament to Camilla's genius. Despite my joy in the work, my mind kept wandering away, posing questions. Why did Elena Castellan take her cat to the vet? Why did she need a "cover story" for the disappearance of Luis? Was she having an affair with Joe Piper? What were the men at Plasti-Source up to? Was everyone at the Stafford plant corrupt? Was there any corruption at all, or was that an illusion? Could there somehow be an innocuous explanation for Luis's disappearance, despite the car with blood inside? Could he simply have had an accident? Bumped his head, bled a little, and wandered away, confused?

I looked up to find Adam studying me. "Something on your mind?"

"All sorts of things. But mostly I'm admiring these lovely covers." When we finished, half an hour later, there were thirty-five canvases leaning against one another.

"Good," Adam said. "Let me just call Enrique and

Peter to take away these boxes." He went to the door and spoke to someone in the hall. "Can you send my busboys here for a moment?"

Enrique and Peter, both about twenty years old, appeared a moment later. "Did you want us, Adam?"

Adam took the knife out of my hand and handed it, and his, to the boys. "Guys, can you spare about ten minutes to carry these boxes out to the recycling dumpster and break them down?"

A light of interest gleamed in their eyes. Men loved doing jobs with tools. "Sure, Adam. No one's close to being finished eating right now, anyway."

"Great! Thanks."

The two started carrying out boxes, tucked underneath their arms. Adam looked back at the standing covers. "Now the question is how to display them. I have about ten easels, so we can stagger some out in front— maybe the most recent ones? But I was thinking the others could be hung right on the wall. I have a fair amount of wall space if I temporarily take down the sconces. The nails are already in place, so we could maybe get six per wall. That's twenty-four. Plus, another ten on the easels is thirty-four. So where do we put the last one, along with the author picture of Camilla?"

I thought about this, then walked to the door and peered down the hall. I turned back to him. "Why not in the hallway? One on each side. People have to travel down there to get to the bathroom, right?"

"Yes, I had considered that. You think that's all right? Not—tacky, to have them there?"

"No. It's wall space, and people will want chances to study the art up close, wherever that may be."

He clapped his hands together. "All right, then! We have a plan. The food is covered, the guests have RSVP'd, Allison has her music list, I hope?"

"Yes, I sent it to her last night."

"Good. She's a talented girl. Camilla loves to hear her sing."

"So do I. It will be great, Adam. You don't have to worry."

He shrugged. "It's the first party I've ever thrown for her. I mean, I've gone to her birthday parties for years. But I've never been in charge of one. Certainly never expected to be planning one as her husband." The awed look was back on his face, and I gave him a quick one-armed hug.

"She will have the best time ever. Now, let me sort these. Did you want them in chronological order? That would make the most sense, right? If so, *The Lost Child* can go on the north wall, and we'll snake around from there."

"Good. You order them for me, and I'll dig out the easels from my storeroom. Be right back."

He left, and I started stacking. North wall, west wall, south wall, east wall. The easels and the hallway would hold the most recent twelve novels. I lifted the canvas of *For the Love of Jane* and walked to the west-wall pile. I held it for a moment, contemplating the cover, recalling the complex plot that had assaulted me with surprises, one after another. Camilla's plots were famous for that rapid-fire, chapters-long denouement. "Huh," I said, distracted by a thought. In the book, Jane's husband had disappeared, just as Luis had disappeared . . .

Adam came bustling in. He was never happier than when he was working on a project. "Okay. You've been a lifesaver, Lena. Now I'm going to give you a pad of sticky notes, and if you'll number them according to the order they were published, that will be great. Do you actually know that by heart?"

"No. I can tell you what decade they all came out, but not what year. I've been double-checking on my phone. There's a website that lays them all out in order."

"Wonderful." He walked briskly over and kissed the top of my head. "I have to go check some things in the kitchen. When do you need to get back?"

"Just within the hour would be great. But you know what? I want to walk over to town to get a couple things. Can you pick me up outside Sullivan's Drugs in half an hour? I can stroll over and wait for you out front."

Adam's hands went to his hips. "No, I *cannot* do that. Do you think I want my wife to divorce me a day after our wedding? Because that is what she would do if she knew I let you wander out alone while men are looking in your windows and following you in cars."

This was true, and not a happy thing to contemplate, but his expression made me laugh anyway. "Okay, geez. And don't think I don't see through you, Adam. You're the protective one; you're as transparent as my dad. He was always blaming things on my mother. 'You have to be home by ten or Mom will worry.' 'Mom gets concerned when you don't spend enough time on your homework.' I'm pretty sure he hadn't even consulted my mom before he made some of those speeches."

Adam shrugged. "I am protective, and I am unrepentant about that fact. After this summer—" He broke off ruefully. Adam had saved my life back in July, and we had become much closer since that day.

I lunged forward to hug him. "I know, Adam. I love you, too."

He squeezed me tightly for a moment. "I don't mean to be a lecturer. But you are young, and like my own children, you tend to feel immortal. I don't think you can help it—it's probably woven into your DNA. But I am far enough down the path of life that I can look behind me and see the pitfalls. It's my job, as I see it, to keep you young ones out of those pitfalls."

"Adam. No wonder Camilla loves you." I went to the wall with my pad of sticky notes, then paused. "When did you propose to her, anyway?"

"Last week. We were walking the dogs, crunching over the leaves on the bluff road, and she had been to the dentist, remember? She was murmuring that she still felt woozy, and what if a heroine were to be abducted while under sedation?"

"By an evil dentist?" I said dubiously.

"That's what I said, and we both laughed. She never stops plotting, that one. And I just—it overwhelmed me, in that moment, how much I love her. I said, "How about if you marry me, Camilla, at long last?""

"Oh, Adam. That's so romantic. When I think of your years of devotion! Did you fall in love with her at first sight, the way James did? Was it just an instant thing, way back when she came to Blue Lake?" I was putting numbers on the notes now, and adhering them to the proper covers.

Adam shook his head. "No, it was long before she came to Blue Lake. She and James wrote letters, as you now know. Sometimes he let me read the ones she wrote. Often, she simply related things about her day—what her mother said, how she'd seen a gray kitten in the road, how her sisters were annoying but she loved them anyway, things like that. And you know better than anyone that she has a way with words. I—fell in love with her voice, long before I saw her face."

I paused on the verge of adhering a note to the canvas of *On London Bridge* and studied his handsome face. "You are just too perfect. Both of you. You have to tell that story at her party; you'll have people in tears. Allison will be all over you, probably while singing some saccharine love song."

Adam laughed heartily at the thought. "Maybe not, then."

I turned to glance out the window behind his desk. "Oh, yuck. Look at the weather! Wasn't the sun shining when I got here? Now it's overcast, and that looks like freezing rain."

"Welcome to autumn."

"Yeah, blech. Okay, last five. One, two, three, then my beloved *Salzburg Train*—the book that brought Camilla and me together—then *Death on the Danube*. And we're done!! Although I understand we're going to see the tentative cover for *Death at Delphi* any day now."

"We'll leave that to people's imaginations," Adam said. "As it is, Camilla will complain about all of these, asking what in the world we're supposed to do with them all."

"I have an idea about that. You know that long hall that goes from her front door to her kitchen?"

"Yes."

"We could give it a fresh coat of paint—white or cream—and then hang these as though it's a little gallery. It would make that hall look bright and beautiful instead of dark and uninviting."

Adam beamed. "A great idea. We can do it while she's off at some appointment. It will be a secondary birthday surprise."

"Exactly." I looked at my watch. "All right, now we really should go. Make a quick stop and then see what's happening at the house. Those developments Camilla texted you about. Things keep happening—"

"As ever," Adam said. "Right, let me talk to them in the kitchen, and then I'll get my keys."

WE DROVE OUT of the lot, tiny ice pellets clicking on the windshield. "I'll have to stop for gas, too," Adam said. "Sorry about that."

"No problem. Are you going to Bentley's? I'll run next door and grab some cat food; then I won't need Sullivan's Drugs. Sam's kittens are going through my usual stash."

Bentley's was one of two gas stations in Blue Lake, up the hill from Wheat Grass on Green Glass Highway. Next door was a tiny grocery store where Camilla and I sometimes stopped for staples on the way home from some event or other.

"Sounds like a plan," Adam said. Ever the gentleman, he pulled up in front of Highway Convenience Mart to spare me from the worst of the rain. "I'll get some gas and come back here in a minute."

"Got it. I'll wait just inside the door." I waved and darted through the cold rain into the store, where I searched for the pet aisle. I walked past the dairy section, where a man was peering into a carton of eggs. He glanced up at me and we both froze. Joe Piper clearly recognized me and saw that I recognized him. His brows came down in a scowl and I'm sure my face grew red. I looked away and forced myself to find the proper section, to grab a bag from the shelf with slightly shaking hands, and to move briskly to the front of the store. I had the vague sense that Piper was still standing by the eggs, murmuring into a phone; I barely heard the young man in front of me when he held up the cat food and joked about the cute face of the feline on the bag. I muttered my agreement, keeping Piper in my peripheral vision. He had ended his call, and now he stared out the front windows of the store, seemingly watching for something. The attendant rang me up and told me to have a nice day.

I thanked him and went to the door, peering through the cold spray to find Adam's car. Someone loomed up in my periphery; I had one second to wonder if it was Joe Piper before he moved behind me and pushed the door open by reaching over my head. I had no choice but to move out into the rain because he was tall and broad, and he was pushing me forward. "Hey! Stop it!" I cried.

Then his voice was in my ear. "We need to talk, Lena," he said, just as a dark car pulled up next to me and a back door opened. "Get in," he said.

"What? No, I—"

But again, his bulk and strength were moving me forward against my will, pushing me into the car, where Elena Castellan sat glaring at me. Joe got in on the other side; I was effectively trapped between them. "What— what is this? I don't even know you!" I protested.

"We don't know you, either, but that hasn't stopped

you from following me all over town, has it?" Elena asked in a voice as icy as the rain that pelted the windows. "To my shop, to the vet, to this store."

"I don't know what you're talking about."

"Save it," she snapped. "Drive, Tommy."

Another man sat at the wheel, and now the car moved forward, away from poor Adam, who was probably still filling his tank and worrying over those pitfalls that lay in wait for people like me.

18

How she regretted ever climbing into the car!
—From *Danger at Debenham Station*,
a work in progress

THE MAN CALLED Tommy pulled onto the highway and drove for about a minute before pulling off again onto a tree-lined road that led to nothing but a deserted barn. Sam had pulled into the same spot once when we were driving home from a trip to Chicago and he found (he said) that he couldn't wait to kiss me . . .

I didn't want to be on this lonely rutted lane. Was this how it had been for Luis? They had driven him somewhere and said, *This is the end of the road*?

"I don't understand why I'm here," I said, my voice shaky. "Let me go, before I call the police!"

Elena snorted. "Oh yes, your police friends. I just bet they'd be happy to haul all three of us away, wouldn't they? Lock us up and throw away the key so that no one ever knows about this meeting."

I reached for my phone in my jacket pocket, but Joe

Piper leaned over and wrested it from me. "Give it back!" I cried. "Give me back my phone, and let me out of here!"

I lunged toward the door on Elena's side and tried to open it; she tore my hand away, and the two of us were suddenly wrestling, gasping, almost spitting at each other in our fury.

"Let me go!" I cried, trying to tear her clawlike grip from my arm. "How dare you?"

She squeezed harder, her face mean. "You've got a lot of gall, lady. How dare I? Why don't you tell me why you came to my coffee shop? Why you were outside the vet when I came out? Why you seem to be spying on me for them every chance you get?"

"I'm not spying for anyone! I went to your coffee shop because I wanted coffee."

"Right. God, I am sick of the lies in this town. Even little Pollyannas like you lie right to my face! I can't stand it anymore!" Her eyes glittered with some dangerous emotion.

A pulse of anger burst through my fear. "If you don't commit crimes, people tend to leave you alone!"

She snorted. "I don't need lectures from you, a freaking double agent!"

I stared at her. "What does that mean?"

She said nothing; her jaw was tight with anger.

I tried to tone down my panic, to reason with them. "I can assure you that you will be in very big trouble if you don't take me back to the store this instant. Adam will be looking for me, and the security camera will provide your license number."

Elena and Joe Piper exchanged a grim glance. She stuck out her chin. "Then I guess you don't have much time to tell us the truth." Her hand was still clutching my arm, and the grip seemed to tighten. The threat in her tone made me even angrier.

"To tell you the truth? You haven't told the truth to *anyone*!"

"What?" Her voice was cold.

I hesitated. What the heck? I didn't have anything to lose at this point by putting my cards on the table. "You want the truth? I know you're lying about your husband. I know you know what happened to him, and that you have a cover story. I know the two of you probably hurt him, and he was a good man." I glared at her, and then at Joe Piper. "And if he's dead, you'll have a lot to answer for, no matter what you do to me!"

Her hand dropped away from my arm, and in the next instant I found myself unencumbered, wiping at my furious tears. Elena's eyes looked almost black as she pondered my words, her face blank and white. "What? What did you say?"

I still knelt on the floor, facing Elena and her lover. "I know that you killed Luis. I know about his car, his blood. Everyone does—it was in the darn paper. And I know that you lied to the police, and to Carl, and to the man who came to your coffee shop to fill out an application. You've lied to everyone, because you hurt your husband. You and your conspirator from Plasti-Source, your hulk of a boyfriend here. I suppose you did it together."

Elena's eyes sparked with a sort of interest. "You think I killed Luis?"

"*Yes*. Are you telling me you didn't?"

She studied my face closely, leaning in to do it. She turned to Joe Piper, seemingly sending him some unspoken message. He shrugged at her and handed me a handkerchief from his pocket.

I wiped my eyes and blew my nose. "What's going on?" I said.

Elena sighed and leaned back. "You write those books, right? With Camilla Graham."

"Yes."

"I've read about some stuff you did. In the paper. But I had thought—" She shook her head. "No, of course that doesn't make sense."

She looked at Joe Piper again. "She helped catch that psycho from Greece. She helped put him away."

Joe nodded, then looked at me. "And you helped prove Sam West wasn't guilty, right?"

"Again, I will ask you what is going *on*? Why am I in your car? What do you want from me?"

She nodded. "Let me introduce myself to you. I'm Elena Castellan. Luis is my husband."

"I know that." My voice sounded bitter, even to me.

She pointed at Joe Piper. "And this is my *brother*, Joe. He helped Luis get the job at Plasti-Source."

"Your brother." My brain felt dull, full of cotton. The car shook with the onslaught of the cold wind.

She nodded. "Tommy's my brother, too. They've been helping me since this whole thing happened."

"*What* whole thing?"

"I think I've been all wrong about you, Lena London. But I think you're wrong about me, too. I apologize for the rough treatment. Joe, give back her phone."

He handed me my phone and I took it, scowling, still kneeling at their feet. "Please take me back to the gas station."

She shook her head. "In a minute, but first we have to talk. I need to set you straight about a few things, and you're going to want to hear them."

"Why is that?" I glared at her.

She didn't answer; she looked out the window and said, "You're friends with the cops, right?"

"A couple of them, yes."

"Be straight with me. Are they dirty? Are Blue Lake cops corrupt?"

I barked out a laugh. "That is the pot calling the kettle black, Elena. Doug Heller and Cliff Blake are as honest as they come. They've been trying to find your poor husband even though you didn't report him missing. Who sounds corrupt in *that* scenario?"

Her dark eyes slid back to meet mine. "How did they know he was missing if I didn't report it? See, that's why I wonder about Blue Lake cops."

Was this woman for real? "Because Carl *Frailey*, who is a good friend to Luis, reported him missing. Even though his wife and his boss conveniently decided he wasn't. Cops tend to think things like that are fishy. Which they are."

To my amazement, she smiled. A real smile, an almost happy one. "Carl *Frailey*!"

She looked at Joe, who smiled as well. "Little Carl, man. He's the fly in the ointment. He and Luis do have a bond."

Elena pointed at my phone. "Go ahead and text your friend. Tell him there's been a misunderstanding and that you'll meet him at home. But there are a few last things I want you to know."

"Like what?"

"Like this: I love my husband. I always have and I always will. Joe there is one of his best friends." For the first time her dark eyes softened and filled with tears. "And for the life of me I cannot imagine who would want him dead."

AFTER SOME WRANGLING, I convinced the three Piper siblings that the "meeting" Elena wanted to have should take place at Camilla's house, where we had used our roundtable of great minds to work through problems more complex than this one.

They agreed, reluctantly, and I made some calls. First to Adam, with an apology and a brief summation of what had happened; then to Doug, to suggest he might want to be present for the meeting; then to Camilla, to explain why I wanted to bring Elena Castellan to her house.

I knew Carl was already installed in his safe house, and Belinda was working, so it would just be the police for now.

We drove to Camilla's place, where the four of us were greeted at the door by two protective German shepherds and a scowling Adam. I held up a hand, a nonverbal encouragement to hear us out.

Adam backed away from the door, and I encouraged the three visitors to enter. Both of Elena's brothers had to duck to get through the doorway. Elena looked around her with a dazed expression. I doubted she had planned my abduction; Joe must have texted her from the convenience store when he saw me enter. The fact that they had seized me suggested a certain desperation, and now they found themselves here, unexpectedly, following Elena's instincts.

Camilla strolled down the hallway, and all three of them

looked slightly shamefaced at the sight of her. Camilla did not have the look of a conspirator; rather, she looked like someone's friendly, attractive aunt. She seemed to sense the ambivalence of everyone in the room. "Why don't we come back into the sunroom? I've got a space heater in there, and Rhonda whipped up some hot chocolate and cobbler. We can clear the air while you get warm."

Doug and Cliff arrived just then and came stomping up the front porch stairs to join us in the foyer. They were in uniform, and Elena pointed at Cliff. "You," she said. "You were at the vet." Her eyes went to the shepherds. "With one of those dogs, I'm guessing."

"Yes, ma'am," Cliff said. He stuck out his hand. "I'm Cliff Blake."

She shook her head; she still looked both uncertain and suspicious. "I must be an idiot. I know who you are—you're the long-lost brother of Sam West. I saw your picture in the paper."

"True, that's me. And I did go to the vet with Rochester there. The truth is, I have a crush on the veterinarian. I asked her out, and she said yes. We're having dinner tomorrow."

Elena was no fool. "That's not the only reason you were there."

Doug stepped forward. "No, Mrs. Castellan, it's not. He wanted to get a read on you. We all did. Because our information suggested that you might have something to do with the disappearance of your husband."

"Your information?" she said, her voice scornful. "I'm sorry, but I'm still not sure I trust you, or your source of information. For all I know, you could be on someone's payroll."

Doug found this interesting; he cocked his head slightly as he considered her words. "Who do you think would be paying us? And for what, exactly?"

Joe Piper put his hands on his hips. "Listen, we know that people at Plasti-Source have connections in this town. I know it, for sure. We just don't know how deep those connections go. So we're not going to trust any cop who comes to Elena's door, or any amateur detective who follows her"—he paused to look pointedly at me—"or anyone else who comes sniffing around."

I leaned in. "Is that why you lied to the boy applying for a job? You told him Luis cheated on you."

Elena stiffened. "His question seemed a little fishy, didn't it? Saying he really wanted to meet Luis for old times' sake? Suddenly all these strangers saying they want to see Luis. Even Carl—he showed up at my door asking where Luis was—how could I know who sent him?"

Doug and Cliff exchanged a glance; their police antennae had picked something up. "Wait a minute," Doug said. "Why are you so worried about people looking for Luis? You should be looking for him, too."

Something clicked then, and my pulse rate increased. "I know why you're not," I said. "You had Camilla's book in your coffee shop. *For the Love of Jane*. You read it, didn't you?"

Elena spun toward me, surprised. Then she allowed a little smile. "Aren't you smart."

Camilla came closer. "You read that book? I see. Oh my goodness!" Her eyes were bright. "Carl will be so pleased."

"What am I missing?" Doug asked, irritated.

I was still looking at Elena. "Luis is still alive, isn't he? And you know where he is."

·━◆· 19 ·◆━·

In her fourth week of captivity, her "aunt" left to do
some shopping, warning her to remain out of sight.
Celia knew instinctively that the tide had turned,
and hope surged within her.

—From *Danger at Debenham Station*,
a work in progress

ELENA SHRUGGED, THEN nodded. "I thought I was being so clever, but I guess I shouldn't have borrowed a plot written by someone who lives right here in town."

"I'm so relieved," Camilla said. "I was truly worried about that boy."

"You and me both," Elena said.

Doug and Cliff gaped at us, trying to follow our conversation. Camilla said, "Come to the back, everyone. We'll all help to explain things to one another."

We followed her, an obedient and unlikely gang, the dogs padding behind us. When we reached the sunroom, we found that the cats had joined us, too, and they all jumped up on the wide window ledges to observe the proceedings. Tommy snagged Geronimo and started petting him. Geronimo purred appreciatively.

Doug looked at his watch and accepted a cup of hot

chocolate from Camilla. "I don't even know where to start. Why does Camilla's book have anything to do with this?"

I looked at Camilla, who nodded at me. "*For the Love of Jane* is about a woman whose husband disappears. Remember I told you about it, when we were driving to the cabin? For a long time, she fears he is dead, but eventually it's discovered that he's faked his own death in order to keep her safe. There are dangerous people after him, and he doesn't want them to try to use his wife as leverage, so he arranges his death, which appears in all the newspapers, and she is safe. Of course, she learns all this eventually, and so she must hunt down the people who wanted him dead. And they have a romantic reunion at the end."

Just then Sam walked in, and all three visitors stared at him with interest. "Hello," he said. "What am I missing?"

I patted the seat next to me. "A whole lot. And I forgot to wake you from your nap because of it. Sam, this is Elena Castellan, and her brothers, Joe and Tom Piper."

"Her brothers," Sam said, his brows raised.

"Yes. I understand you thought Joe was my secret lover at Plasti-Source," Elena said, looking at Sam, and then, amused, at her brother.

"Well, not just me," Sam said. "So—what brings us all together?"

"Well, they, um—detained me earlier," I said. The Pipers looked chagrined. "But they did it because they thought I was in some kind of Blue Lake conspiracy against them and against Luis."

Doug held up a hand. "Let's get back to this. You had read Camilla's book, and you decided to use the plot to hide Luis. Why? Who did Luis have to hide from?"

"I don't know," Elena said.

"What?" Cliff stared at her, confused.

She looked at all of us in turn, then at her brothers.

Then she sighed and said, "Here it is. One night at Plasti-Source, someone tried to kill Luis. He doesn't know who it was, or why they tried to do it. He got away, but obviously he didn't go back to work. Then, just when he thought there might be some other explanation, or he might have misunderstood, they tried again. This time by attempting to run him down in the road. He came home really scared, and that's when we decided this. I didn't know who to trust. Those guys who run Plasti-Source have powerful connections. Luis says Mr. Grange is even friends with the governor. So—we needed to buy time."

"So you went out with the car and deserted it. I assume that's Luis's blood spattered on the windshield?"

She nodded. "He cut his hand, and I used my kitchen whisk to sort of flick it on the glass."

"Very resourceful," Camilla said.

Elena shifted in her chair and ran a finger down the smooth handle of her cup. "Then we got into my car, which held a bag for Luis, and we drove him to—an undisclosed location."

"And you're sure it's safe?" Doug asked.

"I think so. I took away his phone and destroyed the SIM card, so no one can track him on that. I check on him now and then through an intermediary. I can't go myself, because the other day Joe found a tracking device on my car."

"Really," Doug said, leaning in.

"I took it off," Joe said. "But then I realized that might have put Elena in danger, too. It tells someone we're on to them, I guess. I just hated the idea of them keeping tabs on her. We thought it might be you, actually."

Doug shook his head. "We don't do that, Mr. Piper."

Now Elena pushed her cup away, put her palms on the table, and leaned forward. "Yeah, well, someone did, and they want Luis bad; I just don't know why, and I don't know who. He said there's been no sign of anyone where he is, so that's good, but I've been really paranoid. How did I know that you weren't going to turn him in to some rich Plasti-Source guy when you came asking all your questions?" She turned to me. "And how did I know that you weren't, I don't know, the girlfriend of the murderer? Everyone who asked where he was, I had to be suspicious."

"That makes sense," Cliff said, nodding. "I think you did the right thing. Except when you held Lena against her will."

"I'm sorry," Elena said. She looked sorry, too, pale and sad. Some of her defenses were falling, and emotion was creeping in. "When Joe saw you in the store, he thought you followed him there. Followed us. And he just got mad. We were tired of not knowing."

Camilla said, "Dear, I'm going to have to insist that you have some hot chocolate. You look a little done in, and a bit of sugar can help."

Elena politely lifted the cup in front of her and took a sip. "Thank you," she said. "That's good."

"Tell me more about the attempted murder," Doug said. He had his phone out and was typing in some information.

Joe Piper spoke up. "Luis doesn't know why he has a target on his back. But I've known for a while that things were weird at work. There would be secret meetings, mostly run by Phil Enderby."

"What do you mean, secret?" Cliff asked.

"I mean, normally I'm part of all the administrative meetings, but I would find out that Phil had been talking with people in his office. I'd say, 'Did I miss a meeting?' And he would get all weird and say no, he was just talking with some inspectors or something."

"And who was usually in these meetings?"

He shrugged. "I didn't always see. Sometimes it was guys from the plant, and other times it was guys from Crandall Construction. They're out of Chicago, so they're not always around. They're—kind of rough-looking guys."

"And what about Edward Grange?"

"He was at some of the most recent meetings. He's been away because his wife died. But now he's back; I'm not sure if he knows what's going on. If Phil is up to something, he might be working alone."

Doug rapped the table. "Back to the attempted murder."

Joe nodded. "Yeah. Well, one evening Luis was working late. There had been some kind of computer glitch and people couldn't access the Internet or something. Luis is the head IT guy, so they told him to stay until it was resolved. He was in a basically empty plant, running back and forth between the server room and the executive offices. He said he was in this long hallway leading up to the offices of the top brass. There are smaller offices along the way, with glass panels in the doors so you can look in and see people working. Luis was moving along, and he tripped over the carpet runner. There's this plastic runner on the carpet, and it had bunched up somehow, and he tripped, and it saved his life. He heard glass shatter, and he looked up, and there was this fresh bullet hole in the window above him, right where his head had been."

Camilla gasped, her gaze riveted on Joe.

"Well, he whipped his head around and saw no one at all. But he knew it was a bullet, and he knew it was meant for him. He kept running, past the executive offices and to the south stairwell. He said it felt like he took those stairs about four at a time. He got to his car, shaking and trembling and fumbling for his keys. The whole time he was expecting another bullet. He sped home and told it all to Elena, and then they called me."

Doug speared him with a glance. "And you don't have any idea who could have done it? Do you have any sort of grudge against Luis Castellan, Mr. Piper?"

To my surprise, Joe didn't get angry. "Number one, Luis is my friend. I got him the job there, although we kept our relationship secret so people didn't cry nepotism. Number two, I was home in bed with my wife when Elena called to tell me what happened. You can ask Beth. We were—occupied for a few hours before we fell asleep."

Elena nodded. "It wasn't Joe. I know when my brothers are lying, and he's not lying. I told Luis not to go back to work for a while, but he was still running little errands in town. After the second time, though, when someone tried to run Luis down in the dark, we tried to pinpoint—what did he know?"

"He knew something," I said. "He said as much to the guys at Blue Lake Games."

Her eyes widened. "That's where he was when the car tried to hit him. That's the night we decided he had to disappear." She looked at Camilla, then back at me. "What did he say?"

Camilla said, "He mentioned Uriah Heep. A Dickens character who pretended to be helpful and subservient but was cheating and stealing money. Did he mention any suspicions to you about his workplace?"

Elena bit her lip. "He knew that there was something going on. The Anemone guys were there all the time, but then there was this whole other construction group."

"Crandall," Sam said.

The Pipers nodded, and Doug said, "The question is, why the need for two construction companies. Perhaps a secret pipeline project?"

Joe's face held some bitterness. "I'm plant manager," he said. "And I have no idea what we're doing with Crandall Construction. Although . . ." He squinted, thinking.

"What?" Cliff prompted.

"I did hear someone saying something once in the hall, outside my office. Just a quick something, I didn't catch much, and then later I couldn't pin Phil down about it."

"As much as you can recall, please," Doug said, his hands poised over his phone.

He shrugged. "Just something about how we didn't need a new pipeline, we just needed to repair the one we found."

"The one you found?" Doug and Cliff exchanged a glance. "I don't know of any pipelines in Blue Lake, aside from basic water pipes. Could they have been talking about the Stafford plant?"

"I guess. But Blue Lake is the site of our construction."

Camilla spooned into her cobbler. "Why is the construction halted?"

Joe sighed. "We have to jump through some hoops for the EPA inspector. The company has had issues in the past—chemicals from the plant getting into the local water supply in small amounts. We paid a fine, fixed the problem, or so Ed tells us. I didn't work at the Chicago plant. I was hired on in Stafford. Anyway, locals have done their research and they're demanding safe water, which is fair. But Ed and Phil have been pressuring me and Gino to get EPA approval so we can move on with construction."

"That's Gino Perucci?" Doug asked.

Joe sniffed and looked at his brother. "Yeah. You guys are really on top of this, aren't you?"

"Only because of Carl," I said. I was looking at Tommy. "Do you work at the plant, too?"

He smiled and said, "Nope. I manage a Walmart in Blueville. I'm just here for *familial* support." It was the first thing he had said all day. His voice had a pleasant twang, almost like an accent, but it was really just his sardonic tone.

"I need to think about this for a minute, and I'm going to eat cobbler while I do," Doug said, digging with a fork into the bowl in front of him. It was blueberry cobbler, still warm, with a dot of whipped cream on top.

Encouraged, the Piper men started to eat theirs, too, and Tommy moaned. "This is good, man. I didn't have lunch today."

"Oh my goodness. We have all sorts of things to feed you," Camilla said. "Adam, do you—?"

"I'm on it," he said, and he left the room. When he returned a few minutes later, bearing a tray full of sandwiches and little bowls of Rhonda's potato salad, everyone had finished the cobbler.

"They say you should eat dessert first, which we have done," I joked.

Adam put food in front of everyone like an adept waiter. "You're amazing," Cliff said.

Camilla watched him fondly. "Adam worked as a waiter all through college. He never lost the skills. That's when he decided he might want to own a restaurant one day."

Elena perked up. "Oh—you run Wheat Grass, don't you? It's really good. Luis and I eat there on every anniversary. We have one coming up." Her dark eyes grew sad again.

Doug tapped on the table, staring at his sandwich. Then he looked at Elena. "There's no way around this. I'm going to have to talk to Luis. We need to know what he knows, and we need to ask enough questions that he might come up with a fact, an idea, that he didn't have before."

Elena shook her head. "No way. He's safe where he is. You can't go there, or they'll know. You're a cop. They might even be watching us now, which means they know we're comparing notes, right? If they think Luis is alive, despite our little ruse, then they'll follow us all."

Doug was starting to get his cop look—tough and unyielding. "Then it won't be one of us who goes to get him."

"There's nowhere in this town to hide him," she said. "I'm not risking his life."

"There are many safe places. We could keep him at the police station, for one thing."

"What, in a cell?" She scowled at him. "No, thanks."

Something blinked on in my mind—an idea, fully illuminated. I smiled. "No, but maybe something *like* a cell. Something super private, secluded, away from the world, where no one would ever think of looking. Somewhere quiet, and even soundproof." I looked at Camilla, and then at Sam, and I saw that they both knew what I was thinking. Sam nodded his approval.

"Elena," I said. "I think I might have the perfect solution."

"What are you talking about?" she asked.

Doug and Cliff had caught on, too. Cliff said, "Lena's referencing the currently unoccupied home of Nikon Lazos. It has been vacant and for sale for several months."

"My friend Allison is pals with the real estate agent," I said. "I'll bet she would cooperate."

Tommy had finished petting Geronimo, who was looking drowsy. He set the little cat on the windowsill, and Geronimo promptly curled into a ball and went to sleep. Tommy looked back at us and frowned. "Didn't a bunch of people get shot in there?"

"Not a bunch," Doug said. "Just Cliff and me." They exchanged a look—cop solidarity.

"Oh wow—you both got shot?" Elena said.

Cliff looked slightly defensive. "You had to be there."

"They saved my life," Sam said. "And Lena's. But more to the point, we got very familiar with the layout in his basement. He had very comfortable living quarters down there; he hid in the place for months without anyone ever being the wiser."

"There would be no reason for whoever wants Luis to think he would have any connection to the notorious Lazos house."

"And we could even let him have a friend in there," Cliff said. "We're currently keeping Carl in a different safe house."

Elena's brows rose. "Carl? Why?"

Sam leaned back in his chair, one hand on his stomach. He had eaten almost all the food people had put in front of him. "He hacked into Plasti-Source computers. They have not reported the fact to the police; Carl is afraid they might want to silence him. Doug and Cliff there were kind of afraid of that as well."

"Oh my gosh, that kid," Elena said, almost grinning. "He's such a pain, but he really grows on you. Luis just loves him."

"He loves Luis," I said. "He's devastated. He thinks Luis is dead."

Elena looked at her brothers. Tommy said, "Do it, Lainey. He'll be closer to you and the cops will be keeping tabs on him. Let's get this resolved so Lu can come home to you."

Joe nodded. "I agree. Let's get Lu into the house. He and Carl can play their precious video games. And he can look for a job. He's obviously not going to want to return to this one." He scratched his head with a worried expression. "I don't know how long any of us will have jobs there if there's something fishy going on."

Doug looked at his watch again. "Where is Luis now? Is he at all nearby?"

Elena sighed. "Not exactly. About an hour and a half away. I couldn't send him to anyone traceable, not to any of my brothers."

Camilla smiled. "How many brothers do you have?"

"Six," Elena said. "These two are the only ones who live near me." She gestured at Joe and Tommy, looming on either side of her like pillars.

"So you sent him—where?" Cliff asked.

"I have this former teacher that I keep in touch with. She retired, and she and her husband have a farm. I don't want to say where."

"Would they be willing to drive him out here? They can go straight to the house in Allison's subdivision. We'll have Allison stock it up and get it ready. No one's watching her. She's not related to this at all," Doug said.

Elena pursed her lips. "I guess it would be okay. Let me know when it's ready. I'll have to borrow someone else's phone to call her. I don't know what kind of surveillance they're using on me or my family. I was calling her on that old pay phone at Bick's Hardware."

Camilla had been mostly quiet, listening to all of the testimony of Elena and her brothers. Now she folded her hands on the table and said, "I see that you drive a dark blue car. Did you happen to be the ones following Lena and Belinda around town? Did you follow them here yesterday after they left Blue Lake Games?"

The Piper siblings all wore the same blank expression. "I worked yesterday," Elena said. "So did these guys. They're only here because it's Saturday. And when Joe saw you in the store—that was just a coincidence. But we were waiting for him outside, so he called, and we pulled up the car."

Doug's eyes were on the lake, and the tree that bent under the assault of the icy rain. "You all just happened to be driving around together?"

"We didn't just happen to. We were still trying to figure out why Lena and Sam West were watching us. Tommy was along because he was going to have dinner with us. Joe was going to cook, and he stopped there for ingredients. And there you were," she said, looking at me. "And it felt like you were following us again. I just kind of lost it. I told Joe to bring you to the car."

Doug stood up. "We have to go, Cliff. Elena, I will let

you know when I've talked to Allison, and to the Realtor, and made arrangements about the house. They will both be sworn to secrecy under fear of prosecution."

"Okay," Elena said. She stood as well. "We should go, too. Camilla—it's really an honor to be here. I have read several of your books, and now that I know you guys aren't somehow plotting against Luis—well, it's really neat to meet you face-to-face."

Camilla nodded. "Thank you, dear. I think things will look up for you now; rather than bearing a secret alone, you have a team intellect working toward its resolution."

"I'm counting on that," she said.

Joe and Tommy shook hands with Doug and Cliff and then with the rest of us. Before they left, Joe sent Doug a warning look. "I don't know who it was following Lena and her friend, but if it's someone from Plasti-Source—well, just be careful."

"We will," Doug said. "And they will—right, Lena?"

"Yes. I'm always careful."

"Somehow that never helps," Sam said. He was standing, too, now, and looking restless in his Sam way.

Adam and Camilla ushered the visitors down the hall and out the front door, and Sam looked at me. "It continues to be an eventful week."

I wrapped my arms around him and rooted into his neck, which smelled faintly of sandalwood. "Mmm. It's so nice to see you up and around."

"Imagine my surprise, after waking from a Camilla-imposed nap, to find the Piper family in her sunroom."

"Imagine *my* surprise at being thrown into a car with them."

"What?" He looked murderous.

"No—all a misunderstanding. Don't look like that. What are we going to do about Carl?"

Sam shrugged, his arms still around my middle. "We don't do anything—that's Doug's territory. But I hope Doug is filling in Belinda, or I have a feeling there will be trouble in paradise."

SAM AND I spent the evening with Camilla and Adam, first watching a movie and then playing a few rounds of charades, before Sam yawned and I suggested he should go to bed. "Camilla, we'll meet in the morning, right?"

"Oh yes!" Camilla said. "And I have some notes for you for the writer's advice manual, if you'd like to look them over tonight. Let me run to my office." She left the living room and returned two minutes later with a small sheaf of papers.

"I will happily read this. And in return I will have a stab at an opening page for *Danger at Debenham Station*. I'll send it to you when I get upstairs."

"Perfect," she said. "Good night, dear."

"Good night." I hugged her and kissed Adam's cheek.

Sam said, "Camilla, Adam, congratulations on your wedding. I'm very happy for you."

"Thank you, dear," Camilla said. Sam shook Adam's hand.

Then we climbed the stairs together (with two kittens at our heels, though they seemed to think they were invisible). We went into my room, where Lestrade already lay on the bed like a lazy lion. "Our family," Sam said indulgently.

I laughed. "You go ahead and get ready for bed. I'm

probably going to work over here at the desk for a while. It has a built-in light, so the rest of the room can be dark and you can get some rest."

Sam went into the bathroom; I heard him brushing his teeth. When he emerged he looked both tired and young. "I was hoping you would tuck me in," he said.

Laughing, I jumped onto the bed and got under the covers as Sam climbed in the other side. "Just for a minute," I said, as his warm mouth met mine. The rain had finally ended, but a cold wind still battered the window, and it was as if time had returned to the moment when I had first kissed Sam, the cold wind blowing around us as we stood in front of the tall pine at the foot of his driveway. That had been a year ago, and now we were going to be married . . .

"It's nice and warm in here," Sam said near my ear.

"It's the flannel sheets."

"It's also because I have a warm companion." His words were flirtatious, but his eyes were closed.

I kissed his nose. "I want you to go to sleep now. Your warm companion will still be here in the morning, along with various felines."

"Mmm," he said. I waited until he was fully asleep, watching the gradual relaxing of his features. His face bore some lines from life's harsh blows, but it retained its basic character and sensitivity. It was a courageous face. I kissed him gently on one cheekbone and then slid out of the bed. I still felt alert, partly because I was eager to see Camilla's notes about her book.

I went to the corner and flipped on the light in my desk. I opened my laptop and studied what I had written. I had tried to mimic her style, which was all at once nostalgic, wise, and suspenseful. My first line: "Once she got to Debenham, Fiona intended to tell her aunt everything it had been too hard to say in a letter; in fact, she climbed aboard the morning train feeling confident that any miscommunications between them would be cleared up that evening, when her aunt met her at the station."

A pang of regret surged through me. "Too wordy," I murmured. "And not suspenseful enough." I found myself suffering from the common writer's malady of hating what I had previously liked.

With a sigh, I thought about other options for beginning the book. Perhaps the focus did not initially need to be on her destination, but on the train itself. Perhaps Fiona would have some sort of experience on the train that would become significant later. Might she meet her love interest there? Might he be going to Debenham as well? Or perhaps he would disembark slightly earlier, so that the reader and Fiona temporarily forgot him?

Or what if there was some sort of clue on the train, some object that Fiona might notice over and over again, but only unconsciously. Later perhaps that object would become significant.

"Hmm," I said, liking this thought.

I deleted the first sentence and changed it to "The train wasn't particularly crowded, but somehow the red suitcase two seats ahead of her managed to block her view of both the passing scenery and the front of the car."

A red suitcase? Seemed too obvious. And how would it end up being significant later?

With a sigh, I deleted that sentence and retyped the original one. "Camilla will know," I said to Arabella, who had daintily jumped onto the desk and begun to wash her one black paw. I scratched her little ears, then attached my document to an e-mail and sent it to my mentor.

I pushed my computer away and pulled out her notes for the writer's advice manual. She had tentatively titled it "A Writer's Guide to the Story Within." I scratched a note on this. "Isn't every story within until we bring it out? Is that the point you're making? Or should you be using second person to include the audience? What about 'We All Have a Story: Camilla Graham Helps You Find Your Life's Narrative'?" I stared at the paper. "But that doesn't indicate that this is also a memoir." I said this to Arabella's fuzzy face, and she seemed to contemplate what I was saying. "Your story is very interesting, Arabella. Kind of a rags-to-riches tale. With that benevolent king over there taking you into his castle. The question is, how did you get up on that bluff in the first place, back when he found you and your brothers?"

Arabella wasn't telling. Her eyes were half-closed, and she purred with pleasure at receiving my attention.

"What a weird day," I said. Arabella's eyes opened long enough for her to climb up my arm and settle on my chest. I scratched the ruff of her neck and leaned back in my chair.

Really, life had been strange since Sam and I had received Doug's call, back when we were innocently making wedding plans on the bluff. That had led us to Carl, who had led us to Luis, who had led us to Plasti-Source.

"What an ugly name," I said softly to the sleepy cat. "Harsh and hard. But I guess that's appropriate for plastic." I sighed, got up, and set Arabella next to Sam. Geronimo and Lestrade were already pressed against his left side. More warm companions. I grinned, then returned to the desk. I was still awake, and Camilla's notes awaited.

I sat down and picked up a purple pen that Camilla had given me in August—she said it matched my purple chair. I began to scratch my notes on the paper, aware of my own gratitude: Camilla's writing was always a pleasure to read; Sam was on the mend and tucked safely into a healing sleep; the kittens were all safe from the elements; Carl and Luis were both safe; Camilla and Adam were married; Belinda was safe and back with Doug, who loved her. The repeated theme there, I realized, was safety.

Nothing else mattered, really, if one wasn't safe.

I looked at the dark window. Even in the blackness I could make out the motion of trees, tossing in the cold, windy night. The weather in Blue Lake, I had learned from experience, could be cruel and relentless.

An image came back to me, unbidden, of a man at Camilla's dining room window, scowling, full of menace. He had nothing to do with Elena or her brothers. Who was he?

And what did he want from the people in Graham House?

The question kept me wakeful for another long hour.

✦ · 20 · ✦

*The dark night. The ominous feeling. The ghostly
pursuer.*
   *All of these combine to create what we all seek
in a Gothic suspense tale.*
                    —From the notebooks of Camilla Graham

I WAS SEEING Luis Castellan—really seeing him—for the
first time. Of course, now I remembered him from the
book group discussions, but we had learned so many
more dimensions of his life that it was like looking at a
long-lost friend.

Doug had made the arrangements he had promised,
installing both Luis and Carl in the old Lazos home in
the middle of the night. Now Luis sat in front of a computer, Skyping with the members of law enforcement in
Camilla Graham's home so that, Doug said, "every darn
piece of the puzzle can be accounted for" by the people
who all knew one bit or another. Crammed into Camilla's office, besides Camilla and Adam, were Doug, Cliff,
Sam, Belinda, me, and Elena Castellan with her brother
Joc. Luis had been told in advance whom to expect, but

he still smiled wryly at Belinda and me. "Maybe we could do a quick book discussion while we're here," he joked.

"I'm game," Belinda said, smiling.

Luis's eyes went to Elena. "Hey, babe," he said.

"Hey, babe." Her eyes filled with tears as she waved.

"How you holdin' up?" Luis said.

"A little better now that we've got a bigger team," Elena said, dabbing at her eyes with a handkerchief Adam provided. "These guys have been great." She gestured vaguely at all of us.

Luis nodded. "Yeah, I have to say these are classy accommodations. We've got everything at our fingertips. The advantage of staying in a millionaire's lair, right?"

"Billionaire," Doug said.

"Even better," Luis joked.

Cliff looked restless. "We've got some questions for you, Luis. Are you all settled? Is it okay to get started on those?"

Luis grew more solemn. "Yeah, absolutely. Let's get to the bottom of this so I can get home to that lady there."

Doug and Cliff consulted each other briefly, then said, "Let's start with the night that someone tried to shoot you. You didn't see anyone? No sign of anything we could investigate further?"

He shrugged. "No. I've been going over it in my head. I just—it still doesn't feel real. I mean, why me? I'm just an IT guy." Carl appeared beside Luis, holding a cup of coffee. He offered it to his friend, and Luis claimed it and set it down, then pulled Carl onto the bench beside him, wrapping an arm around Carl's shoulder and giving him a hearty half hug. "This guy! He's like my little brother. Went around town looking for me when Elena killed me off."

Carl grinned; he looked about twelve years old. "I knew you wouldn't walk out on her," Carl said. "I was right."

"You were right," Luis agreed, looking at Carl. Then he turned back to us, his brown eyes smiling. "Carl made me a breakfast so delicious I almost cried."

"Mmm," several people said at once. So many of us had now sampled Carl's cooking that we understood exactly what Luis meant.

Doug sat up straight in his chair. "Anyway, about last Monday night."

"Yeah. I finally fixed the problem on Phil's computer. He's the one who had told me to stay late. He said it had been acting up all day. The guy constantly abuses his computer, and then he gets upset when it doesn't work right. Drives me nuts." He scowled at the memory of Phil's abuse. "So it was maybe eight o'clock. The plant was empty except for maybe a cleaning person or two; there was a vacuum cleaner running somewhere."

I glanced around. Everyone's eyes were riveted on Luis, except for Adam's, which were fixed on Camilla; he smiled slightly. Of course, he was appreciating the fact that she got to sit up front at a real-life mystery. Adam was always looking for gifts to give Camilla, and he hadn't even had to arrange this one.

"How did you know it was a bullet that broke the glass, and not something else?" Cliff asked.

Luis focused in on him. "When my brother and I were kids we sometimes got to take my dad's shotgun, under supervision, and shoot stuff in the woods. One time we shot an old window from a shed we tore down. The hole looked just the same. The window in that shed was pretty thick, to keep out weather and varmints. And the window in this door at work was a pretty good thickness, too—it's an older building and stuff was built to last back then. So it's not hard to see when a bullet hits glass like that. You get the central hole, and then a lot of webbing effect around it. And of course there's that sound, that little *chick* sound. I never had a doubt. I bent over, I heard it and then saw it, and my brain said *run*."

Doug leaned in. "Did you have the sense that someone was chasing you?"

"I did. You know how, when your adrenaline is high, you just know things? I knew two things: that someone was shooting at *me*, and that that someone didn't want to be seen. So I mostly ran, but a couple of times I dared a look backward. I never saw a thing, except one time I thought I caught a shadow as it darted behind a pillar. That was when I was already on the factory floor. There were a couple night-shift guys down there, so I think the person chasing me gave it up at that point."

Cliff scratched his head and blinked in a sudden sunbeam. "Anything happen that day that made you suspicious? Any interactions with people that might make them hold a grudge?"

Luis nodded. "Nothing I thought would get me killed, but yeah. First of all, when I worked on Phil's screen there was a weird e-mail. He told me straight up not to read his e-mail, just to fix the computer. But he also reminded me that all of his stuff was privileged administrative information, blah blah, and I could be fired for sharing anything."

"Way to be subtle, Phil," Joe Piper said. "There's no doubt that guy is up to something; I just don't know what."

"What did the e-mail say, Luis?" Camilla asked.

"It was from a guy at Crandall Construction. They're building the waste disposal system for the new plant. Our quality control guy, Gino, was looking at the blueprints a couple weeks ago. But this e-mail seemed to be about something else. The guy said something like 'I know you have a timeline for inspection, but if you're trying to avoid the Feds and Blue Lake officials, we're going to have to work at night.'"

"Work at night," Camilla murmured.

"That's interesting," Doug said. "Anything else?"

"I had talked with Joe in the past about the fact that Phil seemed to be shady. We had agreed that if we got wind of what he was up to we would go to Ed. But Ed was gone for more than a month because his wife died. Then he came back and he looked kind of thin and sad, and we didn't want to bother him unnecessarily."

"It hasn't been a great situation," Joe said. "Gino is on the verge of quitting. He's supposed to guarantee the safety of everything and he said that lately he's basically not even consulted."

Luis took a sip of his coffee. Carl studied the side of his face, absorbed in his story. Luis smiled at him, then looked at Doug. "So even before I saw the e-mail I noticed that Phil was looking at some alternative chemicals; they had gotten in trouble in Chicago for some of the stuff they used in production, and Ed's goal was to move toward less toxic materials."

"What do you mean?" I said.

Luis looked at me. "Well, we—sometimes additives

can be incorporated into polymers, if you have the goal of improving the basic quality of your plastic product. They had used one chemical, I guess, that the local health board in Chicago didn't like. So Phil had samples from some companies, and I know he and his team had done some limited testing on a few of the new products. I jotted down the names—this was maybe three, four weeks ago. Then I went home and researched them. As far as I could see, none was an improvement on what we had gotten in trouble for in the past, and one was really bad. It was called Dythnocan HT. If you look it up you can read stories of people having terrible reactions to it, just breathing it in. People having asthma attacks, people vomiting. In one case someone died. You could imagine if somehow it was ingested, although I guess in smaller doses it wouldn't have an obvious effect. Except that you'd probably eventually die."

"So of course they wouldn't choose that one," Adam said.

Joe snorted. "The company line is, lots of chemicals are toxic. We use them in a safe, controlled environment, so they're fine. Do you know there are laws that protect companies from having to reveal all the toxins in their products?"

"It's disgusting," Elena said. "When Luis was reading this research, he was getting really mad. He said he had to look for a new job."

Luis held up a hand. "But first I wanted to make it clear what was happening. I went to Ed. He was just back, still looking kind of out of touch and pale in his office, and I felt bad bothering him. But he's the president, for gosh sakes. And besides, his wife was an environmentalist. He was concerned about stuff like that, because of her." Luis shook his head for a minute, thinking back. "So I went to him and put some of my research on his desk. I said, 'I know this is a bad time, but we're going to be in production in a few months, and this stuff is toxic.'"

"Was he on board? Did he acknowledge your concerns?"

Luis picked up his coffee and held it in both hands. "He looked surprised. He was sitting there, reading the articles like he hadn't ever heard this stuff. I mean, he has guys he pays to do all this research. I think he was just dialed out—he probably shouldn't have come back so soon. I said, 'Ed, you and I both know that if you put this stuff in water it would be deadly.' He sat there for a minute kind of frowning at the articles, and then he asked me if Phil knew. I said I didn't know, but that I wasn't privy to the meetings Phil Enderby attended."

Joe cracked his knuckles, scowling. He looked at Doug and Cliff. "I was privy to a lot of them, but believe me, those guys weren't talking about public health concerns," Joe said. "Luis was stirring things up more openly than I was, but I had been looking into things, too. Our plant is pretty equally divided, I think, between employees who care about people and employees who care about profit. Those top guys seem to care about profit. Even Ed, although I think he cares about the average Joe."

I looked at Belinda and saw that she felt my distress. Blue Lake, our Blue Lake! What if it were sullied by the chemicals from the monstrous Plasti-Source? The executives within could take their money and run, but we had to live here. We frolicked in the lake in summer, and there was our water to consider, Blue Lake water, fresh and delicious. It all came back to the water, in the end. Could we as people manage not to contaminate our basic source of life?

"Lena's getting depressed," Sam said, holding my hand.

"It's all so unbelievable. That people could be so crass and callous. So uncaring about the welfare of others. So irresponsible," I said.

"Hey, we don't have evidence of anything," Doug said. "Let's not get ahead of ourselves."

Cliff said, "Let's get back to the timeline. They shot at you, what, a week ago?"

Luis thought. "More than that. It's been nine days."

"Then you came home and told your wife."

"He was really shaken up about it, as you can imagine," Elena said. "I told him no way was he going back to work."

Doug looked sternly at the screen. "Funny thing is, Luis, I have no record of a police report about the shooting."

"No, you don't." Luis lifted his chin. "This might be paranoia, but when I was driving out of the parking lot, a cop car was driving in. Really fast, but with no light on. I tore out of there and never looked back, but it got me thinking: Did whoever was inside call a pal on the police force? Did he ask him to come and hunt for me? Why else would that car have been speeding to an empty Plasti-Source parking lot?"

Doug and Cliff exchanged a glance, then laughed. "Because Chip Johnson is an idiot," Cliff said.

"What?" Luis looked at him blankly.

"Chip is young and hungry. He likes action. Sometimes he goes to parking lots to practice his driving. For when that big chase comes along." Cliff glanced at his watch. I wondered if he had arrangements to make for his big date. "Okay, that explains why you didn't call the cops. You were paranoid. And it explains why you didn't go back to work. What was your plan, then?"

Luis sighed. "I talked it out with Elena that night. Once things settled down, and my heart rate went back to normal, I started thinking, it couldn't have been what I thought. Why would someone shoot at me? In a place of business? And why would I never see that person chasing after me?"

Elena turned to look at us. "I believed Lu when he came home; he was obviously terrified and traumatized. But the more we talked, the more we said—it just doesn't make sense. We figured we'd have him call in sick. Meanwhile, he called Carl and asked him to take a look at the window in that first-floor office."

"I just told Carl I thought I noticed it was broken, and I asked him to tell me if it was."

"I knew you were lying," Carl said. "But I thought you broke the window."

Luis let out a bitter laugh. "If only my problems were that simple. Carl called me back the next day at lunch. He left a message the window was intact, no break at all. So either I was totally losing it, or someone had worked to make sure that window was repaired before any employees got to work. Which suggested either someone in charge, or someone with keys."

"It was a new window," Carl said.

"How do you know?" Cliff asked.

"The smell. It had that glue smell of whatever they

caulk it with. It didn't smell that way before." Carl looked out at us with his canny green eyes and I felt a chill, even in a room full of warm bodies.

"Who all has keys?" Doug asked.

"Not me or Carl," Luis said. "I guess all the top guys. Ed, Gino, Phil, Joe. Some other executives."

Everyone pondered the information for a moment. I said, "I have a question. When Luis disappeared, Carl said that his bosses weren't concerned about it because Luis had a reputation for this sort of thing. But we know that Luis doesn't. So who started that rumor? Or was one of the bosses just lying to Carl?"

Joe Piper cleared his throat, looked at Elena, and raised his hand. "I did that."

The attention of those assembled shifted to him. "I didn't want anyone looking for Lu, so I told his boss, Gary, that Luis had a reputation at his previous job for just not showing up for weeks at a time. I said I had warned him not to do it here, but apparently he was up to his old tricks."

"And Gary believed that?" Doug asked.

"He did. So much so that he complained to his bosses about it. I told him on Tuesday—the day Luis didn't show up—and they started interviewing other IT people a day later."

"But at least one person probably knew why Luis was gone," Camilla said. "Luis, I have a question, too. Why did you go to Blue Lake Games if you were in hiding?"

Luis shrugged. "Saturday morning, I had calmed down a little. Elena said no way was I going back to Stafford, but we were both starting to think it was an isolated thing. Maybe a security guard was drunk, or maybe I surprised a burglar or something. We really couldn't believe that anyone would be shooting at me personally. Even though that's exactly what we thought the night before. And I realized I couldn't just hide in my house forever. So I went out and about. I got groceries and brought them home. I raked some leaves. I kept an eye out on my street, but nothing was unusual. Then Carl called and asked if I wanted to go the game store. I said sure."

"Why did you talk about Uriah Heep at the store?" Camilla asked. "Were you still thinking of Phil Enderby?"

Luis's eyes darkened. "Yeah, I was feeling bad vibes about the whole situation. How some of the bosses were probably corrupt, and how I still felt weirded out about the whole shooting thing. And the police car. So, yes, corruption and fakery were on my mind."

"And after you left?" Doug said.

"Carl and I talked for a while on the sidewalk. We said good-bye, and he walked down the block to where his car was. I looked at some games in the window of BLG, and then I started to cross the street to my car. I heard it coming." He looked right into the camera, his eyes wide with the memory. "I felt it, you know? That it was bad. And I heard the guy hit the gas. So I dove, and he missed me by about a foot."

"He came home shaking like a leaf. That's when we decided we had to be drastic, and to kill him. We had no idea who we could trust," Elena said.

"That must have been so scary." I sent her a sympathetic glance.

She nodded; then she folded her arms and looked at Doug and Cliff. "What do we do now? How do we get Luis out of hiding? How are you going to get these guys?"

Doug sighed. "It's not as simple as storming the plant and shutting it down. We need to have some reason either to search their premises or investigate their records. I'll certainly be talking to the top guys again, and Cliff and I plan to look more deeply into Crandall Construction. But the problem is, the people at Plasti-Source are going to lie to me, the way they've been lying to me all along. I need something to use as leverage. Something to pry them open with some honest information."

"This could take forever," Elena said, clearly on the verge of tears.

Belinda had been quiet for some time, tapping on her phone. "I have an idea," she said.

Everyone turned to look at her. "I get Plasti-Source e-mail alerts; at some point I signed up with them so I could keep track of the plant's progress. There's a new alert this morning saying that there's an open tour at the Stafford plant tomorrow evening. Apparently, it's for all those citizens concerned about safety. They're going to take people through the plant and answer questions. Blue Lake residents are welcome as well." She read this off her phone, but now she looked up at us and pushed her glasses up on her nose.

I stole a glance at Doug, who looked besotted.

"Brilliant," said Cliff. He stood up and looked at his watch. "Who wants to go to an open house?"

Everyone in the room raised a hand.

Doug shook his head. "Elena, you're not going. That would raise suspicions—people there know you. That wouldn't necessarily be a bad thing, but since they don't know what happened to Luis, they might assume you're there with a grudge."

Elena looked at Joe, who nodded. "They'd certainly have questions about me being there. I guess we're out."

"The rest of us have valid reasons to be there. We're either law enforcement officials or members of the community. Even if someone at Plasti-Source has been keeping tabs on some of us, they have no reason to think this wouldn't just be an innocent fact-finding mission."

"You'd be surprised," Camilla murmured. "But as a newly married woman, I can certainly say that my husband and I would like to ask some questions at the Stafford plant."

"What?" Doug said. He stared at Camilla, his face shocked. "What did you say?"

Camilla's eyes widened. "Oh, Doug, I'm sorry—I thought Belinda or someone would have told you. Adam and I were married a few days ago."

Doug stood up, grinning from ear to ear, and went to embrace her. "Congratulations, Milla! I am really happy for you."

"Thank you, dear."

Doug shook Adam's hand, still grinning.

Adam said, "Where Camilla goeth, there go I. We can certainly look the part of concerned retirees at this tour, rather than sleuths looking for dirt on Plasti-Source. Should I smoke a pipe?"

Doug barked out a laugh. "We don't need anything out of central casting. Let's just go, be ourselves, listen to questions, and look around. And when I say look around, I mean poke into things. If anyone complains, we can say that we thought open house meant we could look at whatever. Right? Peek into offices, jot down serial numbers of machinery, whatever you feel like doing."

I had been mulling things over. "I'm just wondering— why have this open house at all? Didn't they just have a meeting in Blue Lake that was meant to answer residents' concerns? It was written up in the paper, right? And the Stafford plant has been around a long time."

Doug lifted his shoulders. "In response to complaints, maybe. People in Blue Lake who still aren't thrilled with the idea."

Sam raised his hand. "Lena and I saw a sign protesting the new plant. It was signed by some group. What was it called, Lena?"

"Something with ecology," I said, trying to remember.

"That's it. The Blue Lake Ecology Commission. It sounded like a fancy name for just a few ticked-off townies. But maybe this group is putting pressure on Plasti-Source," Sam said.

Doug nodded, thoughtful, and made a note in his phone.

Cliff's eyes were on the monitor. "Luis, Carl, will you be okay there for a while? I think you're pretty well stocked. Is there anything you need?"

Luis and Carl exchanged a glance. "Well, there is one thing," the older man said. "I can't have Elena pick up my new copy of *Blood World* at Blue Lake Games because then they'd ask her where I was. But if someone could smuggle us a copy—well, between that and Carl's food I'd be pretty much set. This Lazos guy has a primo gaming system here that no one has touched."

A chill fluttered down my spine. I remembered the claustrophobic feeling of Nikon Lazos's basement lair, beautiful as it was, and how I feared I would never leave that place. I tried never to look at it when I visited Allison, but sometimes my eyes would dart across the street and remember the horror of that house. On the other hand, we had found treasure in that cave-like dwelling: Baby Athena. And we had the joy of reuniting her with her mother. The pendulum had swung back . . .

"It sounds like my dinners will be a real disappointment after Carl's cooking. I had no idea, Carl!" Elena said.

Carl shrugged. "I watch a lot of cooking shows," he said. It seemed to be his mantra, and it made me smile.

"Carl, I'll need you at Wheat Grass very soon. That gives us incentive to resolve everything quickly," Adam said. "Andre can't wait to meet you."

Carl looked pleased. He nodded, then walked away with Luis's empty coffee cup.

Doug said, "Luis, thank you very much. We'll be in touch. I'll leave you to say your good-byes to your wife."

He went into Camilla's front hall, where I found him checking his texts. Belinda joined us. "I have to go," he said, slipping an arm around her. "Cliff and I have work to do. But I'll see you tonight." He kissed Belinda on the cheek. "How about if you drop me off at the station? Cliff can drive the other car back."

"Okay," Belinda said, pleased.

"Go start the car, I'll be right there; I just want to ask Lena something."

She waved at me. "See you tomorrow."

After she had gone out Camilla's front door, Doug said, "Who's going to be here tonight?"

"Full house," I told him. "Camilla, Adam, Sam, me."

"Keep your eyes open."

I edged closer to him. "What's going on?"

He tapped his phone a few times and then held it out to me. "Is this the man you saw in the window?"

I gasped. "Yes! Oh my gosh—who is he? How did you get that picture?"

Doug looked grim. "His name is John Driscoll. He works at Crandall Construction; from what I can tell he doesn't have actual training in the trade, but he's a sort of general dogsbody. He's got a record; he served time for breaking and entering. I've got an APB out on him, but he hasn't been seen since he appeared in your window Sunday night."

"Huh." I stared at the photo; it was a mug shot in which Driscoll was scowling, so his expression was pretty much just as I remembered it. "Okay, now you have me nervous."

"I just want you to be vigilant. I'm guessing he won't return, but this whole thing with Luis, and Plasti-Source, and a spy on your property—it's giving me bad vibes."

"Okay. We'll lock up tight. We've got two German shepherds and four smart people. Adam, as we have all learned, possesses a gun, despite Camilla's reservations." I didn't add that Adam had saved my life with that weapon, but Doug and I both remembered that drama quite well.

He said, "That's really cool that Camilla and Adam got married. I've known them both a long time."

"It is. They're both so happy." We looked over as the couple in question strolled out of the office, conversing with Sam and Cliff.

A horn tooted outside: Belinda letting Doug know she had pulled up to the door. Doug said, "I've got to go. Remember what I said." His gaze shifted to the other cop in the room. "Cliff? I'm going with Belinda—see you at the station." He waved and moved out the door.

Cliff said something to Camilla, gave his brother a quick hug, and walked past me.

"Ready for your date?" I murmured.

"Ready as I'll ever be," he said with his charming Cliff smile. Isabelle was going to fall hard, I was sure.

He strolled out the front door, whistling under his breath.

Sam appeared at my side, and I felt his forehead. "You might almost be healthy," I said. "You feel good."

"So do you," he said, squeezing me against him.

I giggled.

"What was Doug saying? He was wearing his 'concerned father' face."

"He found the man from the window. An ex-con named Driscoll who is currently on the loose."

"Of course he is." Sam sighed. "So he wants us to batten down the hatches?"

"Yes. He has bad vibes."

Sam was quiet for a moment. My head was still resting on his chest; I could hear the rhythmic beating of his heart. He put his nose into my hair and murmured, "We need to live in a monastery or something."

I stepped away from him, reluctantly. "Nowhere you can go that human evil can't reach you."

He studied my face. "Are you okay?"

"Yeah. I probably just need some lunch."

His eyes left mine to find Adam and Camilla. "What sounds good for lunchtime?" he said to them. "Should I order something for everyone?"

Camilla came closer. "Rhonda has us covered. Adam and I are going to take the dogs out for a minute, and then we can regroup."

"Stay close," Sam said.

She and Adam understood; they had seen me talking to Doug.

"We will," Adam said. Elena and Joe came out of the office, and Camilla walked them to the door, speaking graciously to them. Elena hugged her in a sudden burst of emotion, and then she and Joe disappeared down the steps.

Camilla returned and looked at me, reading my mind in her Camilla way. "Everything will be fine," she said.

I wanted that to be true. I wanted to get back to the preparations for her party, to sit with her and talk about her new book projects. I wanted to walk the dogs with her and share Blue Lake gossip without fear that somehow we were being watched, or that the very water we drank might be contaminated.

Camilla understood all this, and she squeezed my hand. "Mark my words," she said. "By the end of the week, this will all be over."

21

*In a Gothic tale, there must always be a terrible
structure. It is the embodiment of evil.*

　　　　　—From the notebooks of Camilla Graham

STAFFORD WAS NOT a pretty town, but it had a certain
dignity, thanks to some antique architecture and a rather
grand town hall. The Plasti-Source building was on the
outskirts, between a gas station and a used-car dealer-
ship. It sat on a huge lot like a gray metal spider, and
when we pulled off Blandings Road at six o'clock, we
found many available parking spaces, since the factory
workers had left at five.

　　Sam and I had doubled up with Adam and Camilla in
Adam's car; Doug and Belinda had driven on their own
in Belinda's Mazda. Rusty had found himself short-
handed, so Cliff had to work.

　　We walked toward the building, which, in the waning
light, looked more black than gray. It blotted out the twilight with its hulking form; it was not a welcoming place.

Camilla tucked her hand in the crook of my arm and murmured, "Welcome to Thornfield after the fire."

I sniffed my agreement.

"More like Castle Frankenstein," Sam said.

"But without the Gothic charm. This thing looks like it was designed by a kid with Legos," I said. "And this is what we have to look forward to in Blue Lake."

Adam had given it a more objective scrutiny. "Luis said this building was old, didn't he? But it doesn't look well maintained."

I followed his gaze and saw that, even in the dim light, the building looked as though it could use some care and maintenance. The minimal landscaping was overgrown, and parts of the gray siding seemed to be bulging away from the frame.

We went through two large main doors into a factory lobby with cement floors. A woman in a lab coat met us there; she wore a name tag that said "Barbara." In all, the tour group only had about twenty people, including the six of us, which surprised me. What about the angry citizens? Wouldn't they have drummed up support for this event?

"Thank you for coming to Plasti-Source," Barbara said. "Please refrain from taking any photographs during our tour. I'll be happy to answer any questions you may have, so feel free to raise your hand at any time. I'm sure you'll be fascinated to learn about the patented process we use to create plastic sheeting, containers, and strips."

Belinda stood behind the group, typing away at her phone. She was more adept than anyone at pulling up significant information with just her cell phone. Leave it to a librarian to use a phone as a mini card catalog. Moments later she stood beside me and said, "Plasti-Source does not have any patents on file with the US Patent Office. Lie number one."

Barbara glanced at us to see if we had a question, but we merely smiled at her, so she finished her introduction. "If you'll follow me, I'll lead you to the factory floor." Two silver-haired men in suits walked swiftly past, and Barbara pointed at them, her face euphoric. "Oh, what an honor, everyone! This is the president of Plasti-Source, Edward Grange, and the vice president, Philip Enderby! They'll be available to answer questions after our tour."

The men paused briefly to send a friendly wave to the group, looking like politicians in a campaign commercial. I realized where I had seen Edward Grange before: he was the man who had been buying camping supplies when I bought Sam's medicine. Today's suit transformed him into a corporate look-alike, but I recalled the sadness and vulnerability of the man in the store. Perhaps he had been thinking about this wife.

As they walked toward a side door, I thought Edward Grange caught my eye; perhaps he recalled our meeting as well. I followed the small crowd, wondering what Grange's environmentalist wife had thought of Plasti-Source overall as a career choice for him.

I looked at Sam, who had narrowed his eyes at the two men. "He looks shady," he said.

"Who, Grange?"

"No. Enderby. Did you notice the way he didn't make eye contact when he waved? He looked over our heads."

I hadn't noticed that. My gaze moved to Camilla and Adam, whose hands were joined casually as they moved along, looking as if they were genuinely enjoying the tour.

In the factory, Barbara instructed the foreman to turn on some machines, after which she had to yell at us. "You'll probably be surprised to see how many sophisticated robotics we use here in the factory! We have robots that load and unload injection molding machines, kit our plastic components, and even pack our finished products for shipping."

We watched dutifully, trudging along the line as metal arms toiled over the various tasks of making plastic. At the end of the giant factory floor, it was a bit less noisy, and some people ventured to ask Barbara questions about production. Who bought the plastic products? Did they remain in the US? How expensive were they? Were they filled with dangerous chemicals?

Barbara had clearly been listening for that last question, because she gave it special attention, speaking soothingly with euphemisms that made even Belinda blink in astonishment. "Our plastic products are made with the utmost care and under careful supervision by no fewer than ten line inspectors. As you can see"—she gestured around the factory floor, which gleamed dimly in the fluorescent light—"we have impeccable standards of cleanliness and keep a safe, sterile atmosphere."

"Does she want to operate on someone?" Sam asked quietly, his mouth on my ear. His proximity was close enough to be exciting; I sent him a glance that held some sexual suggestion. His lips curled up on one side, and his hand slid around my waist.

"She didn't answer the question," Belinda insisted in a tiny whisper.

"Excuse me," said Camilla's gentle voice. She had truly dressed for the part of a frail elderly woman. She wore a blouse with a Peter Pan collar, a white sweater, and a long navy blue skirt. "I think you forgot to answer the part about the toxic chemicals. Do you have some safety precaution for the workers who might inhale them? And how do you dispose of any chemical runoff?"

Barbara smiled thinly. "When I spoke of our clean environment, I meant that we apply the same careful standards to our containment of chemicals. We've had no workers reporting any ill effects from working on the factory floor, and we have a very particular containment and disposal process which is overseen each year by several environmental regulators."

"Does that include the EPA?" Adam asked.

"It does; we have an EPA investigator scheduled to visit next week, and that person will also be looking at our new construction in Blue Lake."

Sam said, "Why was the building halted at the Blue Lake site?"

Barbara offered him a toothy smile. "These things often happen in the construction world, as you all know. We expect to resume work early next week. If you'll all follow me, we'll take the elevator up to our office suite, where Mr. Grange, Mr. Enderby, and some of our other executives will speak with you in the meeting room. Did all the guests sign in? If not, please do that now." She held out a clipboard that we had all signed. "There will be light refreshments offered upstairs."

It struck me suddenly that no one else in the group had asked questions. They had merely followed along, occasionally smiling when Barbara made some mild joke. Belinda edged close to me. "I can't find any mention of this open house on the Plasti-Source website," she whispered, looking at her phone. "That's so odd."

I glanced at her, surprised, but our small group was already following Barbara, and Doug pulled Belinda away from me to murmur something in her ear. I moved along dutifully; Sam's eyes found mine, and I imitated Barbara's fake smile, which made him laugh. The guests had to take turns on the elevator, so when Sam and I stepped out into a carpeted lobby, we waited until the entire group was assembled, and then we began to follow Barbara down a long hallway with offices on either side. I imagined the hallway in darkness, and Luis running for his life past the shadowy offices. Which of these tinted windows had been pierced by a bullet? Who had been pursuing Luis, and why?

I stole a glance at Sam, who was clearly thinking along similar lines. Barbara was chatting away with that special tour guide's gift for gab, noting the design of the building and the floor plan, which allowed for a view of the factory floor at both ends of the hall.

We reached an intersection with another large hallway; this one seemed to hold restrooms, a janitor's closet, and more offices. Sam turned left, seemingly in search of a restroom. Since he and I were last in line, only I saw that he kept walking and studied the names on office doors. I caught Doug's eye; he was closer to the front of the group, near Adam and Camilla. He, too, had been scanning offices and names on doors. Belinda was near the middle of the crowd, occasionally tapping her phone. I feared that Barbara would pounce on her and take it away, or demand that it be turned off. Doug nodded at me, which I took as encouragement, and I followed Sam down the gray hallway, not illuminated as the main one was.

Sam had reached the end of the hall. He peered at the final office and gave me a thumbs-up. I jogged toward him, my feet silent on the industrial carpeting, and arrived to find that the name on the door was Philip Enderby. Sam tried the doorknob, which turned easily under his hand. "Doug said to assume that if doors are open they're encouraging us to wander around," Sam said.

I looked back; there was no one in sight.

I turned and followed Sam into the room. Sam found a light switch and flipped it on.

PHIL ENDERBY'S OFFICE was larger than one would expect from the outside—spacious enough to house a giant credenza against one wall, holding two abstract sculptures and several stylish file holders, along with a wide crimson bowl filled with what looked like candy.

A gray desk dominated the room and sat squarely in front of a window that looked down on the various robots in the factory below. Sam went to the window and looked down, but my eyes were drawn to the desk, which held an assortment of files and a newspaper. It was a *Chicago Tribune*; I recognized the logo and the large blue lettering, but I also recognized something else, even upside down . . .

In a bolt of adrenaline, I hurled myself forward and looked at the paper. "Sam."

"You would think that a place this giant would have more security on the main floor," he mused, still looking down. Someone in the factory was switching off lights, one by one.

"*Sam.*"

He turned, surprised, and looked where my finger pointed.

"Uh-oh," he said.

The date of the paper indicated that it was from January, when a reporter named Jake Elliott had written a long feature about Sam, which had then been picked up by several papers. The story included several pictures of Sam, some of which included Camilla and me, and one that highlighted Doug Heller. On the front page was a picture of Sam, with me behind him, my arms wrapped protectively around his neck. The caption read, "Sam West with his new love interest, Lena London."

"Why is this here?" I asked. "Why is Phil Enderby reading an article about us?"

Sam shook his head; his eyes moved to the office door and widened slightly before I saw the shadow fall across the desk.

A voice behind me said, "And my question is, 'Why are Sam West and Lena London so interested in Phil Enderby? Why do they even know his name?'"

I swung around as Phil Enderby stepped into the room and shut the door behind him. "So I guess maybe it's time we cleared the air."

22

*She knew that if she was going to run, she would
have to do it now.*

—From *Danger at Debenham Station*,
a work in progress

"THAT'S A GREAT idea," Sam said. His voice betrayed
nothing beyond a mild interest. "We certainly have a lot
of questions."

Phil Enderby looked older than he had in his picture,
or even in the factory; he was perhaps sixty, with gray
hair and a slightly defeated look. He gestured to a small
couch near his desk, and Sam and I sat down. Sam took
my hand in his in a casual, affectionate gesture.

Enderby said, "And again I must ask: Why do you
have questions at all? Who are you to me, or me to you?
We don't know each other, as far as I recall?"

"And yet our photograph is in the center of your desk,"
Sam noted.

Phil sat down behind his desk. He donned a scholarly
expression. "I like to keep up-to-date with events in Blue
Lake," he said. "I live there, in fact."

"You're woefully behind the times," I said. "That's a very old paper. At this rate you'll catch up to the present in about nine months."

Enderby smiled thinly. "Well, gosh, we could go back and forth like this all day. So let's put our cards on the table. I had a man following you. He learned that you were all very interested in Plasti-Source. Why? What's the point of spying?"

"Asked the man who sent a spy," Sam said. "And an ex-con spy, at that."

Enderby paled slightly. "So your cop friend is also in on this. I wondered about that." He pushed a button on his desk. "Sherry, ask Barbara to send Mr. Doug Heller and Ms. Camilla Graham to my office. Thanks. And tell Barbara to wrap up the tour and lead people out when Ed finishes speaking."

I looked at Sam. Were we about to get answers, or was this something more threatening? Doug Heller was a police officer. Surely Enderby was intimidated by that fact?

Moments later Doug arrived, with Belinda close behind him. Doug looked around and said, "What have we here? Mr. Enderby, didn't I just talk to you earlier today?"

Enderby motioned to some chairs along the wall, and Doug seated himself and Belinda across from the desk. "Camilla and Adam will be here shortly. She wanted to use the restroom," Doug said.

I turned to Doug. "Mr. Enderby just admitted that he had someone spy on us, and that Driscoll is his man."

"Driscoll," Enderby said. "You all have me at a disadvantage. You seem to know something I don't. How exactly did you know that Mr. Driscoll was—making inquiries about you?

Belinda and I laughed. "He wasn't making inquiries. He stood in Camilla's window like a Peeping Tom and scared us to death. Then he ran away, like a criminal," I said. "And now we learn he was sent by you."

Enderby sighed and leaned back in his chair. "Miss London, Plasti-Source is a forty-million-dollar-a-year business, and it is expected to grow in revenue over the next few years. We must guard our interests at all costs. Mr. Driscoll caught all of you trespassing on the Blue Lake site—

"We weren't trespassing. We were sitting on the road, looking at the building," Sam corrected.

Enderby continued as though Sam hadn't spoken. "He caught you trespassing, so he took note of your car and did some research."

"Translation: he copied down Lena's license number and illegally linked it to the owner," Doug said, his face hard.

Enderby shrugged. "It's not illegal; our lawyer has told us that—"

"I'm sure your lawyer will say a lot of things if the price is right," Doug shot back, scowling.

To my amazement, Enderby merely smiled, as though we were all at a tea party. "Ms. London, Ms. Frailey, is it?" Belinda nodded. "I'm sorry if Mr. Driscoll was unorthodox in his methods. He was not instructed to frighten you in any way, but to learn why you were so interested in our company."

"So—asking us was out of the question?" Sam said.

Enderby sighed. Clearly we were trying his patience. "Why were you so interested in Plasti-Source in the first place?"

"It's simple," I said. "It's an ugly monstrosity of a building, we don't want it in our town, and we wanted to pull over and look at it for ourselves."

"Hmm." Enderby studied the tip of a pencil on his blotter. "And why did Driscoll hear you talking to Carl Frailey and mentioning Luis Castellan—both of whom worked at this plant and have since disappeared from our ranks?"

Belinda lifted her chin. "You fired my brother. He didn't disappear, you fired him."

Enderby nodded. "We could do a lot more than that. Because like you, he was digging into things that were none of his business. So again, I'm wondering—why? What are you all looking for? Haven't our press conferences and events like today allayed your concerns? What deep dark secrets do you think we have at this respected place of business?"

"And if you have no deep dark secrets, why do you care? Why aren't you prosecuting Carl?" Doug asked.

Now Enderby was irritated. "Well, I can see that nothing productive can come out of a meeting in which we just keep firing questions at each other."

"I have another question for you," Belinda said. "Why do you have contracts with two different construction companies?"

For the first time Enderby looked disconcerted. "What—we—Anemone Construction has a long history in Blue Lake, and they were a perfect choice to—"

"What about Crandall Construction? What can they do that Anemone can't?"

He recovered quickly. "It's about timelines. We need to be finished by the date we set out to finish; Crandall can work solely on our waste-disposal design."

"May we see the design?" Doug asked.

"No, that's top secret at this point."

"Why?" Sam asked.

The door opened, and Camilla and Adam entered. "Have we missed much?" Camilla asked with a mischievous smile.

"Not really," Sam said. "We are at an impasse."

"This is all ridiculous," I said. "You need to tell the police why you would hunt a man down, threaten his life, when he did nothing to you. What did he find out, anyway?"

"What? What are you—? Are you referring to Luis? Listen, I know the poor boy disappeared and that the papers suggested he met with foul play, but we had nothing to do with that. Good Lord, this is a place of business. I assumed—perhaps he was involved in drugs, or some kind of gang, or something."

"You worked with the man. Did he seem like he was in a gang?" Adam asked, standing near the doorway with his arms folded.

Enderby pounded on his desk. "This is a moot point! I certainly had nothing to do with the death or disappearance of Luis. He was a good worker. He is not related to the discussion at hand except that you have somehow linked him to your own inquiries into my business."

"*Your* business?" Doug said, raising his brows.

"I have a stake in it, yes." Enderby's face reddened slightly.

"I assume you've been running it, while Grange was away?"

"Yes. I'm second-in-command."

"Command?" Sam said. "You talk like a military man."

Enderby straightened. "I served. US Navy, eight years."

Doug let out a loud sigh. "Listen, I'm getting tired of these conversations. You gave us the runaround when we asked you about Luis Castellan, and you're giving us the runaround now." He stood up. "I ought to arrest you right now, Enderby."

Enderby's mouth dropped open. "For what, exactly? I'm running a business here."

Doug pointed at him. "What does Crandall Construction need to do at night in order to avoid detection?"

"What?" He stared at Doug for a moment; then his eyes darted back and forth among the rest of us, perhaps hunting for some inspiration. "What do you—?" Something seemed to dawn on him then. "So Castellan is alive. He talked to you."

"Were you hoping he wasn't?" Doug asked, moving closer. His hands sat on his hips, ready perhaps to go for his cuffs.

Enderby lifted his hands in entreaty. "Whatever he told you was taken out of context. Our workers do sometimes have to work at night."

"Why?"

"Well—because—sometimes during the day we don't want to—upset traffic patterns, or—disrupt the busy flow of things . . ." He seemed to barely know what he was saying.

"In Blue *Lake*?" Sam asked, his tone skeptical.

"Where are the plans for the waste-disposal system?" Doug asked.

"I'll have to consult Ed. It's up to him what you see or don't see, and he is busy with the tour."

"What does it entail? Is it a pipeline?"

"What?" Now Enderby's eyes were wide. "I—we have

secure barrels and a way to transport them to a licensed waste-disposal site."

"Then why does that require construction?" I asked.

Enderby dabbed at his forehead with one hand. "You can take all this up with Ed. I do my job. If you want to arrest me over some alleged safety issue, then be my guest."

Doug still loomed over him. "Why did you think Luis Castellan was dead?"

"I—because it was in the paper. As we discussed. Before that I thought he was just being—lazy, I guess."

"Even after what he read on your computer?"

"Why would his reading my computer make me assume he was *dead*?" Enderby looked genuinely confused.

"Did you replace some glass in a door last week?" Doug edged closer.

"Wha—? Yes. It was broken. The janitor had to repair it when we came in for an early morning meeting."

"How did it get broken?"

"I don't know. We assumed it was the cleaning crew, or some accident caused by someone leaving Friday. No one owned up to anything."

"You didn't question why it looked like a bullet hole?"

"It didn't look—" Now Enderby paused, and for the first time he seemed to take stock of the situation. "What's going on?" he said quietly.

"Mr. Enderby, did you know that Luis Castellan went to Edward Grange about the chemicals you were sampling for use on the factory floor? He felt they were highly dangerous, potentially toxic to workers."

Enderby's eyes narrowed. "Many chemicals are toxic. That's why you must be careful."

Doug leaned over the desk. "Tell me why I shouldn't haul you in right now for attempted murder."

"Attempted murder of whom?" Enderby's eyes were wide and, as far as I could tell, innocent. Doug saw it, too, and he backed up.

"What did Luis Castellan say to you before you left Monday night?"

"Nothing. Just that he would look at my computer. It was frozen, and I needed to get to it before the Tuesday meeting."

We sat in silence. Phil Enderby certainly had something to hide regarding Crandall Construction, but he didn't seem to understand any of the references to Luis Castellan.

Belinda spoke, her soft voice sounding almost loud in the quiet room. "Why was tonight's event not advertised on the Plasti-Source website?"

Enderby's face became furtive. "I'm not sure how it was advertised. You'd have to ask our publicity department."

"You have a publicity department?" Sam, sounding skeptical.

"Not our branch specifically. That stuff comes out of the head office."

Belinda's green eyes widened. In that moment I was struck by her resemblance to Carl. She opened her mouth, then shut it again, sending an urgent glance to Doug.

Enderby cleared his throat and straightened the newspaper on his desk; his body language said that he was trying to reclaim authority over this meeting. "In any case, I have answered your questions, but you have not fully answered mine."

Doug laughed. "You absolutely have not answered our questions."

The two of them bickered for a while, accusing each other of withholding information.

I looked at my lap, trying to work things out. Who might have a grudge against Luis? Did he anger a security guard? They had guns, after all. Did he have a feud with a co-worker? He hadn't said anything to anyone, except to tell Edward Grange about the chemicals Enderby had been testing.

He had implied that if the chemicals got into the water, they would be toxic.

What had he said? *"If you put this stuff in water it would be deadly."*

For some reason I thought back to Sam's illness and my unfounded fears. I had worried over poisoning because the idea of toxic chemicals had been planted in my mind. I had feared that someone would actually put something into Sam's food or water and choose to kill him for some insidious reason. I had pondered the dangers of consuming something without being aware that a deadly substance had been added to it. How terrible, how permanent, how invisible, was poison.

An ugly thought bloomed, huge and monstrous. "Oh my God," I said.

Camilla's eyes met mine. "What?"

"Luis said that if the chemical was added to water, someone could die."

"So?" Enderby said. "I told you, we have safety—"

"I'm not talking about your safety procedures," I said. "I'm thinking about the fact that you've been running things because your boss was on bereavement leave."

"Yes." Enderby's mouth was grim. "I can assure you, I have kept everything according to Ed's standards, and—"

"Phil," I said, impatient. *"How did Ed Grange's wife die?"*

Phil stared at me; Doug swung around quickly, his face tense as he studied mine. Phil said, "What? Why do you—it happened quickly—some kind of undetected heart ailment. It was unexpected because she was only sixty. Ed was devastated; he still is."

The room was silent for a full minute, but I knew that everyone's thoughts were churning, like mine.

"Maybe what looked like devastation was actually guilt," Camilla said. "Lena might be on to something here. Luis said that Ed Grange looked sad and lonely. But if Grange was guilty of his wife's murder, and if he in fact put something toxic in her food or drink, then certainly he might jump to the wrong conclusion when Luis told him about the toxic chemical. He might think that Luis was calling him out on his crime."

"Luis said that he spoke to Ed directly. If you think about it, the words could be interpreted as an accusation. Didn't he say, 'We both know'? Something like 'Ed, you and I both know that if you put this stuff in water it would be deadly,'" Doug quoted with a musing tone. "It is true that people with guilty consciences tend to think that other people see their guilt."

Enderby was livid. "This is *ridiculous*. What, are you trying to end up in one of *her books*?" He pointed to Camilla with a certain disdain. "Now I see. You're trying to shut down this company any way you can. You said you hated it and found it ugly. First you go after me, now you're going after Ed in his time of grief. You need to leave the poor man alone. This is outrageous beyond belief!"

Doug sat back down next to Belinda. "Do you know if Grange was happy in his marriage?"

"His wife was an environmentalist," I said. "What if she knew something that could be devastating to the company?"

Enderby stood up. "We're done here. My employer is a respected man in this town, he is a widower, and he is my friend. You can just take yourself right out of here. Direct any further questions to our company lawyer."

A voice behind us said, "I'm afraid they can't leave, Phil." We spun around to see Edward Grange, thin and pale and holding a gun, like a terrible phantasm in the darkening hall. "And neither can you. I have far too much to lose to let any of you go now. And that is truly unfortunate. As if I don't have enough on my conscience."

His haunted eyes found mine. "I'm sorry," he said. "I'm going to need you all to line up against that wall."

$$\cdot\ 23\ \cdot$$

*The drama of the Gothic climax! We find it rather
like a soap opera. We might laugh, except that we
are so absorbed in the details, and so determined
for light to win against dark. We are lured into the
architecture of both building and plot.*

— From the notebooks of Camilla Graham

SAM STEPPED IN front of me and I hugged him around the
waist. Enderby sat at the desk, his mouth open, like an
emoji of surprise. Doug moved forward, alert as a cat.
"Listen, Grange, let's talk about—"

Grange came into the room and pointed his gun at
Belinda, who still sat on the couch, her face pale and
frightened. "You're a cop, so I'm guessing you have a
gun. Slide it here so I don't have to shoot her."

Doug didn't hesitate; he removed the gun from the
holster under his jacket and slid it over to Grange. "Don't
do anything you'll regret," Doug warned. On the surface
he was calm, but his skin had gone five shades paler. I
wondered if he was going to faint. "There are people in
the building. They would hear the shots."

Grange still pointed his gun at Belinda; he shook his

head. "The tour is over. Barbara ushered them out, and she left herself."

Camilla's eyes were on Grange. "This was a lure, wasn't it? Belinda said it wasn't on the website. You didn't care about the public's questions. You hoped we would come, or at least some of us. You sent an e-mail just to her."

Grange nodded.

"And then you told poor Phil there to see what he could find out," Adam added.

Phil found his voice. "Listen, Ed, I know you've been under a lot of strain. Let everyone leave here now, and we'll get you some help."

Grange's sad expression was more frightening than anger would have been. He seemed resigned to the idea of killing us. "I'm afraid I'll have to take a loss, Phil. Once I lock you all in here, we're going to suffer an accident. The good news is that we're insured. The bad news is that it will take some lives."

Belinda gasped; her green eyes filled with tears. That made me angry. I looked at Camilla, who was calmer than anyone else in the room. I frowned, sending her a question, and she nodded at me. Her look held some reassurance.

Grange bent to pick up Doug's gun, his eyes scanning all of us. He turned to Belinda. "Go and get everyone's phone and bring them all back here."

Belinda stood and moved shakily across the room, and one by one we handed her our cell phones. She brought them back to Grange, who had pocketed Doug's gun.

"Why did you kill your wife?" I asked.

Grange looked at me with mournful eyes. "Carmen was a good woman. Too good for me, and too good to keep my secrets."

Camilla, her eyes flashing, opened her mouth to speak, and Adam sent her a quelling look.

Grange, still aiming his own gun at Belinda, who in turn still held all of the phones, said, "You go first." He pointed at the hall. Belinda sent one regretful look toward Doug before she went out into the dim corridor. Grange backed out of the room. "I'm sorry," he said again, as he shut the door. We could hear something sliding into place.

"What sort of accident is he planning?" Doug asked Enderby.

Enderby shook his head. "I don't think there's anything he can do with the machines—they all have fail-safes in case of danger. I can't imagine what he's thinking."

An image of Grange in the store came to me: the clerk telling him he had too much kerosene. "A fire," I said.

All eyes in the room went to me. "What?" Doug asked.

"I saw him once at Sullivan's. I didn't know who he was, but he was buying a gallon of kerosene. He said he was going camping."

Adam stared Enderby down. "Is he likely to start a fire?"

Enderby shrugged, clearly in shock.

Camilla said, "Lena's information makes it sound like he was going to start a fire anyway. He says he's insured for it. He was buying supplies. His company must be in trouble. Burning us down with it is probably something he didn't plan until today. Until Lena figured out that he was a murderer." Her voice shook slightly, and Adam slid an arm around her waist.

Doug's eyes darkened with intensity. "Why does the door lock from the hall side?"

Enderby shook his head with a helpless expression. "It doesn't. He must have brought something."

"Then we can break it down," Sam said. He lunged forward and slammed into the door; nothing happened. "Oh wow, that is solid," Sam said. He turned back toward us. "Any other ideas, before this psychopath burns us alive?"

Doug looked at Adam. "You didn't happen to bring your gun?"

Adam was mournful. "Camilla dissuaded me."

Camilla stepped forward, holding out her purse. "But then I changed my mind," she said. "I decided to trust my husband's instincts." She handed the purse to Doug, who rummaged inside and retrieved Adam's gun.

"Thank you, Milla!" Doug said. "Bullets?"

"There's a box in there," she said.

Adam took her hand in a grateful gesture.

Doug was busy with the gun. Then he said, "Everyone step back and cover your ears." He aimed at the lock beneath the doorknob, firing once, twice. Then he tried the knob; the resistance seemed to be higher up on the door, so Doug shot there, once, twice. The door splintered and Doug kicked it open. He turned to us. "This hall is dark, and he has a gun. We can't all go rushing out, or he could pick us off one by one. But I don't want us to stay in here long, either, not if he's planning to start a fire. Let me go down this hall; if I call out to you, you can come as far as the main hallway."

Phil raised his hand. "If he plans to start a fire, he'll probably do it on the factory floor so that he can say one of the machines malfunctioned. We had a problem with one of them last week—he'll do it there."

"Where's the machine?" Doug asked.

Phil went to a window overlooking the factory floor and pointed to the south corner.

Doug nodded. "Stay here for a minute."

We stared after him for a blank moment; not all of the evening's events had sunk in.

Adam stepped forward, his face calm. "Let's get organized," he said. "We'll want to travel together and keep track of one another. No one gets left behind. Not to sound like a camp counselor, but everyone needs to find a buddy."

Sam took my hand, and Adam took Camilla's. Phil Enderby looked at me and said, "You two can follow me; I know my way around this place." He had managed to summon some courage; his chin lifted and he stood up behind the desk. "All right. We can do this. I still can't believe Ed would actually—"

We heard a gunshot ring out, and I moaned. We ran to the door, and Adam called softly down the hall. "Doug?"

We waited a tense moment but heard nothing. Had Doug been shooting? Had Grange shot Belinda? The second possibility had me feeling faint with horror.

Adam said, "Doug or Belinda might need us. We have to go."

Slowly, the five of us moved into the shadowy hall. Enderby walked in front; he led us to the end of the hall, then turned right.

Camilla whispered, "Phil, how many staircases are there?"

"Two," Phil said. "One down there, by the conference room, and up here where you came in, near the elevator. That's where we need to go; I think Ed would have taken the other one."

"Why didn't Doug call to us?" I said. "I have a very bad feeling."

Sam held my hand. "Likely Doug didn't want to expose his location. There's safety in numbers. I'm guessing Grange won't harm any of us. Because if even one of us got away, he would go down."

"Or he'll want to harm all of us for the reason you just said." When I heard my own grim voice in the dark hall it generated a burst of fear.

Enderby said, "I'm sending the elevator down. That will signal that we're already free and at large in the building. It should intimidate him."

"But it will also tell him our location. Do we want him to know?" Adam asked.

We contemplated this; on the lower floor another gunshot rang out. A gray, dismal feeling grew inside me. I said, "Where are the phones in this place? We can call for help!"

Enderby shook his head. "I tried the one on my desk; it was dead. He must have cut the line. I think he's actually insane. This is nothing like the Ed I know."

Adam said, "I'm going down the stairs. We need to know who's shooting and if anyone is hurt. Let me go first." He darted through the stairway door before any of us could protest. Camilla stood looking after him, her face pained.

"Someone should go down the other stairway," I said. "We should divide and conquer. Sam?"

"I'm with you," he said.

"Camilla, Phil, you follow Adam in a few minutes. He should be able to fill you in when you reach the bottom of the stairway."

Just as Sam and I were about to turn away, we heard a lurching, humming sound. The elevator was on, and coming up. "What do we do?" Phil yelled.

"Stand on either side of the door, out of sight," Camilla said, flattening herself against the wall. "If he steps out, we have time to jump on him and knock his gun out of his hand."

With little time to think, we did as she said. The rising elevator made a terrifying sound, and we shared a living nightmare in the dark hall, waiting for the opening of the doors that might bring Grange back into our midst.

I stared down the dark, shadowy hallway of the mammoth building, a hall as silent as a crypt, and hoped that it wouldn't become our tomb.

The elevator stopped. Sam's hand gripped mine. The doors opened; for a moment nothing happened. Then Adam's voice said, "Don't be afraid; it's me. I've got Belinda, and she's hurt."

We swarmed the elevator, relieved and eager to help. Belinda leaned against Adam, who was holding on to her arm; it was dripping blood. We helped them out onto the floor, and the elevator doors closed behind them.

"I ran away from him," she said. "I know he would have killed me soon, because I wasn't locked up like the rest of you. I threw the phones in his face and ran. He shot me." Her eyes were wide with shock.

I took off my sweater and said, "Camilla, Sam, help me." We tore the light garment into strips and began winding them around Belinda's arm. She winced but submitted bravely to our ministrations. "I'm so sorry," I said.

"This was my brilliant idea," Belinda said, her teeth

chattering. "To come here." She giggled weirdly, clearly in shock.

"They targeted you," I said. "They somehow traced your e-mail to you and realized they could use it to their advantage."

"What was the other gunshot?" Sam asked.

Adam said, "I think Doug has him cornered. At least I hope so. I didn't get far before I found Belinda."

Phil had gone into an office and brought out a swivel chair; he helped Belinda lower herself into it. She was shaking but managed a brave smile. I had a sudden image of her coming around the corner at the cabin in Michigan, blond and pretty, holding a bouquet of leaves. And of Doug spinning her around, laughing up into her face.

"We need to make a plan," Adam said. "We need to get back downstairs."

Belinda shook her head. A piece of her blond hair, damp with sweat, was matted against her face. She closed her eyes and leaned her head back on the chair. "We can wait here. Just wait it out."

"Wait what out?" Camilla said, smoothing the lock of hair away from Belinda's face.

Belinda opened her eyes and looked at me. "Before I threw the phones at Grange, I dialed 911. I had the volume down, but I'm sure it went through."

"Oh thank God," Enderby said. "I just want to go home and never come back here."

"We can't wait. We have to go down," Adam said.

"Why?" Camilla asked him.

"Because I smell smoke."

She was free of the house. She had no plan but to run, to put distance between herself and the place that had been her prison. On the dark path that led to the road, she saw a silhouette moving rapidly toward her: a large, hulking, fast-moving body that would in moments collide with hers.
—From *Danger at Debenham Station,*
a work in progress

ADAM WASN'T WRONG; a moment later the scent of smoke, thick and terrifying, carried to all of us. Enderby said, "Let me run down the stairs and see where he set it. I'll come back."

He disappeared into the stairwell.

Sam said, "I'm not sure that we can trust that man."

Camilla tucked against Adam's side. "There's always the chance that he will find nobility in a moment of crisis."

We all stared at one another, wrapped around Belinda in a protective circle. Our mouths moved when we talked, but the scene was dulled into a dreamlike reality, as though we were inhabiting the bodies of others to whom this was happening. And was it my imagination that the air was growing denser, foggier, around us?

Enderby came bursting back through the door. "We can't get through down there. We'll have to use the other stairway, and we need to run. I don't know how many fires he's starting."

We moved rapidly down the dark hallway, pushing Belinda's chair while she cradled her arm. I reached out and touched her good shoulder, wanting to give comfort. A loud crack sounded from the lower floor. "Was that a gunshot?" Sam asked.

Another crack, and another. A battle was going on below us; we would be walking through the smoke into the unknown.

There was a surreal silence in the hall as we moved toward our last option for escape. An occasional squeak from Belinda's chair was the only sound that penetrated the darkness, the only thing that broke through the tension and fear.

We reached the stairway next to the conference room. "Buddy up," Adam said. "I've got Camilla."

"Sam, help Belinda," I said. "I'll be with Phil."

Phil Enderby took my hand in a fierce grip. His hand was warm and, despite everything, comforting. Sam lifted Belinda carefully and held her against his chest. She wrapped her right arm around his neck and held on.

We all moved into the stairwell and made our careful way down the stairs, first to the landing, then to the floor. We could smell smoke more strongly now, but it didn't seem to be seeping under the door.

Phil edged forward. "To the right is the exit door. I think Sam should go first, with Belinda, once we determine whether anyone is by the door. I'm assuming your friend Doug has things under control."

Camilla nodded. "I think we can count on Doug. We'll be right behind you, Sam."

Sam looked at me, and I nodded. Belinda was pale, and I feared she might faint. She slumped against Sam. "Okay. Someone open the door," he said.

Adam lunged forward and slung open the door; no intruders bulged out of the smoky room, but we also couldn't see beyond the small area outside the door. A fire alarm was beeping insistently on the factory floor; it was jarring and disorienting. Sam and Belinda disappeared, plunging into the fog of the room.

Camilla took Adam's hand. "Lena, follow us," she said.

"Right behind you," I told her. She and Adam disappeared as well.

I turned to Phil Enderby and studied his sweaty face.

"I feel like we should check on your cop friend," he said. "Do we dare?"

"I think we should, yes," I said. I hadn't wanted to tell the group, but I'd been concerned about the gunshots, and about the fact that Belinda hadn't seen Doug on the factory level.

We stepped out of the stairwell and I said, "Doug?"

There was no answer. I turned to Enderby, and he frowned.

He pointed toward the exit wall. "I suppose we should—" He spun completely around at the same time that I heard another shot ring out, and then he was on the ground.

"Oh my God. Phil? Phil, are you okay?" I knelt beside him, my eyes stinging with smoke, trying to determine whether he was alive. "Phil?" I whispered, fearing whatever evil presence lurked within shooting range.

Phil was not conscious; I found his wrist and thought I detected warmth, and a pulse, but I didn't know what to do. If I left him here, he would die of smoke inhalation or worse. And where was Doug?

Blinking away tears, I grabbed Phil's hands and began to drag him toward the exit, but it was slow going, and I was finding it harder and harder to breathe. I heard Sam's voice calling to me, and farther away, Camilla's. The high pitch of her cries was blending weirdly with the fire alarm.

"Stay where you are!" I shouted to them. I jumped up, trying to catch a glimpse of the door, and the next moment Ed Grange loomed out of the smoke like a demon, half of his face covered in blood.

"Well, hello," he said, raising his gun and pointing it at me.

My scream was choked out by smoke and a dry throat, and I braced myself for the impact, the pain, as a shot sounded, but Grange winced, then buckled, as though he had turned to water, and then he pitched forward and fell on his face a few feet from Phil Enderby.

"Oh God," I croaked. "Doug?"

Doug appeared then, alive but gray and sick-looking. "Lena! Is everyone all right?"

"Belinda's shot in the arm. Sam got her out."

"Dammit." He coughed and wiped at his eyes.

"We have to get Phil out of here."

He dove in and grabbed Phil's right arm. "Yes. I'll pull this arm. You pull—" Then Doug dropped to his knees, his eyes wide. "Lena—the smoke—"

Yes. It had swirled around us, hot and toxic, and the short distance to the door seemed too much now; I couldn't even call to my friends, who were probably not twenty feet away. I thought I heard sirens, voices, but they were too far now, distant in time and space and consciousness . . .

I reached for Doug's hand but missed and toppled forward, worrying that the cement floor would feel hard but then feeling nothing at all . . .

· 25 ·

*His hand was warm in hers. "It will be all right,"
he said as he led her to the train that would take
them both home; and despite everything that had
occurred before this moment, she believed him.*
  —From Danger at Debenham Station,
                a work in progress

FOR A FOGGY time, I was not aware; I gradually became conscious of sounds, which became voices, which shouted my name. "Lena? Can you hear me? Lena?"

I opened my eyes, hot and stinging, and at first I could see nothing. "I'm blind," I said, panic-stricken. Then a liquid feeling on my eyes, and something cool pressed onto my eyelids. A time in shock, when I was conscious of hands lifting me, moving me, but not really engaging with those around me.

Later, someone said, "Lena?"

I opened my eyes, and this time I saw light and shapes. "Who's there?" I said, stiffening defensively.

A face appeared above mine. Cliff, concerned and rumpled. "Hey, kid."

"Where am I?"

"In the hospital. You slept all night, like a little princess. I'm keeping watch over you while they tend to the other cases. Good thing they had a light load last night, because we brought three gunshot wounds and multiple smoke inhalation cases, then some minor trauma victims— that's your whole Scooby-Doo gang."

I tried to clear my throat.

"You need water?"

I nodded, then sipped from a straw he put in front of me. "How did we get out?"

Cliff made a muscle. "I got there just before the fire department, just as Sam was marching back in like a damn fool. Although he had found a mask somewhere in the factory. We found you in a pile of bodies. Typical Lena, right? Like the freaking Trojan War in there."

"How—?"

"I carried you out, and Sam got Doug, then some fire-fighters met me at the door and I led them to the Plasti-Source guys."

Memory rushed in. "Phil! Oh God, is he dead?"

"Not just now. He had surgery. Took a bullet in the upper chest, prognosis uncertain."

"Is Doug okay?"

"Yeah. Complaining as always. He wants to go sit by Belinda, but she had surgery, too, and she needs to sleep. That's what Allison said. Doug's been making the rounds, trying to interrogate people while he's wearing a stupid hospital gown and talking in a voice as scratchy as yours."

"Belinda will be okay?"

"Yeah. I already got to talk to her a little."

I let out a long exhalation, then coughed. "You need to take it easy," Cliff said.

"What happened to Grange?"

Cliff's lips tightened. "He's dead. I hear that you pulled a Nancy Drew in there and figured out he killed his wife. We'll be looking into just how that went down, but I already found out from the station that he had a million-dollar life insurance policy on her. And that they didn't bother to do an autopsy on her, since Grange made it clear she had a heart problem. It also turns out he was pals with the coroner; he had suggested to his old friend that an autopsy would upset him."

"I'll bet it would," I croaked.

I looked down and saw that Cliff was holding my hands in his: a gesture of comfort. Panic tore through me. "Where's Sam?"

Cliff squeezed my hands. "He's fine, spaz. He'll be here in a minute. He wanted to buy you a present. Like you aren't spoiled enough."

"Don't make me laugh; it hurts. Where's Camilla? Adam?"

"They went home last night, but I think they'll be back soon. Allison said they should name a wing of the hospital after you guys, since you always seem to be here."

"You were here, too. For a gunshot wound," I reminded him.

Cliff pursed his lips. "Yeah. That's another thing we tend to do a lot—get shot by people."

I sighed and studied his handsome face. "How was your date?"

He couldn't prevent a smug grin. "It was pretty awesome."

"Are you in love?"

"*She* is," he said, preening.

I laughed. "Are you?"

He shrugged. "I could see myself going down that road."

"She's too good for you," I joked.

He nodded. "I think maybe she is, but I plan to pursue her anyway."

"Good. That makes four couples—five, actually, if you count Camilla and Adam. Perfect for board games and dinner parties."

Cliff put his hand over my mouth. "Stop gabbing. You're supposed to rest and drink your water."

Sam strolled in, holding a stuffed tiger. The last time I'd been in a hospital bed he'd brought me a giraffe; I hoped this was the last jungle animal I'd receive as a convalescent. "Hey," he said. "How are you doing?"

"Okay. Glad to be alive, and glad you're all alive, too."

Cliff and Sam nodded, processing this.

Cliff touched the tip of my nose and clapped Sam on the back. "I have to go check in. I'm in contact with Rusty, and the information is coming fast and furious. I'll catch up later." He strode out of the room, and Sam sat on the edge of my bed.

"Why aren't you in a hospital gown?" I said.

"I never put one on. I stayed under the radar," he said with a little smile. "But I got oxygen, and some medicine."

"Good. I should be able to leave now, too. I didn't need to be admitted."

"They're just observing you, I think. I heard someone say another hour or so." His blue eyes met mine with an earnest expression. "When I heard the gunshot, I was afraid. I didn't know what I'd find behind all that smoke, Lena, and I was terrified. Thank God Cliff showed up and helped me plow through."

"It must have been quite a sight, four of us lying there."

"He carried you out, and I had a terrible moment. I've had enough terrible moments to last into my old age." He handed me the tiger, which was still in his left hand.

"Thank you. This is cute." I sighed. "The pendulum again, huh?" I lay back against my pillow, trying not to ponder some of the more horrifying images of the previous day.

Sam adjusted himself on the bed and stroked my hair, telling me what I had missed. He had a hoarse cough; carrying Belinda, the doctor had told him, had caused him to breathe more strenuously and therefore take in more smoke.

Adam and Camilla had been treated, and Adam had insisted on taking her home, Sam told me. They had both watched over me in my sleep, he said. "Going home sounds good," I said. "I'd like to text Camilla, but as you know, I have no phone. I don't suppose—"

"They were all destroyed. I'll buy you a new one."

We sat together in the quiet room. I touched Sam's face, still slightly gray with soot. "I never thought, when we walked into that hulking Gothic monstrosity of a building, that we would be in danger of not coming out."

"None of us did."

"What was wrong with that man?"

"Desperation," Sam said. "He thought he got away with the first crime. Then we all showed an interest in Plasti-Source, and he needed to find out why—was it about the environment, or was it about his wife? He used poor Enderby like a pawn."

I thought about this. "I think Phil has something to hide, too. He seemed—remorseful."

Sam sighed. He stopped petting my hair and lifted my

hand to study my engagement ring. It was white gold, with an "infinity twist" design around the center diamond, which was—because Sam was incurably romantic—shaped like a heart. I gazed at it often, watching it glint in the light, and sometimes I took it off to read the inscription inside: *Lena and Sam, Always.*

"Sam?"

"Hmm."

"You told me, when you were sick, that you were afraid of being alone. You know you don't have to fear that, don't you?"

He shrugged. "It's more of an instinct than a fear. Just ground in by experience. I know, on a conscious level, that the people who love me don't intend to leave."

"They really don't," I said.

"And yet here we are again—in a hospital."

"But about to go home." I coughed, too, and then I laughed, because Doug Heller appeared in the doorway, wearing a hospital gown and posing seductively.

"Looks great," I said. He came in and sat on the side of the bed that Sam wasn't occupying.

"I feel great. They're done with Belinda and she came through like a champ. They let me talk to her for a few minutes."

"Oh good," I said. "God, I'm so relieved."

"Me, too," Doug said. He punched Sam on the shoulder. "Thanks, man. You got her out of there when I couldn't. I was still stalking Grange, who had the instincts of a predator. Or maybe just a desperate man. I managed to graze him once, but he was elusive. Thank God I found him before he took a shot at Lena."

I sat up straight. "I can't believe it. Any of it. It's bad

enough that he killed someone and was ready to kill more, but how desperate did he have to be to try to burn down his own company? To destroy the livelihood of all his employees!"

Doug's expression grew darker. "Cliff's been looking into this with Rusty. The company wasn't doing as well as Grange and others let on, and it seems the Blue Lake site was stretching his resources thin. He had taken out large insurance policies on both his wife and the company. So it looks like Camilla was right, and he was planning to burn it all down anyway."

Sam's look brightened. "So—there will be no Blue Lake Plasti-Source?"

"Doesn't look that way," Doug said. "By the way, I just had a heart-to-heart with Phil Enderby."

"Oh—he's okay?"

"Weak, but alive. Maybe it was the drugs prompting it, but he apologized. Better than that, he told me the location of an old industrial pipeline, something from a long-gone factory outside Blue Lake. Crandall has been updating it for easy but inconspicuous dumping. Our suspicions were well-founded. Enderby says he'll testify to that effect. He'll probably get a slap on the hand, since no dumping has actually occurred."

"Thank God," I said. For now, in this one place, the purity of the lake would be preserved.

Sam's grip on my hand tightened, and his eyes grew wide. "I don't suppose that location is right around Lake Road and Route 22?"

Doug looked surprised. "Pretty close to there, yeah. Why?"

Sam shook his head, smiling. "Lena and I saw two

men going down a lake path with some tools on the morning Belinda disappeared."

"No kidding?" Doug said.

"They looked villainous," I recalled, returning to Camilla's word.

Doug nodded. "They probably were."

"Hey!" I said. "Has anyone filled in Luis and Carl?"

Doug shook his head. "Too much going on. We need to talk to Elena, too. I think she's about ready to go back to her old life."

"Aren't we all," Sam said. "Now I can harass you with tuxedo fittings."

"I'm cool with that," Doug said, grinning at us.

CAMILLA GRAHAM SAT in a throne-like chair and adjusted her rhinestone tiara, something we had to command her to wear, but which had looked so charming on her gray-white hair that even she seemed pleased to have it there. She had spent the first part of the day greeting guests, several from England, including her mother. Priscilla Easton, at ninety-two, was the most adorable human being I had ever known. I had met her once, briefly, on our London book tour, and now she was staying in Camilla's house, letting me lead her on tours and saying, "Oh, lovely," about everything, and calling me "pet" with continuous, comforting pats on my arm. At one point, soon after her arrival, I had whispered to Camilla, "Can we keep her?"

This had made Camilla laugh; it was clear that her mother's presence had made very happy, and she looked more like the girl she had once been, back when she lived in her mother's house. Now, post-dinner at our Wheat Grass party, Camilla finished opening presents. She had made a short speech in which she said that seventy felt like a gracious gift and that her life had unfurled in beautiful ways over the last year.

"Most notably," she said, "I first found a collaborator who became my dear friend, and I reconnected with an old friend who became my husband." She held up her glass, toasting first me and then Adam.

"And while I have certainly written enough books—"

"Never!" someone cried, and we laughed.

"—I intend to keep writing them for as long as I possibly can." Those assembled in the large dining room clapped their appreciation. Camilla pointed at the book covers that Adam and I had staged carefully throughout the room. "And since my dear Adam and Lena have so kindly reminded me of my entire literary history, I feel more connected to my writing than ever before."

The crowd said, "Ahhh," and clapped some more, and then Camilla sat down and Allison moved in with her microphone, her husband John accompanying her as she crooned to Camilla (at Camilla's request). First, she sang "In My Life," by the Beatles—a slow, beautiful, and contemplative version made truly moving by Allison's velvety voice. Camilla, not normally a teary person, dabbed at her eyes with a napkin. Then Allison brightened things up with "Paperback Writer," which had the audience clapping along, not particularly on the beat. Finally, she sang "For Good," from *Wicked*, and then every other person in the room was wiping at their eyes.

I leaned away from Sam momentarily, toward Belinda, who looked pale but pretty in a gold and green dress. Her arm was in an elaborate sling. "How are you?" I murmured in her ear. "Do you need anything?"

She shook her head. "Doug is waiting on me hand and foot." She frowned slightly, perhaps at the idea of needing help. "I'm having fun. Camilla looks beautiful."

"Can I tell you a secret?"

Her green eyes met mine, curious as always. I recalled the day I met her, when she said she would start some research for me and call it "The London File." "What?"

"Doug told me he's never seen you look more beautiful. He said you look like a mermaid in this dress."

Her mouth curved into a pleased smile. "He didn't tell me that."

"He loves you a lot, Belinda."

"I know. I love him, too. A lot."

"And—does he know that?"

She nodded. "I told him. He was happy."

"What color do you want to wear as a bridesmaid? I don't really care. Although I think Allison is pushing for pale yellow."

"That sounds nice. A super pale one, like lemon ice."

"Great! You two gorgeous blondes are going to make me look dark and severe."

"You could never look anything but pretty. And also noble and good," Belinda said. "I'm glad you're my friend." She pushed her glasses up on her nose in a now-familiar gesture.

"Back at you." I touched her sling. "We seem to have reversed roles."

She sighed. "Yeah. What are the odds? Same arm, too!" She looked around the room. "You know who's a knockout? Your friend Isabelle."

She was indeed. She had entered the room on Cliff's arm, looking like a million dollars in a red dress with a daring neckline. Cliff looked a bit dazed when they walked in, and the expression hadn't really left him. Belinda saw it, too. She said, "Cliff always looks so smart, but his face gets kind of stupid around her." We both giggled.

As if she sensed our discussion, Isabelle floated over to us; her dark hair had been swept up on top of her head, with selected strands artfully hanging down, leaving a clear view of her ruby-look earrings. "Hi, Lena, hi, Belinda. I'm so sorry to hear about your arm, but you look wonderful." She rested a graceful hand on Belinda's forearm.

"So do you," I said. "I understand you had a fun date the other night."

Isabelle rolled her eyes blissfully, as if appreciating the memory of a delicious piece of chocolate. "Who knew, after he blew me off for two months, that he would be so romantic? Oh my gosh, he's amazing!" She pointed at me. "You don't have to look so smug, matchmaker. I know you predicted we would hit it off. Well, you're right."

"He can't stop looking at you tonight," Belinda said.

Isabelle grinned. "I guess that justifies the two-hour preparation period." She shook her head, smiling, then said, "Belinda, Doug tells me the two of you might be looking to adopt an animal. Is that true?"

Belinda smiled shyly. "We're talking about it. Do you have some at the vet's office right now?"

"We do! Some really wonderful little guys, dogs and cats and even a turtle. Come on by, and I'll show them all to you."

"Okay." Belinda beamed. "I might have to wait until my arm is better. I'm going to want to cuddle."

"Fair enough. Oh, I see Elena and Luis Castellan! That was nice of Camilla to invite them!" I followed her gaze. Elena and Luis had joined some other guests on the dance floor; John had switched to a playlist of big band music so that he and Allison could circulate among the crowd. Elena smiled up into Luis's face, and Luis, as Carl had told us all along, looked utterly devoted to his wife. She wore the charm bracelet Luis had given her, the one he apparently had made after I told him about mine.

"It's great. I'm so glad to see them together; what a trauma it must all have been." I opened my mouth to say something else, but Sam returned from his spot against the wall, where he had been chatting with Doug and Cliff.

"Looks like dessert's here," he said.

A Wheat Grass waiter wheeled in a cart with various dessert trays and a large, beautiful cake shaped like a stack of books. Each book was a different color and bore one of Camilla's titles on the spine. The top of the cake looked like the first page of a novel; it read, "Happy Birthday, Camilla Easton Graham Rayburn, Queen of Mysteries and Queen of My Heart."

"Oh, Adam," Camilla sighed after reading it.

Adam held up a hand and the room grew quiet. "I'd like to tell you all that one of our guests tonight was responsible for making this cake and several of the desserts. His name is Carl Frailey, and he is a new Wheat Grass chef."

We turned to look at Carl, who loitered in the kitchen doorway, looking slightly uncomfortable. His eyes darted around as he realized that people were waiting for his response.

"I hope you like it," he said. "I just like to cook. I watch a lot of cooking shows."

Belinda beamed at him, and Camilla cut the cake. Moments later, we heard the appreciative sounds of people who were enjoying Carl Frailey's food for the first time. I groaned my appreciation as well. My piece had the word "Camilla" on it, and I didn't even want to cut into it, but once I took one bite of the light, delicate, orange-flavored cake with cream cheese frosting, I couldn't stop eating it.

The music started again. Sam put his mouth against my ear and said, "They're playing our song." He pulled me onto the dance floor and I finally recognized the music: "Unforgettable."

"I never realized what a good dancer you are," I said.

"We'll have to do more dancing. In the kitchen, after we do dishes. We'll have to put Geronimo in the other room or he'll get under our feet."

"Sam?" I looked into his blue eyes, creased with amusement and tenderness. "You're perfect."

He pulled me against him and spun me around the room, and for the first time in my life I felt dizzy with love.

HALF AN HOUR later Camilla approached me; her smile was wide, her skin glowed, and her tiara was slightly askew. She wore a silver-white dress and a pink rose wrist corsage from Adam, and she clutched her silver bag against her as though it held a secret. "I wonder, Lena, if

I can ask you to be a stereotypical female and accompany me to the bathroom?"

"Sure," I said, laughing. "Lead the way."

In the cream-colored Wheat Grass ladies' room there was a little lobby with a couch and a coffee table, then a long mirror with a counter and stools for those who wanted to adjust their makeup. Camilla went straight to the couch and pulled me down next to her. "First," she said, her purple eyes on mine, "thank you for this party. It is wonderful to feel so loved."

"You're welcome."

"Second." She opened her bag, took out a little pad and a pen, and snapped the purse shut again. "I had an idea for the Debenham novel."

"Wonderful. Let's hear it."

"I was dancing with Adam. He's quite graceful, isn't he, for a man of seventy-one? And then I thought, what a romantic thing a dance is. The lights are low, the dresses glimmer, everyone has a certain mystery. And every woman is transformed into Juliet at the masquerade."

"So that's where our young woman can meet the man who will help her?"

"Of course. She's been forbidden to communicate with people by these captors, but for reasons we will have to explain, they all have to attend this dance. She's been ordered to stay in the shadows, but a man spies her—perhaps he's watched for her since he saw her at the train station?—and he sweeps her into a dance."

"And she pours out her heart? Or will she give him only tantalizing clues, afraid to say too much?"

"You see? We can play with it, but it would be good, yes?"

I sighed and leaned against her. "Yes. It would be very good." I felt suddenly sleepy, there in the warm room. Across from us were our own reflections: Camilla, crowned, was in her shimmery gray-white dress. I was in a dress Sam had bought me for the occasion: a purple bodice and a black tulle skirt. On my wrist was the bracelet from Sam, something I rarely took off. I had never seen Camilla and me this way, reflected side by side, caught in a moment of love and perfect companionship.

"Camilla, did you see that?"

"What, dear?"

"Just for a minute—I looked like you."

She put her head on my shoulder. "One or two people tonight have asked me if you were my daughter. I told them you had a wonderful mother who is here with us in spirit. But if ever someone had a daughter of the heart—" She paused to dash away a tear.

"I know, Camilla. I feel the same."

"Ridiculous, how much I've ruined my makeup tonight."

"You look amazing. Now, pick up your pen and let's jot down these ideas before they fade away."

We bent our heads over her notepad; I stole one more glance at the mirror, at the perfect moment captured there, and then, with Camilla, I got to work.

Sender: Cliff Blake
Recipients: Sam West, Lena London, Doug Heller, Belinda
Frailey, Allison Branch, John Branch, Camilla Graham, Adam
Rayburn, Isabelle Devon

Hey, gang! Lena and I went running today, and guess what?
They've started demolition of the Plasti-Source Gothic skeleton.
I'm sure the stories in the paper have our Blue Lake Fathers and
Mothers in a big hurry to yank that thing down. Not to mention
the *Blue Lake Ecology Commission*, whoever the heck they are.
And, perhaps as penance, now that everyone knows about the
near miss with toxic dumping, there's talk of them building a park
there, instead. I'm cool with that.

By the way, Lena and I were joined today by the dark-haired Isabelle, who runs like a gazelle. Probably because I was chasing
her like a lion. She and Lena told tales out of school, and I
learned that Lena London had a poster of that dude who played
Harry Potter on the inside of her locker. None of us should let her
forget this.

Sender: Sam West
Reply All

Lena continues to harbor a secret lust for Harry Potter. Sometimes she asks me to pretend I'm putting a spell on her—but enough about our love life. ;)

I can't tell you how glad I am that the Gothic monster is coming down. We have been reprieved, and the rising sun will still be ours for the viewing.

On another note, Geronimo is getting so big that he can barely have adventures. I'd put him on a diet, but he's still a growing boy. Arabella continues to tattle on him, but she's obviously his biggest fan. Well, she and Camilla.

Sender: Camilla Graham
Reply All

I must confess I am a Geronimo fan. He has a mighty spirit. I miss the days of him living at Graham House, but I realize that Sam House is his home. Even Lestrade and the dogs miss him, I think. Perhaps we should buy one big castle and dwell in it together with our animals.

That gives me an idea for a children's book.

Sender: Adam Rayburn
Reply All

Camilla continues to blossom. First, she branched out from fiction to autobiography. Now, perhaps, children's literature?

Sender: Isabelle Devon
Reply All

Camilla, if you write a children's book about people who move in together so that their pets can share a house, I will sell it in the vet's office. Every vet would want to carry it. Please invite me to the book signing for that one.

I would also like to thank Lena and Cliff for letting me join their running club. Their route is spectacular, with views of the lake for the whole last leg. But the best part is seeing Cliff in his tight running clothes. If I had known that he wore spandex leggings to go running, I would have been a spectator long ago.

Sender: Belinda Frailey
Reply All

We would also be thrilled to feature Camilla's children's book in the Blue Lake Library. Sounds like a great choice for story time.

Sender: Doug Heller
Reply All

Sam and I have occasionally been spectators (translation: hecklers) of Cliff in his spandex. I once used a Blue Lake police vehicle for a full five minutes of harassment of Cliff on his day off when I saw him capering down Route 41. Luckily Cliff is immune to sarcasm.

Yes, it's good that it will be coming down, and I intend to be there to watch the last dark support beam fall. Anyone want to join me? I think they plan to finish up on Friday.

Sender: Lena London
Reply All

I'll be there. This is the next happiest event in this town since Camilla's birthday.

I can already imagine Gabby's joy (she's Camilla's publicist) at the thought of Camilla branching out into children's literature. Although I think it should be a children's mystery. Let's get them started early on the best stories of all.

Cliff, I'll have you know that the picture in my locker was of Daniel Radcliffe, a talented and versatile actor, not of Harry Potter. Although I do have a Professor McGonagall wand in my drawer at Graham house, and Allison and I used to spend long hours trying to determine our most appropriate Patronus.

And I think you look very athletic in your running clothes.

Sender: Allison Branch
Reply All

Lena finally decided her Patronus was a cat—big surprise. Mine was an otter. John says hi!

Sender: Belinda Frailey
Reply All

You're all invited to Warm House after the viewing. But first, since we have a lot to celebrate, maybe we should all take a shoe down to Shoe Corner, in true Blue Lake style. Then we'll be in high spirits, and that calls for spirits. And maybe some appetizers made by Carl, If he's not working.

RSVP to me or Doug.

Love you all!

Ready to find
your next great read?

Let us help.

Visit prh.com/nextread